ALSO BY ROBIN PORECKY

A PATHLESS LAND (2009)

978-1-90560-958-1

In 1897 Martin Janow sets out to rescue Tempest, a mad evangelist, from the wilds of Swedish Lapland. His motive is not entirely unselfish, for Mary Warmouth has promised herself to him if he succeeds.

But why is she so eager to save the priest, and is Tempest really mad? On the increasingly frightening journey homeward the layers of truth are gradually peeled back and Janow must fight for his own sanity and his survival.

CRITICAL ACCLAIM

"The plot resembles both Conrad's *Heart of Darkness* and Henry James' *The Ambassadors,* but is none the worse for it. The scenes in Lapland are superbly eerie; and what Janow finds at the end of his voyage of discovery suitably disturbing."

Alexander Lucie-Smith, *The Tablet*

"A gripping, erudite and highly original journey into the heart of Nordic Darkness. Porecky explores issues of spirituality, culture and fanaticism with the flair of a born storyteller."   Liz Jensen, author of '*The Ninth Life of Louis Drax'*

"There are echoes of the great Australian novelist Patrick White's 'Voss': the same epic feel and sense of inevitability. I felt plunged into a powerful place..... and was swept along." Piers Plowright, *Triple Prix Italia winner and Radio 4's 'Saturday review' critic*

LONGLISTED FOR THE AUTHORS' CLUB BEST FIRST NOVEL AWARD 2010

FOOL'S ISLAND (2011)

978-1-84963-075-7

In 1759 the young and wilful Franulka leaves her castle home for Warsaw, where she attracts the attentions of the King's son. Eighteen months later, with her Fool and maid, she vanishes. A closed carriage in the early morning, with an armed outrider, suggests disgrace and exile.

But nothing is as it seems. Caught up in a deadly conspiracy, only the Fool can save her. But is the price too high?

Shifting between Poland, Russia, Venice and an Adriatic island, this is a gripping historical mystery, a passionate love story and a moving study of the painful growth of self-awareness.

"Here's a novel that grabs you by the ear and eye and plunges you into the life of 18th century Poland: court intrigues, love sacred and profane, jealousy, rage, adventure, comedy and danger. And your guide is that wisest of men, a professional 'fool'. The journey to his island is a thrilling one." *Piers Plowright, Broadcaster and Critic*

"A born storyteller." *Liz Jensen, author of 'The Rapture'*

"Powerfully written, impeccably researched." *Elizabeth Carter-Jones, Reviewer*

COME INTO MY ARMS (2012)

978-1-84963-166-2

Magnus Trygg is a happy man. He loves his Swedish wife, his two young children and his home in the sparsely populated northern county of Jämtland. He is proud of his job as a junior policeman in the local force and, though half-Thai, he has always thought of himself as fully Swedish.

Then a young Kurdish girl is found in the forest, tied to a stake and shot. Magnus, waiting with the body throughout the long summer night until an Inspector is available, discovers the murder weapon. It suggests an honour killing, and he is ordered to bring in the father. But Magnus knows Hashmet Nazif, likes him, and is reluctant to believe he would harm his daughter. Unsettled by the sudden explosion of anti-immigrant feeling, he decides to use his local knowledge to uncover anything that may suggest a different truth. It is a very dangerous decision.

"Tremendous pace, a lot of tension and a thoroughly gripping climax."   *Piers Plowright, Critic and Broadcaster*

Robin Porecky is of Polish origin but was born and brought up in England. He now works in Sweden as a maker of customised knives.

This is his fourth novel, following 'A Pathless Land' (2009), 'Fool's Island' (2011) and 'Come Into My Arms' (2012), and is the second in the Magnus Trygg series of Swedish crime novels.

The Devil's Field

Robin Porecky

The Devil's Field

AUSTIN MACAULEY
PUBLISHERS LTD.

A CIP catalogue record for this title is available from the British
Library.

ISBN 978 1 84963 167 9

www.austinmacauley.com

First Published (2013)
Austin Macauley Publishers Ltd.
25 Canada Square
Canary Wharf
London
E14 5LB

Printed & Bound in Great Britain

To Chris, a true friend

DAY 1

CHAPTER 1

August Frisk looked down at the dead man, confident he'd done all that was immediately necessary. Sorting it out had been an unwelcome interruption to his early morning routine. As so often in his life before, it had been a situation that needed managing; and there were still arrangements to be made to ameliorate what he couldn't alter. But that would come later, when he'd called the police. For now it was more important for him to continue his daily walk.

It was a perfect summer morning, the sun still low in the sky, the sea glossy and quiescent. He went down through the trees at his usual steady pace until he was close to the pebbled shore, and then he walked right out to the tip of the headland. Two hundred centuries earlier a layer of ice three thousand metres thick had crushed the area during the final ice age. It depressed the earth's crust there like a giant's thumb pushing into a freshly-baked bun and it had already taken ten thousand years for it to rebound. During that time it lifted shingle beaches onto areas that became forested around them; and the coastal rise would still take five more thousand years to reach its former level.

Squaring his shoulders he fixed his eyes as always on the rock, glaring at it balefully. It was like a cancer growing up through the liquid flesh of the Gulf of Bothnia. It had broken the surface of the water a hundred years before, a pimple first, then a wart and finally, now, a creased and knobbly boil rising into the air. It grew eight millimetres each year; and, as it rose, it spread across the narrow water, forming an island which already almost blocked the only inlet to his fishing wharf. Soon it would imprison the water, making it an inland lake and ending half a millennium of fishing from such a natural harbour.

His grandfather, Anders, had been a young man of twenty-six when the tip first appeared, a tiny spear of rock which simply needed to be noted. But with so much open water either side there was no concern about the safety of his herring boats, few at first but steadily increasing in number. By the time of his death in 1934, when August's father Abel took charge of the family business, the rock was broader and higher. But it was still no threat to the experienced fishermen who manned his larger fleet and fished the Baltic for whitefish, herring and, when the breeding conditions further south were favourable, for cod as well. As a precaution Abel painted the rock red, a warning to any visitors who didn't know the waters as well as he did. But it proved to be a fateful decision, for from that moment he felt his eyes drawn inexorably to the obstruction, and he couldn't rid his mind of it. When August, his only child, was born, Abel began to brood upon it more and more. He became obsessed it would deprive the boy of his rightful fishing heritage; he started to drink, and by the time of his early death the size of the fleet had dwindled. Reacting angrily against what he saw as his father's weakness, August built it up again, stubbornly refusing to countenance what all around him now acknowledged, that, as the land continued to rise, their way of life must change.

Each morning, early, he visited the rock. He'd watched it slowly become an islet, and then the more substantial island it was now, colourfully clad with moss and wild flowers, and dotted with a scattering of stunted trees. The sides reached ever closer to the twin headlands of the channel leading to Frisks. The wooden jetties were there, the workshops and the stores, the extensive areas for drying nets, the slipway where the boats were winched up for repairs. Frisks was the oldest family fishing business in the area, and it was a matter of pride that their name was also their address. 'Frisks, High Coast' was quite sufficient for any correspondence, covering not just the little harbour but the land as well, and the houses all around it. But Frisks, once the dominant force in the community, was now reduced to just a single boat, and only August could safely slither it over the rock beneath the diminishing open water.

Though he concerned himself with Frisks alone, August knew the whole sixty kilometre stretch of the High Coast was affected. Many inlets were already lakes, off-shore islands had joined the mainland, and before the process was complete the whole coastline would be altered. Easy access to the Baltic herring had given the family their earlier status; but now, at sixty-four, his son Daniel already dead, August knew there would be little enough to leave to Jon, his only heir, aged eight.

He was not a despairing man. He'd lived so long with the inevitable, and though he'd never accepted it, and never would accept it, he'd weathered the many storms along the way, setting his bulk against the wind and refusing to be flattened. He'd assumed the character and look of the aged pine trees above him on the upper shingle, reaching down deep roots around the rocks and stones, gripping hard, starting straight but becoming thickened in the body and muscularly twisted in the limbs, rough skinned, a little pitted, but seemingly indestructible. So much of his life had been a battle, against the sea, against the elements, against the changes in the land and the resulting changes in the society where he lived, against the tragedies which scar most lives, against the problems his own stubbornness created in his family life. He'd clashed frequently with his father, who'd clashed with his, and he'd learnt early on that families were hard and often painful in the shaping. Now, suddenly, late in his life when the sap no longer flowed as fast, this new unexpected squall was threatening to bring him down.

It was still early in the morning, cloudy, fresh and cool before the day's summer heat, the resin smell of conifers mingling with the brackish scent of the sea. It was the time between his invariably early rising from his bed and the later drinking of the eagerly awaited first cup of coffee which Hanna, Jon's mother, Daniel's widow, would hand him on his return. He needed this time each day, alone with his thoughts and plans; a time to brace himself, now he was not as resilient as he once had been, for what the day would bring. At his feet the grey water stretched smoothly to the far horizon, but its flatness was deceptive, for there was a vigorous swirl around the flat rock where he stood, and the occasional little wave lashed it with surprising strength, streaking the grey edge with white. It was a treacherous sea, and life around it seemed treacherous as well. Why else had it waited until he'd been weakened by the hard knocks he'd received already, and only then swung a harder blow at him?

He sighed, then drew himself upright. Though he believed in God he relied upon himself. His God was a powerful force, appearing in the storms which sprang up suddenly at sea, in the hail and the lightning; but he was not a God who involved himself too much with the people he'd put upon the earth. They had to cope as best they could, and Frisks, as a community, had always coped best by going its own way and not becoming involved in much beyond its own immediate boundaries. The forested land, the fishing, the houses on the hill behind him; those were what mattered. If others attached themselves to Frisks, as many had across the generations, they were absorbed, becoming lesser members of the family, but family nonetheless. But for the rest, outsiders, prying busybodies, ill-intentioned gossips and those who claimed to have authority, they'd never been welcome, and were not welcome now. When his great-grandfather had settled by the inlet in 1862, there'd been few to trouble him; and when his grandfather built up the fishing business and increased the land he held, he made it forcefully clear to the other settlers that Frisks was self-sufficient, and the uninvited would not be well-received. The huge tree trunk blocking Frisks Way, the track which led up to their clearing, had been felled by his grandfather; his father had added the chains which fixed it in place; and he himself made its message more explicit by adding the painted notice, 'FRISKS. KEEP OUT.'

He drew the sea air into his lungs until he felt himself expand, new strength and resolution coursing through him. If Daniel had lived he might have been able to share the burden of decision, but now there were many more years of leadership before him until Jon would be of age. He took a last look at the island, almost as if he expected to catch it in the act of rising from the sea. He'd erected a fishing hut upon it, but it hadn't tamed the rock, or made it part of Frisks. Instead it accentuated the rock's increasing height and girth, a stone log lying across the water, not keeping others out, but hemming the family in.

He turned and clambered up towards the distant house, conscious of his early morning stiffness, the dull ache in one hip. He passed the several large stretches of rounded pebbles, now lichen-covered but once successive shore-lines; and he nodded familiarly to them as old friends. It was very quiet, and he'd be surprised if anybody was stirring yet, except perhaps his daughter-in-law, heating the coffee kettle in his house. At the highest level was the oldest shingle beach, mixed with remains of the original moraine and forming the largest clearing in his forest. The dead body was sprawled where the stones gave way to earth and trees again. He'd been tempted to carry the corpse with him and throw it in the sea, and years before he might have done it. But now he knew the science backing any police investigation was too advanced for such crude solutions. Though there was only one policeman assigned to the whole High Coast, and he was a man he'd known for years, dragging off a body to dispose of it elsewhere would simply ensure official scrutiny, suspicion and investigation. That would involve Frisks with the outside world, which was precisely what he wanted to avoid. Better by far to be the one who called the police, then try to stay peripheral to what must follow.

As he'd expected he met no one as he walked from the forest onto the cleared slope below his house. The fragrance of meadowsweet welcomed him, not strong so early in the day but full of childhood memories of innocent freedom playing among the drifts which covered the open areas. Beyond it loomed the house his grandfather had built, imposing still though showing the shabbiness of time and the neglect which lack of money caused. It was two storeys, three if you included the spacious loft with its diamond windows. The roof was tiled, pale red in the early sun; the gable over the closed-in porch was tiled too, and the central chimney was made of bricks fired from clay of the same colour. The tall windows added to the impression of a strong and solid house, substantial, a family home for people of consequence despite the faded reddening of the wood and the cracking paint on doors and windows. Beyond this main house, well beyond and well spread out, were the single storey houses where the others lived, though some were empty now. He went into his house, holding himself proudly to show he wasn't worried at all and that all who lived at Frisks could still rely on him. As he'd hoped, Hanna had come down from the upstairs rooms he'd set aside for her and Jon, and was in the kitchen. She handed him his coffee and he took it into his comfortable den where he did his paperwork, closing the door behind him. Arvid, the policeman, was an early riser just as he was, and though he couldn't be called a friend, for August was a family man and had no need of friends, he was someone who held similar views on all that mattered. The seven years between their ages never seemed important, for August felt young and Arvid seemed already old. He was more thoughtful than many in the police, more understanding, knowing the ways of small communities; and though he was often slow to act he was as effective as the area required. August knew he'd listen carefully, without interruption, taking his time to ponder the real import of the words reaching him through the earpiece; and though he wouldn't defer, for he was an experienced man, he'd hear what August said and, approving of the speaker, he'd be influenced. August seated himself in his favourite armchair and drank his coffee slowly, savouring every swallow and preparing in his mind exactly what to say. Then he reached out for the heavy black old-fashioned phone he still preferred to anything more modern, and slowly dialled the number.

CHAPTER 2

Magnus Trygg took the call, and realised at once the caller had expected Arvid, and so was temporarily at a loss for words.

"Arvid's been rushed to hospital," he explained. "Some sort of emergency, deep-vein thrombosis, I think, but I may be wrong. I'm Officer Trygg, his replacement until he's better. How can I help you?"

He waited patiently during the long pause which followed, thinking it likely the caller would ring off, preferring to say nothing than to converse with a stranger. Inspector Amrén, now officially announced as the designated Superintendent in charge of the Sundsvall police, had told him about the community feeling in the area, warning him he was unlikely to achieve much contact until he was better known. But his caller seemed to rally, and the voice, when it came, was firm and authoritative, the voice of someone used to being in charge, of someone who'd prepared, and probably now revised, the words he was going to use.

"I'm ringing from Frisks. There's a body on our land, a man, stabbed in the back. You'd better come over."

Magnus noted the time and a few hasty details. "And you are…?"

"August Frisk."

"Did you find the body?"

"Yes."

"There was no doubt he was dead?"

"No."

"Do you know him?"

"No."

"And you rang as soon as you found him?"

"Yes."

"I'll be straight over."

A sigh was audible. "As you're a stranger I suppose I have to give you directions?"

"I know where Frisks is," replied Magnus, looking optimistically at Arvid's area map on the wall above his desk. "Don't let anybody touch anything, keep everybody well away."

He rang off and, to his relief, found the position of Frisks was clearly marked. He hadn't expected to be involved in anything serious within a week of his arrival but, always happier when he was active, he welcomed the challenge. He thought it was his mother's Thai blood in him which made him so eager to be busily involved. She's been mail-order bride who immediately set about defying the slur implied in such a label. She established herself quickly in her new country, learned the language, and, profiting from her few mistakes, set herself to be beyond reproach as a wife and mother. His Swedish father had been a more deliberate man, slower moving, knowing precisely what was necessary on the small Jämtland farm, and pacing himself through those necessities, without hurry or neglect. Loving his wife and son, content that each farming year entailed essentially the same tasks, he had none of the occasionally rash impetuosity that drove Magnus, and certainly none of that ambition to excel. Magnus their only child grew up to feel entirely Swedish; and now, his parents dead, this feeling was bolstered by a Swedish wife, two Swedish children, and a satisfying Swedish police career.

He'd visited the High Coast before, with Sonja, as tourists giving Angelica and Johan a day out and enjoying it themselves. But he'd been taken aback when Inspector Ragnar Amrén rang him. He'd worked quite closely with him a couple of years before on an apparent honour-killing case involving both the Sundsvall and Östersund police districts. Now he was offering him the job of temporary replacement officer with responsibility for the High Coast.

"Sundsvall can't really spare anybody, we're short-staffed as usual in the holiday season, and I've had permission to try to get somebody from the Östersund force. It'll be good experience for you, you'll be on your own with a lot of responsibility, which I know you like. I imagine you've heard nothing more about your promotion?"

"Not a word," answered Magnus, failing to add that his relationship with his immediate superior, Inspector Hermansson, had soured since Magnus discovered a key piece of evidence had been planted, and Hermansson was implicated.

"If you do well in the High Coast, and I'm sure you will, I want you to request a transfer to Sundsvall. I'll be in a position then to recommend you for Inspector training and when you've finished that you can probably take over my old post as Head of Homicide here. We cooperated well together last year, and I'm sure we will again."

Magnus was flattered, excited, glad of the chance to make a fresh start in a new force, and too stupid to realise he should have consulted Sonja before enthusiastically accepting the High Coast post and all it implied. His delight was rapidly punctured by her furious outburst, telling him exactly what she thought of a posting which would leave her and the children in their present house while he lived in bachelor quarters more than a hundred kilometres away. As for a promotion that would require her to uproot the children and move to town away from everything she loved and valued, her bitterness cut him like a freshly-sharpened knife.

It was their first really serious row, and when he left for the High Coast he and Sonja were farther apart than they'd ever been. Angelica, who was eight and adored him, sobbed inconsolably when he left, and Johan, who at six didn't fully understand the tension in the house, cried because his sister did and begged Magnus to hurry back that evening and go on with a bedtime story which was still unfinished.

The area police station he'd dreamed of during the long drive turned out to be an empty shop front in Nordingrå converted, he assumed, by Arvid himself, for it was roughly done. The quarters at the back were cramped and basic, and he understood why Arvid had lived out in a more modern house nearby. Even when he'd cleaned and aired the rooms, and tried to create a greater sense of order in the office, it remained depressing and he was very lonely. For the next few nights he slept badly in his narrow bed, lying awake for long periods and trying to come to terms with a Sonja who'd so suddenly changed from the sweet, warm-hearted girl he'd adored since they'd been college lovers, into the loud and vituperative woman who seemed to scorn his burning ambition to do well. But was his ambition as admirable as he thought? Though he didn't find it easy, for he wasn't given to introspection, he tried to consider the matter as honestly as he could, looking into himself and not altogether liking what he found. Always proud of his optimistic confidence, it now seemed to mask an uncertainty, not just about his marriage, but about the money needed to bring up a young family; and there was a new consciousness that he was not perhaps the complete Swede he tried to be. As for his ambition, it might be a more complicated beast than he'd supposed, having economic claws, social-integration wings, and a body composed mainly of personal pride. Though he didn't want to think about these things too deeply, he could no longer deny he'd been partly, even largely, to blame for what had happened, and it didn't help him find peace of mind enough to sleep. Mostly he gave up the attempt, gulped an early breakfast, and immersed himself in office-work, preparing himself for the job. Now, squirming guiltily as the thought came, he even felt relieved that something as dramatic as a killing would at least take his mind off Sonja and his own shortcomings.

He telephoned Amrén, a hundred and twenty five kilometres away in Sundsvall, explained there was a possibility of foul play and was delighted when he received permission to undertake the preliminary investigation. As he drove towards Frisks through sunshine which was already bright he began to realise there was more to the High Coast than the popular tourist resort which attracted one day visitors, campers, caravanners and yachtsmen. Once he was away from the marked tourist trails there were no brightly painted cafés, no expensive fish restaurants, no camping sites, open-air swimming pools and gift shops. The land was wilder, full of the signs of economic hardship, decaying barns, neglected farms, empty houses, dirt roads pitted with holes, and dark forest which hadn't been thinned. He passed silted lakes which had once been harbours, and became increasingly aware of the silent emptiness. It was all such a contrast to the busy roads and laughing people in the best known villages which had changed from working fishing ports to small service industries supporting the Swedish Tourist Board. His destination seemed a long way from anywhere, and when he finally turned into Frisks Way he was taken aback to spot three bull elk climbing a slope above the road, their large ears twitching and the lappets beneath their necks swinging violently as they tossed their massive palmate antlers at attacking horseflies. He was used to them inland, at home in Bispgården, but it had never occurred to him they would be roaming so near the Baltic. When he finally pulled up at the chained log he realised the sea was even closer than he'd expected, clearly visible below him, a short way through the trees. He studied the unwelcoming notice and then, when nobody came, he pressed his horn.

A large, slow-moving man appeared from behind a tree as though he'd been waiting there. With his shock of grey hair and full curly beard he might have been an Old Testament prophet stepping out of the wall painting in one of the sixteenth century fishermen's chapels which dotted the High Coast. The dark sombre eyes with which he stared at Magnus enhanced the feeling of someone who knew his mind, was not afraid to speak it and was righteously certain there was no need to change it.

"You can leave your car there, and I'll lead you to the body."

"Are you August Frisk?" asked Magnus, not doubting that he was, but anxious to seize some sort of initiative.

The man nodded, and then stood waiting, as if he was used to waiting and accustomed to getting his own way.

"I'll drive in," said Magnus. "I have equipment in my car I'll need when I examine the body, so I must park as close as I can without disturbing any evidence."

August Frisk continued to stare at him. He'd not been prepared for the foreignness, the smooth bronze features which made the policeman seem almost a boy, and he found it frustratingly difficult to read the impassive face which watched him with interest but without showing the slightest inclination to leave the car.

"I can't move the log, it's chained," said August, showing no impatience.

"Do you have a helicopter?"

"No," replied August, startled by the question.

"Then I assume you have a car, so I'll come in the same way you drive out." His face lit up with a warm smile to show he was not taking offence at August's obduracy, but rather enjoying the game.

"There is another way in, further back," conceded August. "Back up about twenty metres and you'll see a narrow track going off on the right between two trees. It's a bit bumpy, but if you drive slowly you'll be all right. I'll meet you along the way and show you where you can park."

"You don't welcome visitors, do you?"

"We keep ourselves to ourselves at Frisks, it's the way we like it. That's why we don't make the way in too obvious. This is a working community." He spat disgustedly on the ground, adding, "There are no tourist attractions here, and there never will be."

Magnus reversed, found the less visible track on a corner, cleverly angled between two huge Norwegian spruce which almost concealed it, and followed August until he indicated a clearing some distance from the houses he could now see.

When he got out of the car August noticed Magnus was taller than him by half a head, and despite his slimness he looked extremely strong.

"Is that where you live?" Magnus asked, taking out his notebook.

"Yes."

"Alone?"

"My daughter-in-law and my grandson have part of my house. My uncle and his wife live in that cottage, my cousin Elin has the neighbouring one, and Olof Petter and Gubbo, who run the fishing with me, live in the one over there, on the edge of the forest."

"Do they know about the body?"

"I told them all."

"I'm surprised they aren't out here. Most people are curious about death."

"I told them to stay inside and give you space."

"And they do what you tell them?"

"Yes," said August, and he led the way towards the forest overlooking the sea. "The body's down here on the Devil's Field."

"That's an odd name to give a field."

"It isn't a field, it's a beach stuck up here among the trees. I suppose you do know the land round here has been rising from the sea for thousands of years and that's why those bloody interfering UNESCO bureaucrats named it a World Heritage Site?"

Magnus nodded, noting the furious disgust in August's tone. "But I didn't know about the Devil's Fields."

"The first settlers called them that when they broke their ploughs on them. They thought hiding beaches in fertile land miles from the sea could only be a trick played on them by the Evil One."

The body was of a fleshy man of similar size to August but considerably younger, seemingly in his thirties. He was smartly dressed in a dark suit, with an open-necked midnight-blue shirt. The knife in his back had a hilt of polished horn, and though none of the blade was visible it seemed to have done its work extremely efficiently. There were no signs of body movement or scrabbling hands or feet on the ground to suggest he'd lived on for a while after the knife had gone in.

"You don't know him?" Magnus asked again.

"No."

"You've never even seen him before?"

"No, but I take little notice of tourists."

Magnus looked up, interested. "What makes you think he's a tourist?"

"Look at the clothes and shoes. No working man dresses like that."

"Have the others seen the body?"

"I let them all look, but I kept them from coming too close. Nobody recognised him."

"Why did you think you ought to let them see him?" Magnus asked curiously.

"I wanted to discover if anyone knew him, or anything about him. This is my place, and I like to know what's going on."

"How old's your grandson?"

"Jon's eight."

"Did you let him see the body?"

"I already told you everyone saw it."

"You didn't think he was too young, that you might have spared him the sight?"

"I've never left him out of anything," replied August proudly. "He's a sensible boy, old for his years, and he's seen death often enough before because I take him with me hunting."

"But not a human death?"

"People die, as animals do, and he has to get used to it. So I saw no reason to treat him differently."

"And his mother didn't mind?"

August seemed surprised by the question, as though he'd never considered it. Finally he said dryly, "We usually agree on what's best for the boy."

"And she agreed this time?"

"Yes."

Magnus stood up. "I'm going to call up some specialists now. I'd be grateful if you'd go back to your house, and I'll come and take statements from you and the others as soon as I can. I don't need to tell you that murder is a very serious matter, and this is now a crime scene. Perhaps you would spread the word that no one must come near it for any reason at all."

August did not move.

"Is there a problem?" asked Magnus.

August shrugged. "I thought you might have been interested to know who did it, but you didn't ask me."

Very deliberately Magnus took out his notebook again. "Since you'd never seen the victim before I'm afraid it didn't occur to me you might know the murderer. Please tell me now."

"It's a Lapp knife in his back, handle's made of reindeer antler and the decoration's their style. And there's been a Lapp round here. Sami we're meant to say now, but they're still no-good Lapps to me."

"You don't like them?"

"I didn't like this one. He wintered his reindeer herd in my forest and kept them there a lot longer than I'd agreed before transporting them back to Lapland. He was tricky about paying, too, and I don't care for that."

"Surely he didn't keep his reindeer here until now?"

"He finally took them away a couple of months ago, but he must've been back visiting yesterday because I'm sure I saw him, or his double if he's got one. And he always wore a knife like this one dangling at his side, sort of badge of office for a reindeer herder."

"But why should he kill this man?"

"He was a quarrelsome sod, especially when he'd been drinking. He was devious as well, trying to cheat me all he could, and if he did it to me I'm sure he did it to others. That leads to bad blood and fights."

"You're suggesting he'd quarrelled with the dead man, and came back yesterday to settle accounts with him?"

"How the hell should I know?" answered August irritably. "It's your job to find out what happened, not mine. All I'm saying is he had a knife like this, he was a cheating bastard and he was here yesterday."

"What's his name?"

"Paulus."

"Paulus what?"

August snorted. "Who can tell, with them? Paulus of Jokkmokk, that's the only name I had from him."

"Thank you," said Magnus gratefully. "That information could be extremely helpful, and I'll put out a call so that we can at least question him. You can give me more details when I take your statement."

August turned away and walked stolidly up to his house. Magnus noticed he didn't even glance at any of the other houses, though the people there would almost certainly be watching him with eager curiosity; and he noticed too that as soon as he went in the door closed firmly behind him.

Magnus turned back to the body, took out his mobile and, grateful the recently erected mast allowed him to use it, rang Amrén.

CHAPTER 3

Amrén told him what he feared he'd hear. It was summer, his people were on holiday, Västernorrland and Ångermanland were on skeleton staff, and he could spare no one.

"You like working on your own," Amrén said persuasively. "You've done the photography course, you can check for fingerprints, you've got a sharp eye and there's a roll of tape in your car to mark off the restricted area. What more do you need?"

"Pathology and forensic."

"A retired police doctor, Axel Burman, has got a summer cottage out your way and he's still sharp enough for what seems like a pretty straightforward knifing. My neighbour was talking to his wife on the phone yesterday, so I know he's there. I'll get in touch with him and he should be over in the next hour or so to ascertain the time and cause of death. Give me the exact location."

Magnus did so. Then he asked him about forensic, and noticed the hesitation in Amrén's answer.

"Hillevi Zander is probably your best bet. Retired, of course, that's all you'll get at this time of the year. She lives in Kramfors, but she can use the facilities at Härnösand, though I seem to remember she's set up a lab at her home, does a lot of private work. Talk to Axel about her, and then you can contact her if you both think it's necessary. It may just have been the unfortunate outcome of a drunken brawl – we haven't had a murder in the High Coast for years."

Magnus told him about Paulus of Jokkmokk.

"There you are then. The Sami have used that area to winter their herds since time immemorial, but they resent having to pay for what they think of as their right. A quarrel, a loss of temper, and suddenly it's all gone too far. You'll soon sort it out. Meanwhile I'll put a call out to Lapland to pick him up and question him, but it would help if you can find out his family name. Whoever rented him forest must have records of the deal, there was probably even a contract and his full name will be on that. As for the overall investigation, you know the procedure. Prosecutor Vessberg will be officially in charge, but in practice you'll report directly to me and he's unlikely to interfere unless there are complaints or we make a cock-up. He's due to retire at the end of the year, he's in considerable pain from his arthritis and he's trusted me a lot in the past and knows I haven't let him down. But he's honest, he's not a fool, and it's essential to keep him fully informed. So you'll have to keep me in touch, daily, and follow it up with a written report every three days. I'll pass everything on to him, together with my own comments, of course. When you get beyond the background investigation, taking statements, that sort of thing, the prosecutor will expect to make the major decisions, but he's sure to discuss them with me first. "

Amrén rang off, and Magnus understood he'd been embarrassed by his lack of resources and had been deliberately playing down the possible difficulties in an effort to encourage him. But he remained concerned about August's claim that nobody at Frisks knew the dead man, remembering his further statement that everyone on his land did what he said.

He taped off the crime scene, took photographs of the body and the surrounding area, and then went down on his knees and began a painstaking and painful search of the forest floor where the body lay, including the shingle ground beyond. He found nothing, but he was fascinated by the map lichen which turned the stones green and yellow, and illustrated them with charts, occasionally having the semblance of Australia or Africa, but mostly showing weird unknown continents, as if the whole area were an atlas of an undiscovered world. He was still peering at them, and wondering if, as they were in the Devil's Field, anyone had ever taken them to be the map of hell, when he heard someone approaching.

"I hope you haven't touched the body," said a testy voice, and he looked up to see a spruce old-fashioned man with a clever but choleric face below such obviously false hair that Magnus was, as always, astonished at the happy blindness of the vain.

"Burman?" asked Magnus, carefully rising to his feet.

"*Doctor* Burman," the man corrected him. "Have you touched or tramped around the body?"

Magnus looked into the sharp bright eyes which belied the Doctor's age. "I haven't," he said quietly.

"Thank God for that," Burman answered briskly. "I've had a lifetime of idiotic policeman trampling over everything before I arrive." He held out his hand and Magnus thought he detected the faintest twinkle in his eyes. He was surprised, too, that the fingers he touched, though thin, were still strong. Burman lifted the tape and stepped carefully towards the body, though Magnus was uncertain whether he was setting him an example or protecting the highly polished shoes and spotless trousers he was wearing below the snugly fitting fawn cotton jacket.

"What have we got here?" Burman asked as he put on surgeon's gloves, but since he was clearly addressing himself, Magnus said nothing. "A single stab, can't be suicide unless he's a contortionist. It's not accidental, either. Not too recent, at least twelve hours ago I would guess." He stared at the ground around the body. "Killed right here, and he's a big, powerful chap, so it must have been a lucky strike or he'd have been able to defend himself." He turned and spoke directly to Magnus. "Back stabbing's easy, but killing that way takes skill or good fortune. Cutting the throat is much more certain."

Suddenly he gave a cry of excitement and crouched closer to the body. "Look at the shoes," he said enthusiastically. "They're masterpieces, hand-cut, hand-stitched, custom-made for these feet. Italian, I'm sure, but better than anything I've ever seen before. What a lucky, lucky man to be able to afford such wonders."

"Not lucky enough to stay alive in them," Magnus replied.

Burman ignored him, now closely studying the suit and shirt. "All of a piece," he murmured admiringly. "Probably

Italian too, the finest cloth, real button holes on the sleeves, silk lining. He wasn't from round here."

He rocked back on his heels, then stood up, rubbing his hands in enthusiasm. "Heard everything I said, did you?" he asked, peering at Magnus as if to check he was still awake and paying attention. "Well, there's not much more I can tell you yet. I would guess this happened yesterday evening, and I would think he was taken completely by surprise. I'll know more when I've got the knife out, but your fingerprint people will want to go over it first. He is dead, by the way."

This time Magnus saw the twinkle clearly, and he smiled back. "I'm the fingerprint people," he said.

"Short of personnel as usual," said Burman. "RaRa did warn me."

"RaRa?"

"Amrén. Inspector Amrén to you, and the soon to be chief of Sundsvall's police, or so I've heard. I've known him a long time, he's a fine officer, and we're fortunate to have him. And if you're curious about how he got his nickname you'll have to stay that way, because I've no intention of telling you, you're much too young."

Magnus tried to imagine the soft-skinned, shrewd Amrén as RaRa, and failed. Many of his colleagues were reticent about their real lives beyond their work, as Magnus was himself, but in their short acquaintance Amrén had revealed almost nothing of the real person behind the rank. Burman offered to help him with the fingerprint test, but despite Magnus' firm belief that two pairs of eyes are better than one they found nothing, the polished reindeer antler as clean as if it had just been finished.

"May have worn gloves, may have wiped it clean," said Burman. "It's easy enough to do with such a smooth surface. I'll take it out now, and then we can get the body away before the heat affects it."

He eased the knife out very slowly, and it took some effort. Magnus noticed the antler hilt had a slightly swollen top, the borders were decorated with intricate designs, and there was a single star-shaped flower in the centre; but Burman stared only at the blade. "That is real quality," he said, looking critically at the slight curve, the sharp edge and point. "Practically surgical steel, would have gone in very easily." He bagged it and handed it to Magnus. "You can turn him over and go through the pockets now. Do you want me to leave you to it?"

"I'd rather you stayed," replied Magnus. "You've got much more experience than I have."

Burman gave a thin, cackling laugh. "So I should have, I'm eighty years old next birthday."

The search did not take long. There was nothing in the pockets, not even a handkerchief.

"Might have been robbery then," said Burman, "but this is hardly the place for a mugging. More likely emptying his pockets was opportunistic, for if his clothes are anything to go by everything he owned would have been valuable, watch, pen, wallet, quite apart from money and credit cards."

"They missed the gold cufflinks, though," said Magnus. "Maybe whoever did it wanted to make it more difficult for us to find out the identity of the corpse."

"It's possible," said Burman doubtfully. "But a missing person is usually reported pretty quickly. Unless, of course, he's from abroad, and his clothes would certainly seem to indicate that."

"Italian?"

Burman shook his head. "His clothes have style, but the man himself doesn't. Do you like him?"

"He's dead," answered Magnus defensively.

"Do you think you would have liked him if he were alive?"

Magnus considered the features more carefully, staring at the heavy body, the large hands, the dark brows. He did not look Swedish, but without the spark of life it was difficult to get a hold upon the personality and so make a judgement. "I can't really tell," he said finally.

Burman seemed disappointed. "He looks to me like a peasant in rich man's clothes," he said, his dismissive tone indicating he would not himself have liked him. "That makes me wonder what he was doing in a place like this. RaRa told me nobody had recognised him, so you've got a real puzzle on your hands. Now if you'd like to help me get my stretcher we can load him into my car. I'm quite used to carrying corpses in it, and look forward to the day when some smart-ass policeman stops me and wants to search the car."

When the stretchered body had been laid in the back of Burman's Volvo and strapped down, Magnus asked him what he should do if he needed forensic help. "Inspector Amrén mentioned Hillevi Zander," he added diffidently.

Startlingly Burman's face filled with blood. "That bitch," he scoffed, his voice cracking with emotion. "I won't work with her, I'll tell you that. Before I retired I was forced to once or twice, but not now, oh no, I've sworn a solemn oath never to go near her again. Brilliant at her work, certainly, when she's sober enough to be interested, used to have the best mind in the business. But she's not a woman, she's a devil, and she'll eat a young man like you alive." As suddenly as it had come the colour left his face, and he looked a little ashamed to have spoken about a fellow professional in such a way. "We don't get on and we'll leave it at that. But if you do decide to approach her don't mention my name, or she'll slam the door in your face."

He got hurriedly into his car and drove away as if he infinitely preferred the company of a corpse to the mere thought of Hillevi Zander. Magnus, pondering his angry reaction and trying to sort out in his mind the questions he wanted answered, walked up to August's house and knocked on the door.

It was opened by a young woman and Magnus, utterly unprepared, was overwhelmed by such a strong sexual response he could only stare at her. Even in his baggy summer uniform he was terrified his physical reaction might be obvious to the blue eyes which swept over him, and he felt himself redden. She had taken no trouble to make herself attractive, and yet every centimetre of her filled him with desire. It had never happened to him like that before, not so immediately, not even when he'd first met Sonja, and he didn't know what to do with himself. He stared at the tangled blonde hair and longed to comb it out, the bare brown arms which were so touchingly thin he wanted to feed her upon strawberries and cream, spooning them into the mouth which did not smile at him. Even though she looked at him indifferently, he knew a personal complication had entered the case and it shamed him. She was wearing a short vest top which had smudges on the front, and an amber pendant glowed above the plump breasts he could see softly rising and falling beneath the stretched cotton. As she turned to let him pass her the bare skin between the skimpy vest and the low waistband of her jeans gave him a tantalizing glimpse of her tattoo, a lascivious scaly sea-serpent whose voluptuously swollen tail disappeared suggestively down her backbone into the top of her white briefs, making him frantic to ease them off and kiss wherever the tail's point vanished into her hidden flesh.

"I'm Hanna," the girl said.

Magnus nodded, showing her the warrant card ready in his hand and trying to control the tremble. He was not a womaniser, never had been, and though he and Sonja had parted coldly he loved her still, adored his children, had everything in life he needed. But now he wanted something else, and he experienced the sweet awfulness of a feeling so strong he couldn't control it.

"If you want August he's splitting logs outside," she added, regarding him now with some curiosity as he seemed at a loss for words.

"Are you his daughter-in-law?" he asked finally, the disbelief that she could be the mother of an eight year old showing in his voice.

"I could scarcely be anyone else," she replied, but she seemed to have noticed something in his manner, and looked at him more carefully, frankly appraising him. "I'll call him." She stepped outside and yelled his name. Alone in the hall Magnus thought he saw a small movement through a door which was ajar, and wondered whether her son Jon had been watching them. Then August arrived, panting and bringing with him a wholesome smell of sweat.

"In here," he said, and took Magnus into a room opposite the one where he had seen the movement and closed the door behind them. The furniture was old, hand-made, hand-carved, hand-painted and, like the house itself, well-worn.

"Grandfather made most of it," said August, noticing the direction of his gaze. "No TV then, no computer games or videos, so when you weren't earning your living you forged your own tools and made furniture, tables, chairs, cupboards, whatever you required. My father made the dresser there, and the desk."

"Have you kept up the tradition?"

August shook his head. "I'm not much good with my hands, not in the carpentry way. All I've ever made is knives, and that was when I was younger." He opened a drawer in the desk and Magnus saw a pile of them, and a lot of separate leather sheaths. "Not beautiful, but practical," August went on. "I still use them, in the forest, on the boat. They're strong, easy to sharpen, and the tang goes all the way through the grip so I know they won't let me down like a lot of modern crap."

"Why do you leave them loose in the drawer like that, instead of in their sheaths?"

"The acids in tanned leather can spoil the edge if they're left in the sheath for months or years at a time. Better to let the air get to them."

"Have you ever made a Sami knife?"

"I'm not a Lapp."

"Is that a no?"

"It's a big no. And it's not because I'm against Lapps, it's because it's just too bloody difficult. They're wonders at it."

"But some of these knives have horn handles."

"Elk horn mostly, but there's the odd reindeer one among them."

"But the knife in that man's back wasn't one of yours?"

"No, that was a proper Lapp knife, and I can't make them that well." He smiled suddenly. "I needn't have shown the knives to you."

Magnus smiled back. "I'd have got to hear about it, you know that. It's why you got in first, and opened the drawer."

August nodded. "You're young, but you're not a fool and I'm pleased about that because I want this cleared up as soon as possible. Have you put out an alert for Paulus?"

"I need to know his family name."

"I've already told you, I don't know any other name."

"But it'll be on the agreement he signed with you to winter his herd on your land. If you show it to me I'm sure I can decipher it."

August stared at him reflectively, stroking his grey beard. Then he sat down, waving Magnus to a chair opposite him. "I don't believe in written contracts," he said confidingly. "He gives his word, I give mine, we shake hands on it, and that's good enough for me. It may be old fashioned, but it's the way I do business."

"It's a very convenient way, but I doubt if the tax authorities would approve. I assume you made money by letting out part of your property, but if there's no paperwork it implies you didn't declare it."

"And you'd be right, I didn't declare it," replied August with a snort. "I manage my own life here, always have. Are you going to arrest me for tax evasion?"

"That's not up to me. But I'm duty bound to pass the information on, so you'll probably hear more about it. Did Paulus keep to the agreement?"

"Of course he didn't, sneaky little hound. Kept on saying the money was on its way, and then used that excuse to keep the herd here after the snow had gone."

"But surely that just meant more rent for you?"

August looked at him scornfully. "You don't know much about reindeer, do you?"

"I know they eat reindeer moss."

"But only in the winter. It's a sort of lichen, too tough for them unless it's been softened by the snow. Then they'll dig down for it, sometimes as much as a metre or more if we've had a heavy fall, and they guzzle it for all they're worth because it's energy rich, full of carbohydrates. But when the snow's gone they won't touch it and they turn to foliage and twigs, and that's not good for my trees. Any half-decent herder takes them north again as soon as the melt begins."

"And Paulus didn't?"

"He thought he'd got me. I wouldn't let him go until he'd paid up, so he and his damned reindeer just hung around until…"

"Until what?"

"Until I got tough with him," August conceded reluctantly.

"How tough?"

"That doesn't really concern you, does it? He's made no complaint and he won't. But he paid up, got a transporter and had the herd driven back to Lapland."

"When was that?"

"End of May, I can't remember the exact date."

"But you parted on bad terms?"

"We certainly did."

"And he came back yesterday?"

"I don't know when he came back, but I saw him yesterday."

"Where?"

"In the forest, near the entrance to our place. I was driving in and he dodged back into the trees. It was only a fleeting glimpse but I'm sure it was him, I'd almost swear to it."

"What time was that?"

"Late afternoon, about five o'clock."

"Did anybody else see him?"

"You'll have to ask around. Nobody mentioned it to me."

"Was he wearing his knife?"

"Didn't see it, but he always had it hanging from his belt, showing he was a Lapp, I suppose, even though he was wearing jeans like the rest of us."

"Why do you think he came back?"

"To pay me out."

"What for?"

"I told you I had to get tough with him."

"Did you hit him?"

"He owed me money and I made him pay. I'm not saying more than that. It's a private matter."

"It may become a public matter when we pull him in."

"When you do I may answer your questions."

Magnus saw he was going to get no further, and changed his line of questioning.

"You think he may have cheated the dead man too, and he'd come after him and they got into a fight?"

August shrugged. "I've no idea. Maybe Paulus wasn't after me at all, but was using Frisks, which he knew like the back of his hand, for a confrontation with the dead man. But finding out that sort of thing out is your job, I've got worries enough of my own without bothering my head about all that."

"Worries?"

"Open your eyes, look around you. What springs immediately to mind when you hear the words High Coast?"

"Balm for the Soul," said Magnus, quoting the slogan on all the tourist brochures.

"It makes me sick," August burst out savagely. "This was a simple fishing and farming area. We earnt our living by the strength of our arms and the sweat of our brows, and the herring and the trees were abundant enough to give us a decent income. We were free too, free to do pretty well what we wanted within the law. But look at us now, we're a Heritage Site, a designated place of Special Scientific Interest and you can hardly wipe your arse for fear of contravening some new regulation. They're turning us into a sort of theme-park, a frozen snapshot of the picturesque, and all because the land is rising faster than anywhere else, and isn't that interesting? Well, I'll tell you, it isn't fucking interesting for me and many others, it's a tragedy. Our channel out there is nearly blocked, we're reduced to one boat which I have to manoevre round the obstruction, and though Olof Petter and Gubbo still go out, and so do I sometimes, we can't any longer live on the Baltic herring we sell to the *surströmming* factory. So I make money felling the timber, Uncle Henning and his wife keep goats, and Elin makes and sells jewellery. But hard though it is there'll still be something left for Jon and while there's breath in my body I'll never, ever, put 'Balm for the Soul' over my door, tart up the buildings and sell fishing boats in bottles to gawping tourists."

"Jon and his mother share this house with you?"

"Yes."

"So that I don't put my big foot in it when I talk to your daughter-in-law, would you tell me what happened to your son?"

He noticed that the bravado immediately drained out of August, leaving him stricken. He looked away as though the memory was still too painful, and stared broodingly out of the window at the distant open water.

"The sea took him," he said finally. "Hanna was pregnant with Jon at the time, so Daniel never saw him. He was only twenty three, and I still find it's the hardest thing of all, that he was so young." He swung round suddenly and glowered at Magnus. "Why do you need to talk to her?"

"You know I have to get statements from everyone here."

"From Jon?"

"He's too young. There are so many new rules about interviewing children I wouldn't be able to do it alone, I'd have to have a social worker with me and I'd never get one at the moment so I'll wait and see how it all goes, then talk to my Inspector to see if he thinks it's necessary."

"His mother could be with him, you could talk to them both together."

Magnus pretended to consider this, uncomfortably aware he was not going to let anything stop him seeing Hanna on her own.

"I'll talk to her first," he said decisively, "and then the others. If, after that, there is anything I think Jon might be able to help me with, I'll take advice."

"Well, don't upset her with stupid questions about her husband's death," said August irritably. Magnus assured him he would be tactful, but he couldn't help wondering why Hanna should still be so sensitive about something which had occurred eight years before.

"I'll draft your statement this evening, and show it to you tomorrow. If you're happy with it you can sign it then." He got up, and at once felt his stomach tighten at the thought he was about to cross to Hanna's door and be alone with her.

CHAPTER 4

As soon as he heard Magnus enter Hanna's room, August left the house and walked down towards the water. He saw Jon clambering about in the tree house he had made for him, but for once he did not call out or wave to attract his attention. He needed to be alone, and he kept among the trees. The sense of space always filled him with an awe that was spiritually bracing. The sweep of the forest led out to the rocks, and then to the islands off the shore, and finally to the sea alone, stretching out until it blended into the horizon far away where the enormous sky swooped down to meld with it. It was a rugged terrain before him, but it smoothed out at the shoreline and eventually became, on days as calm as this one was, like glass without a blemish. He hoped it was an imitation of life itself, so full of stumbling blocks at first, but, with the final beckoning, unruffled harmony would stretch before him. He had been totally thrown when his phone call to Arvid had been answered by a stranger, and the moment of panic, when he had been unable to speak at all, had alarmed him. Now he had seen Magnus he was less concerned, liking him as much as Arvid, perhaps a little more. He wasn't one of those city pricks, he didn't bluster or throw his weight around, and he felt at ease with him, respected his straightforward attitude and did not for a moment doubt his honesty. He was the sort of man he came across rarely nowadays, the sort of man he would like Jon to be when he grew up, the sort of man, in other circumstances, he would have liked to be himself. But there was a danger in this feeling of affinity and August was alert to it. It dulled the sense of threat he ought to be experiencing, gave Magnus an attractive air of understanding, a sympathetic listener who would respect a confidence. August was a Lutheran and so had never confessed, but had he been forced to do so he had often thought he would find it easier speaking to a stranger behind a grille, someone whose instinctive facial and bodily reactions would be hidden from him. In the same way he felt protected by this policeman's impassive stare, the bronze skin stretched tightly over the high cheek bones. Once or twice in their recent interview he had wondered what it would be like to throw himself on his knees and pour out all the accumulated detritus of his mind. But the impassivity was a snare, as well, for he could not fathom what Magnus really thought and so must tread with special caution. Beneath that bland exterior there was a sharp intelligence and his simple courtesy might mask an inflexible determination to find the truth. Olof Petter would certainly excrete a lot of bile, and none of it would be favourable. Anders, his grandfather, had always welcomed society's misfits, and tried to find them jobs, and at one stage there had been nine of them, working the boats, the land, the forest; and, whatever their mental, physical or alcoholic problems, his dominant personality had bound them to the community and kept them from excess. His father Abel, too, until he had lost faith in the future, had been hospitable to drifters and made use of them; and August himself had tried to do no less. But lack of work had gradually reduced the opportunities, and now there were only two, Gubbo and Olof Petter. The latter took great delight in causing mischief, and this death would be a perfect opportunity for him to sow more seeds of discord. August, who valued his work as skipper of their only boat, 'Frisks 3', still tried to keep a tight control of him and did not doubt he would vent his resentment by damaging him in any little way he could, though without ever putting his own security within the community at real risk. Magnus, if he was as decent and upright as he seemed, would see at once the sort of man he had to deal with; but it did not mean he would not listen and remember.

He'd been mortified when Magnus had raised the question of Daniel's death, and for a moment he'd been unable to face him. He ought to have been over such emotion by now, had thought he was. But the memories had come flooding back and, for some seconds, had quite unmanned him; and, as so often nowadays, the memories, once roused, clung on to him for hours.

It seemed no time at all since he'd strode so confidently through the meadow and across the track to Hammarfeldt's farm. He'd been in his early twenties, cutting a cocky figure in his new suit, the gold watch chain tapping against his yellow waistcoat as he walked so eagerly towards the large farmhouse. Hammarfeldt had done well, the new car parked outside the porch showed that; and his daughter, Amanda, was a catch several of his acquaintances were eager to get into their hands. But August swaggered towards the door because he was certain he'd be the one. Hammarfeldt would never turn down a chance to be related to the Frisks, and Amanda had already intimated shyly that she favoured him. He was welcomed exactly as he knew he would be, and Hammarfeldt shook his hand and gave his blessing, adding with a wink that it must be subject to Amanda saying yes as well. So he went in to her already a conquering hero, and was overwhelmed to find himself, in front of her, suddenly nervous and uneasy. For the first time he realised how much he loved her, and knew he would not be able to bear it if she turned him down; so he was unexpectedly awkward when he asked her, and couldn't meet her eye. But she, unconsciously touching the wealth of auburn hair that was her glory and the object of his secret erotic fantasy, accepted him. And it was a love match, though despite their ardour in the stoutly constructed marriage bed, he didn't become a father until the age of thirty-five; and on that same day he became a widower too. And just as the birth brought him both happiness and grief, so his twenty-three year relationship with his son gave him the same, though the balance was reversed, the grief outweighing any happiness.

Reaching the beach he looked out for the razorbills which bred on the High Coast, on the island where his son had died, but all must have been feeding further out for he saw nothing but the occasional tern. He stared at the familiar pebbles he had collected as a boy, grey-white, purple, some glittering with silica, one, especially large, a duck-egg blue, its open groove still damp and sheltering a washed-up length of bladder wrack kelp. He stooped and picked up a flat piece of the reddish rapakivi granite which dotted the beach and skimmed it across the water towards the island, an action which also reminded him of his childhood. Rapakivi was a Finnish word meaning rotten rock and August wondered if something was beginning to rot in him. The granite was so named because it broke first into squarish blocks, still of some solidity, but over the years the constant wear of time and tramping boots crumbled it into little more than gravel. He shuddered, fearful suddenly that he was crumbling too. But then he shook himself, filled his hands with water and dashed it in his face. This was the moment when he needed to be strong. Always in the past he had known what needed to be done, and he had done it. This had, he supposed, been his morality – if something needed doing, he would do it, even if, in the eyes of others, it might seem wrong. He regretted nothing, he told himself fiercely, but knew it was not true. He wished he had been his grandfather, living in a time of certainty when hard work brought its own reward. His father, Abel, whom he had loved so much before he had despised him, started manhood full of hope, but, as the rock rose from the water, he declined into a drunken sot unable to confront the destruction of his dreams. It was he, August, who had taken a grip on everything again, refusing to face defeat, refusing to become part of the fishing Disneyland gradually growing up around him. He felt his anger rise again and welcomed it. Thinking of the past weakened him; anger at the present made him the more determined to ensure that Frisks survived as something he could pass on to Jon with real pride.

As he thought of Jon, he thought of Hanna, and then of Magnus, chuckling as he recalled his expression when he pretended to resent him seeing Hanna on her own and suggested he might talk to Jon and her together. It was the obstinate look of a little boy determined not to lose his sweet. He had the hots for Hanna, he'd seen that from the first, and though he frequently felt a little protective towards her he knew that she, of all at Frisks, needed no protection. All men were the same about her, but they were putty in her hands. Magnus might be a challenge to him, a greater challenge than ever Arvid would have been; but now, throwing off his depression, and thinking of the many weapons he had to hand, not least his daughter-in-law, he was excited by the test, relishing it. Magnus would be a worthy opponent, and he felt no lessening in his liking for him just because, with Hanna, he was proving himself to be a man like any other.

CHAPTER 5

When Hanna opened the door this time Magnus had himself well in hand, and he was relieved to find he felt nothing for her. She was pretty enough, but she had brushed her hair, put on a little make-up, changed into a top which overhung her smarter trousers, and the animal sexuality was gone. Her face, he saw, was very open and he liked the scatter of freckles and the harebell eyes, but the snub nose seemed too pert, the mouth too small, the chin too pointed, and as he deliberately piled up the criticisms he knew he was concentrating on her face because he utterly lacked the courage to look at any other part of her.

"D'you think you'll be able to remember me now?" asked Hanna smiling, and even as he felt the confusion of being caught out staring at her, he noticed the mouth was not small at all, the nose-tip wrinkled when she smiled and the chin was only slightly pointed. Averting his gaze he went in and took the chair to which she pointed.

"Coffee?" she asked, and he nodded, and while she went to fetch the coffee pot he said to her back, "You know I have to take a statement from everybody here."

"Ask anything you like," she answered, putting down the coffee on the table between them and fetching cups from the corner-cupboard, stretching up to reach the shelf. "I can answer while we're having coffee, and then I'll leave it to you to turn what I say into a statement. I'm no great shakes at writing; I find it hard enough to fill in forms." She sat down opposite him, pouring the dark brown liquid steadily into his cup. "Even Jon's schoolwork is almost beyond me now."

Magnus wanted to tell her about the evenings he used to spend reading with Angelica before he moved here, but knew he must concentrate on checking August's story.

"Were there some reindeer here in the winter?"

"Yes, we nearly always have them here, it brings in money, though Jon and I love them so much we'd happily have them here for nothing."

"Did you ever meet the herder?"

"Paulus? Yes, of course. He was new this year, nice little man, always polite and welcoming when I took Jon down there to see the reindeer. Taught him how to lasso them, even carved something for him from a bit of reindeer horn."

She leant towards him, filling up the cup he could not remember draining. Then she slid out of her chair, went into the next room and after a moment returned with a small carved reindeer.

"It's artistic, isn't it? I know you can buy these things in the shops, but this one's a bit special. What do you think?"

She crouched beside his chair, holding the reindeer out to him, and when he took it their fingers touched.

"Very fine," he said sincerely, then realised he was looking at her as he said it.

"I'm glad you like it," Hanna said warmly, taking it gently from his hands. Their faces were very close and Magnus felt his response to her at their first meeting had not completely vanished, but was being replaced by something deeper; and as if Hanna sensed his emotion she moved back to her seat.

"Did you see anything else he'd made?" he asked when she had settled herself. "Sami often make their own spoons, water dippers or belt knives."

"I'm sure he had a knife hanging from his belt, but I didn't really notice it. I'm not interested in knives, but Jon is, so I'm sure he saw it. You'll have to ask him."

She poured herself more coffee, and then she said, "You need to know whether Paulus was really here, don't you?"

"Everything has to be checked," admitted Magnus. "It's the way we work."

She got up again, and he noticed how easily she moved, so lithe and swift. She returned with a folder of photographs and flicked through them, finally handing him one. It showed Jon in a snowy clearing standing proudly beside a reindeer held by a short youngish man with a dark moustache. It must have been a particularly cold day, for both boy and man were well wrapped up, and no knife was visible.

"Is that Paulus?"

"Yes. You can keep it if it helps, I always get an extra set. You'll see the photo's dated, which might be useful."

She seemed entirely natural, wanting to help him, and with a word of thanks he tucked the photo into his pocket book. "When did Paulus go?"

"He stayed much too long, drove August mad, and I don't think he finally got rid of him until May."

"Was your father-in-law very angry?"

"Furious, and it made it awkward for Jon and me, because we'd got pretty friendly with Paulus and had to stop going to see him so often."

"What was he furious about?"

Hanna sighed. "Money, of course. What else would it be? I don't think he'd been paid on time, and he wouldn't let Paulus leave until he settled up, then blamed him because the reindeer started to damage the young trees. I'm glad I wasn't Paulus, we all duck for cover when August gets in a rage."

"Does he get violent, too?"

Hanna burst out laughing. "Violent? August? He growls like a bear and waves his paws, but he wouldn't hurt a fly."

"But he likes to get his own way?"

"Don't we all? I do, and I'm sure you do too." For the first time since they had sat down she studied his face, interestedly and without embarrassment. Magnus looked down, concentrating on writing in his notebook.

"Did you see Paulus hanging round here in the last few days?"

She shook her head with the unhesitating certainty he was coming to expect. "No. I know August saw him, he told us, but I didn't, and I can't think what he'd be doing here unless he was bringing some more money."

"Did he owe August more money?"

"No, I'm sure August wouldn't have let him leave unless he'd paid everything, he's very tight on money. But he may well have run up other debts while he was here."

"Had you ever seen the man who was stabbed?"

"No. August showed us the body, but he was a stranger, not from round here."

"And did you see or hear anything unusual yesterday evening, raised voices, a cry of pain?"

She shook her head again, and this time he allowed himself to notice how soft her hair was, how it glinted as it flickered about her face. He knew he had nothing else he needed to ask her, but he did not want to go. He sipped his coffee, making it last, then checked his notes and told her he would bring in the printed statement for her to sign, probably tomorrow. Hesitantly, draining his cup, he added, "August told me about your husband's death. It can't have been easy for you, being pregnant, I mean, and not long married. I'm very sorry."

He reddened awkwardly, realising it had sounded crass, but she lent forward and fleetingly touched his arm. "You're a nice man for a policeman. You care about people, and that's not common. But you needn't feel sorry for me. I didn't love Daniel, and he didn't love me. It was a marriage of convenience for us both."

Magnus stared at her, surprised and shocked. Then he stood up reluctantly and she followed him to the door. He wondered if he could kiss her, gently, comfortingly, before she opened the door, before anyone could see them. But while he was still screwing up his courage the door was open and August was in the corridor looking at them; so finally it was Hanna who did the kissing, a soft quick peck upon the cheek.

"That's for being so nice," she said, and he saw her wink at August before she closed the door on them.

"I'll take you over to Uncle Henning, Aunt Ingegerd and my cousin Elin." August said. "Better rub off the lipstick before you get there or Elin will get ideas, something she is prone to do on far less evidence than that. I suppose it's the isolation, but she enjoys imagining the worst."

Magnus felt a fool, but August clapped him on the shoulder and he smiled ruefully, rubbed his cheek, and recovered his good humour.

"I thought you wouldn't mind seeing them all together," explained August. "Uncle and Aunt are quite an age, and Elin, though not much younger than me, is still something of a madcap twenty year old. I shall be surprised if they can help you very much, but you'll have to discover that for yourself. I just thought having them together might save you time. Do you mind?"

"That's fine," answered Magnus, relieved because he had begun to worry he would not have time to prepare all the statements for tomorrow. "If any of them bring up anything important I can always arrange a subsequent private interview."

The little red-stained timber cottage was in better condition on the outside than the main house, and when Aunt Ingegerd opened the door and welcomed him he saw the interior was tidier too. His hostess, plump, white haired and dressed for a visitor, was just as neat and clean as her living room, and his heart sank as he saw the best china and knew he would have to drink more coffee.

"Be patient with Henning," she whispered as she shook his hand. She waited as he slipped his shoes off and left them on the porch, then ushered him proudly in. "He's eighty-six and rather hard of hearing, but he's far from the old fool some people take him for." He liked the way she spoke so fondly of him, then noticed she was peering out beyond him at the tall and eager woman who was hurrying towards them from the neighbouring cottage. "That's Elin," she said pursing her lips. "She and Henning don't get on."

She got him inside before Elin arrived, nudging him towards her husband who stood with his head outside the window, smoking a cigarette with the pleasure of someone who has got an extra one in before being found out.

"I'm not allowed to smoke in here, especially when busybody Elin is coming," he explained loudly, shaking hands without withdrawing his head, then sucking in one last gratifying mouthful before pinching the cigarette out and dropping it carefully among the camouflaging flowers. He was like an old cock, tough and stringy, with watery eyes which peered humorously at Magnus as he turned to face him and a few remaining tufts of white hair obstinately standing up on his sun-browned pate. He looked so like the Jämtland farmers Magnus had grown up among he felt immediately at ease, and was not surprised when Henning spoke about his stock.

"Have you seen the goats yet?" he roared, and, not waiting for a reply he obviously assumed he would not hear, he went on, "They're fine creatures, every one of them, and I make a nice little living selling the milk, cheese and yoghurt I get from them."

"I saw you, Henning, you were smoking out of the window," accused a sharp voice, and Magnus turned to see Elin cantering down on them, her narrow shapely face and glistening teeth giving the distinct impression that if restrained in any way or startled by an aggressive movement she might well bite. "It's a filthy habit, and it's time Ingegerd put her foot down."

"If you mean putting it down and squashing you, I couldn't agree more," countered Henning. "But we've got a policeman here now, and if you don't pipe down he'll probably arrest you for breaking the peace."

Elin sniffed, then introduced herself to Magnus. She was attractive in an oddly individual artistic way, wearing a smart dark red dress, and decorated on almost every visible part of her, ears, neck, arms, wrists, hands, even an ankle, with amber set in silver.

"Elin makes jewellery," said Ingegerd, as if she felt some explanation was necessary.

"She advertises it, too," scoffed Henning.

Elin ignored him. She seemed to have accepted the fact that nothing she wore would ever suit Frisks, and so she dressed to please herself." I've always had an artistic bent," she said to Magnus, "but it's scarcely appreciated in this god-forsaken backwater."

Ingegerd went to fetch the coffee, and when they all sat down Magnus was about to ask some questions when Elin forestalled him. "We are all gathered here," she began portentously, "so that we may tell this policeman all we know about the murder. Now I always keep my eyes open, so in my case that will be quite a lot, but I will allow others to speak first."

It was the beginning of a trying half-hour for Magnus, and at the end of it he'd learnt little more than he'd heard already. All agreed that Paulus had wintered his reindeer in the forest, had fallen out with August over money and had finally left sometime in May. Henning was the only one who remembered he'd had a knife, but his sight was not good enough to be able to say whether it might have been the murder weapon. None of them had seen Paulus again after May, nor had they seen or heard anything the previous night. As for the victim, none had seen him before nor did they have any idea at all of his identity.

"Haven't you questioned that Olof Petter yet?" suddenly interrupted Elin accusingly, as if she knew he hadn't and blamed him for it. "He's a vile man, horrible to that poor dear Gubbo and evil through and through." Her eyes were glistening with vindictiveness, but Magnus noticed the others seemed to be barely listening as though they'd heard it all before. Elin leant towards him, laying her hand along the side of her nose and dropping her voice. "I'm not blind," she hissed, "and I'm not too frightened to tell the truth. You mark my words, Olof Petter will have had a hand in it, and probably so will that tart August keeps in his house."

"Have you any substantiating evidence?"

"I don't need evidence," answered Elin loftily. "I know what I know, and nobody's going to tell me any differently."

Magnus retreated as soon as he decently could, hoping he had not upset Ingegerd by leaving some coffee in the bottom of his cup. Outside he breathed in deeply, walked until he was a short distance from the cottage and sat down on a fallen tree trunk and completed his notes. When he looked up a boy was watching him from the shadow of a tree, staring with fascination at his pistol. He was large for his age, well-built, with an intelligent face, tidy brown hair, alert eyes and a tantalising look of Hanna.

"You must be Jon," said Magnus.

"Have you ever shot anybody?" the boy blurted out, looking abashed as soon as he had spoken .

"Not yet," answered Magnus, "and I hope I never have to." The boy reminded him of his own son, Johan, who, though younger, had the same mix of eager curiosity and diffidence. For the first time he realised they shared the same name, though Hanna's son had the Norwegian derivation. "But I was wounded once when somebody shot at me, and it was horrible. Guns are dangerous things, as I'm sure you know."

"So are knives," Jon answered unexpectedly.

Magnus nodded, wondering whether here, in the open, in full view of the houses, he could ask what he needed to know, and deciding he'd risk it. "Paulus had a knife, didn't he? Did you see it?"

"Yes," said Jon, coming forward slowly. "I asked him and he showed it to me. He said he'd made it himself. It was lovely, and now Grandpa's going to show me how to make one."

"Your Grandpa told me he'd allowed you see the body. Did you look at the knife?"

"Yes," answered Jon, fixing his eyes on Magnus and looking very serious.

"Was it like the one Paulus had?"

Jon hung his head, and then, reluctantly, he said, "Yes, it was a bit like it, but I'm sure it wasn't his."

"You liked Paulus?"

"Very much. I miss him now he's gone."

"Did you see him yesterday?"

Jon looked puzzled. "He's back in Lapland. He took his reindeer there, and he won't be here again until the winter."

Hanna's voice called "Jon,", and he turned towards the sound, uncertain what to do.

"You've been very helpful," Magnus said. He saw Jon was rubbing at a reddened graze around one ankle, and added,

"You'd better get your mother to put something on that, it looks nasty."

"OK," said Jon. "You'll be here for a bit longer, won't you?"

Magnus nodded. "I expect I'll be around for a day or so yet."

"Will you show me your gun like Paulus showed me his knife."

Magnus laughed. "We have a rule you mustn't take your pistol out of its holster unless you're going to use it. But I could show you my baton."

"Now?"

"Your mother wants you, you'd better go."

"She won't mind if I'm another minute or two, she knows I'm with you."

Magnus drew his baton, flicked it out to full extension, and demonstrated a few attacking and defensive movements.

"As soon as Mum's finished with me, I'm going to cut a stick and have it as my baton, and I'll practise what you've shown me."

He ran off towards the main house, leaving Magnus wondering whether Hanna had sent the boy to him so that he could question him.

CHAPTER 6

From his window August watched Magnus with Jon, and was relieved they seemed to get on well together. He was sure Magnus, despite his scruples, would take the opportunity to ask some questions, and though a little afraid Jon might become upset, there was no sign of that. He continued to watch until Magnus went into Olof Petter's house, and then he threw himself contentedly into his favourite armchair. The finding of the body and the coming of the policeman gave them all time off from work, and now he was beginning to relax he felt almost in a holiday mood. He had spoken briefly to Hanna, and nothing she said disturbed him. It was obvious to him she liked Magnus and that was all to the good. He'd been sure the way forward was to maintain the friendly relations normal for bystanders with nothing to hide, and he felt vindicated.

But as he lay back in his chair and let his thoughts wander at will, he found the past intruded more than the present; and disturbingly it had more reality and a greater capacity to upset him. It was, he supposed, a sign he was getting old; but since Magnus had asked him about Daniel he was beginning to brood about him again, and eight years after his death he was weighing anew not just Daniel's failings, but the growing certainty that he himself had been at fault.

Could he have decided, deep down, that Daniel must bear the guilt of his Amanda's death? If so, it had been an unconscious decision, for he always told himself she had given her life to provide him with a son. At first, it was true, he felt greater grief for her loss than joy in Daniel's arrival; but gradually it was the awakening love for his son which enabled him to accept her death. He'd wanted a son so much, and at first the fact of having one was sufficient. Amanda's parents died several years before her own death, and early on he relished the thought that he would be the only one now to bring him up. But slowly, insidiously, he found himself deciding the sort of son he expected Daniel to be, and as the boy grew he never equalled the image of him in his mind. Looking back on it he could see that had Amanda lived so many of the misunderstandings might have been avoided; they would have discussed the boy, and talking to his wife would have provided the balance his own internal dialogue lacked. Amanda, he was sure, would have seen a different Daniel, and in the normal to and fro of parental talk they would have reached some middle point where each, perhaps, would have understood him better. But as a lone and often lonely parent he clung obstinately to the mental image against which, increasingly, he judged the boy; and in time he came to blame him for that difference. The result was that neither, despite their mutual need for love, could understand the other. Daniel, he remembered, always paused whenever August told him what to do, and at first it seemed dumb insolence and he reacted sharply. But gradually the probable cause of such a time-lag dawned on him. Daniel did not seem able to grasp immediately what he was being told to do, nor fathom why he should be told to do it. It was as if the two of them lived on slightly different planes, thought in dissimilar ways, had different sets of values. The pause was simply the time required to translate something so odd it was hard for Daniel to grasp at once; and, having grasped it, to adjust his mind to answer yes, as finally he always did, agreeing to an action which was not, for him, entirely natural.

As Daniel grew August tried to discuss the business with him, the fishing, farming and the forestry, making the point repeatedly that this was what he would inherit and must therefore thoroughly understand. But the perplexity was always there in Daniel's eyes, as if he did not see his future in any of these things, and probably not at Frisks at all. Angrily August would stress the longstanding family connection with the land and sea, how Daniel's great-grandfather, grandfather and now his father had struggled to build it and maintain it. But though Daniel did his best to force an interest which would please him, August saw the blankness in the eyes, as though he heard but could not relate to such obvious ideas. Nor was he ever as physically active as August always had been. He liked to read, to dream, to loll about, utterly content to be alone. And yet, and August knew it now, he tried so hard to be the son August wanted. He worked beside his father, went out with the boat, cut the timber, planted seedlings, helped Henning with the goats. But he would not do everything required of him, and occasionally he drew a line.

As a boy he showed scant interest in the autumn elk hunt so eagerly awaited by almost every male in the area who was strong enough to lift a rifle. In the months before the season commenced men talked about it wistfully, as though they dared not quite believe it would eventually arrive; and when it was over they reminisced about it endlessly, recalling every kill as they gradually devoured the elk meat from the deepfreeze. But once the hunting started it became their life, and all else was set aside for it. Daniel's indifference always galled August, and when he was fifteen he insisted he take part. He took him to the local range where all had to pass a test of accuracy, and to his surprised delight Daniel showed a natural aptitude, scoring well. On the way home he explained the need to keep a balance between a healthy elk stock and the protection of the forests, where they destroyed so many trees by browsing on the young and tender growth. He told him about the annual aerial survey on which was based the number to be culled each year, bulls relative to cows, and so the number of licences issued for each area. They went out together to repair and camouflage the hides, paid special attention to the exercising of the dogs to ensure they were in peak condition, and by the first day's hunting, when they made a very early start, August believed Daniel was so caught up in the bustle and excitement of the final preparations he was certain to enjoy himself. Alcohol was forbidden by the authorities, but August packed a hip flask anyway, explaining to Daniel it was to keep the cold out; and most of the others in the syndicate of seven, all from the neighbourhood, did the same. Each of them had kept an eye on the elk throughout the year, noting their customary paths and building the hides beside them, rough wooden seats raised well above the ground on stilt-like legs, shrouded now in fresh cut branches. August's two elk hounds, an experienced bitch and a younger dog who was learning from her, were frantic to be off, but they were held firmly on the leash until everyone was in place. All were carrying two-way radios so they could keep in touch, and once the others had gone off to different stations in the forest August climbed up into the hide and wedged Daniel in beside him. It was five-thirty in the morning, the breeze was cold and he took a nip from his flask, warning Daniel to stay very still when he saw he was about to shoot. Then he spoke into the radio and once he had assured himself that everything was ready, he gave the order for the dogs to be released.

In his mind's eye he watched them searching out the elk, positioning themselves to drive them toward the guns but never getting too close. A full-grown bull elk weighed a tonne and could use his massive antlers with deadly effect, while cows had been known to kill a wolf with a single kick. But unless they turned at bay they did not usually confront the dogs, preferring to move effortlessly and at surprising speed over the bogs and through the bilberry bushes until they reached their usual paths. Each dog knew its job, keeping the elk moving until its master, sighting the rifle through the screen of branches, brought it down, mostly with a single shot.

August's first kill was a cow, but when he ejected the spent cartridge, closed the bolt and aimed at the calf which had been running with her, Daniel struck his arm, protesting.

"Don't be such a bloody jackass," hissed August. "It can't live without its mother, it has to be shot, that's the rule."

He squeezed the trigger, but he had lost his concentration and had to fire a second time into the bleating, struggling little body.

"Now look what you made me do," he shouted furiously, feeling bad about the fumbled kill but too proud to admit it. But after an interval, feeling remorseful and seeing a fine bull elk approaching in the distance, he handed the rifle to Daniel as a conciliatory gesture.

"Aim carefully," he said. "Those antlers will be a fine first trophy for you, we'll mount them in the living room."

Daniel did not reply, but took his time, his body very still, his trigger finger relaxed, his breathing calm. And then he fired, the bullet splintering a rotten stump just to one side of the bull; and with a swerve and surge of speed it was gone.

"You did that on purpose!" bellowed August, snatching back the rifle and cuffing him. "Get down from here and wait below. There'll be a job for you when the shooting's over, and you'll do it until you drop."

August's anger increased as no more elk appeared though he could hear from the distant shots that others in the syndicate were being more successful. By the time the day's quota was filled he was raging inside, and as soon as he clambered down he opened up the carcases in sullen silence, cleaned them out, skinned them, then took his axe and hacked them into several pieces.

"That's the only job you're fit to do," he said to Daniel, pointing to the bloody dripping gobbets. "Carry them to the truck, you'll only manage one at a time. And when you've done all that, perhaps you won't be quite so squeamish any longer."

The truck was parked half a kilometre away, and by the time Daniel returned for the fifth piece his shirt was soaked in gore, his hair was streaked with it, his jeans were partly red, and even his sweat was bloody. August was calmer now, and ashamed, knowing he'd been waiting for Daniel to beg; so he told him gruffly to rest himself, and he'd carry what was left.

"I'll finish my job," Daniel answered steadily, though he was swaying with exhaustion and almost choking with disgust. "But don't ever ask me to hunt again, because I won't do it." And though August blustered, and said he would damned well do what he was told, he sensed a will as steely as his own and never put it to the test.

As Daniel became a man, and increasingly the work was shared between them, it seemed to August the emotional gap between them widened even more. Sex was the new area of incomprehension, with August boasting he'd been a randy little sod from fourteen onwards in the hope of encouraging Daniel to show a little interest. But, as in so much else, he wouldn't be hurried, and was embarrassed whenever August pointed out a likely girl, or offered to invite some family over who happened to have an eligible daughter. It was only the arrival of Hanna at the settlement which seemed finally to spur him into action.

August stood up and went outside. He didn't want to think about the body of his son washed up on the shore, the boat stuck fast upon a rock. He realised now the presence of the policeman would be no holiday, it would drive him mad if too extended. Work stopped him thinking, kept his memories beneath the surface of his mind; enforced inactivity turned him in upon himself where he did not like to be. He strode down to the water's edge, and all the way along the headland until he reached the point where nothing was before him except the Baltic. Frisks had always harvested the sea, but on that day, eight years before, he had garnered a corpse instead of fish. He struggled within himself, and slowly banished all he did not wish to think about again, forcing it down like herrings in a keg and fixing the lid down tightly. He mustn't let it worry him so much, he told himself. It would be over soon.

CHAPTER 7

"And last of all the policeman comes to us," crowed Olof Petter as Magnus walked up to the open door. He must have been in his thirties, perhaps the same age as Magnus, but with his short and powerful body, bulging stomach and thick hairy legs protruding from long, baggy, multi-pocketed shorts which fell beneath his knees, he looked physically the elder, an impression strengthened by the black socks pulled half-way up his calves and the solidly placed parted feet, thrust into open-toed sandals, emphasising the belligerence of his stance. But above the checked shirt the face showed none of the calm assurance so settled into Magnus' features; instead there was the sneering defiance of an uncertain adolescent. It was a very round face, stubbled, and the thick black hair above was gelled and twisted into spikes; the dark eyes were small and mean, conveying to Magnus an intimation of violence which he took seriously.

"We're just the hired hands, aren't we, Gubbo? We're not rich, or pretty, we can't lay out the finest china and give him coffee, so he leaves us to wait until the end."

Another figure appeared beside him, some ten years older, bigger, just as strong, with a bushy reddish beard and unkempt locks, bare footed, dirty and, as Magnus quickly noticed, smelling strongly of stale sweat. He wore no shirt or vest beneath the old brown leather waistcoat which outdid even Olof Petter's shorts in the number of bulging pockets. But whereas the younger man's face looked unfeeling, his was amiable beneath a small flat cap of pink and blue flowered material which seemed to mark him as a natural fool. He laughed, leaning on Olof Petter and peering at Magnus; and when Olof Petter gave him an apparently playful punch he laughed again as if he was delighted at the attention he was receiving, and rubbed his wrist which bore a red weal, reminding Magnus of the mark he had seen on Jon.

"Well, Mr Policeman," taunted Olof Petter, bowing ironically as he ushered Magnus in, "how can we help you, for we really want to help, don't we, Gubbo?" And when Gubbo laughed again, nodding enthusiastically, Olof Petter said to Magnus, "Don't mind him, he's an idiot, but I look after him."

"I need statements from you both," explained Magnus, looking round the grubby, untidy room.

"You can start with Gubbo then," said Olof Petter, and he made a silly face so that Gubbo guffawed. "Right, that's the only statement you'll get from him," he went on briskly, "so now you'd better take mine."

"I'd like to speak to him myself," said Magnus patiently. He fetched a chair from the table and invited Gubbo to sit. Gubbo looked uneasily at Olof Petter, but when he saw no sign of disapproval he sat down gingerly on the edge, his knees together and his hands in his lap.

Magnus sat down opposite him and took out his notebook and pen. "What's your full name?"

Gubbo looked helplessly at Olof Petter who raised his hand to him and shouted, "What are you called, you loony?"

Magnus stiffened, trying to control his anger but ready to intervene. Gubbo seemed to be becoming increasingly anxious, and suddenly Olof Petter, with surprising tenderness, gave him a hug and told him to go and look at the magazines in his room.

"It's no good," he said to Magnus when they were alone. "Something's wrong in his head, he can't remember anything. He was in an accident before I knew him, and he hasn't spoken since. I call him Gubbo because that's the place I met him six years ago."

"What sort of accident?"

"No idea."

"What was he doing when you met him?"

"Pissing."

"What sort of work?"

"No sort of work. He can't work on his own, that's why he needs me."

"What sort of work were you doing?"

"No sort of work, just like Gubbo. I can't work on my own because I don't see any point in it. That's why I need him."

"He gives you a reason to work?"

Olof Petter glared at him. "I don't expect you to understand, but to look after him I need to work, and because I work, he does."

"Do you know what work he did before?"

"I don't *know* anything, but I'm pretty sure he must've been a fisherman. He knows all about boats, that's why we do the fishing here."

"You take the boat out?"

Olof Petter clicked his tongue at him. "What are you thinking about? *We* can't be trusted to get it round the island, *we're* too stupid for that, only old Shithead can manage that." He spat his disgust on the floor, then rubbed it in with his shoe. "It makes me so mad. I can handle any boat, in any circumstances, and given the chance I'd get it over the end of that rock without scraping it half as badly as he does. But oh no, old Shithead knows best, he doesn't trust me, and like everybody else around here we hired hands have to bend our heads and kiss his arse."

"Old Shithead being Mr Frisk?"

"*Mister* Frisk! My, what a formal way to address a brothel creep."

"Meaning?"

"Meaning, dear *Mister* Policeman, that *Mister* high and mighty Frisk's no better than he ought to be. Soon as his wife was dead he started going to some posh brothel down in Stockholm, regular as clockwork. But when that little fiend Jon was born, of course he stopped, came all over pious, and expected everybody else on Frisks to be holy-holy too."

"How long have you been here?"

"'Bout five years, I suppose. Don't really know why I stay, but it's good work for Gubbo and it keeps him out of the hands of those do-gooders who'd like to try more operations on him so he'll remember what seems to terrify him, the accident and that, and then, *maybe,* he'll speak again. But he's happy as he is, so I protect him from them."

"If you've only been here five years, how do you know what your employer was up to before Jon was born?"

Olof Petter's face adopted an expression of self-satisfied cunning. "I know everything about this place. I'm not much of a sleeper, so I creep about and listen at doors and windows, poking and prying until I winkle out everybody's secrets. I could tell you things about all the people here that'd make your ears twitch."

He paused, waiting for Magnus to ask, but he did not seem put out when Magnus only asked him if he liked secrets.

"I love them," he said with obvious relish. "Knowing about people, knowing they don't know I know, watching them begin to suspect that maybe I do know something, seeing it gnaw away at them, it gives me a real buzz, almost takes the place of sex. And there's not much of that round here for the likes of me, though if I was the telling kind I could say things about that bitch Elin, intimate things, as'd make your blood beat faster. She claims she hates me, and she probably does, but there's one part of me she doesn't hate at all." He thrust his groin forward obscenely and licked his lips.

"If you see so much when you creep about, tell me what you saw last night."

Olof Petter looked sullen. "I didn't go out yesterday evening."

"Why not?"

"Headache."

"Did you hear anything?"

"No."

"Do you know Paulus?"

"Course I do. We used to drink together to keep the cold out."

"Did you see him in the last few days?"

"Fat chance, he's back in Lapland."

"Did you recognise the knife in the murdered man's back?"

"I don't understand."

"Was it like the one Paulus had?"

Olof Petter stared at him in astonishment. "For Christ's sake, you're not trying to pin the killing on that poor little sod, are you? Old Shithead gave him enough grief threatening to shoot his reindeer or hand him over to the police if he didn't pay up and get out, but stitching him up for murder's going way too far."

"Please answer the question. It'll form part of your statement, so think carefully about your answer."

Olof Petter appeared flustered. "I don't know, all those Lapp knives look the same to me. But Paulus wouldn't kill anybody, and anybody who suggests he did will have me to answer to." It was a poor attempt at bravado, but Magnus felt he was genuinely upset. "Who put that idea into your mind?" Olof Petter went on angrily. "Was it that blonde tart, who's no better than she should be? Or old Henning, who's a lot too close to his goats, if you take my meaning? Or dear old Ingegerd who tipples away when she think no one's watching? No, it was probably old Shithead himself, or maybe that darling boy with angel's wings and cloven hooves."

"You don't like Jon?"

"I don't like anybody, I don't even like myself. But that boy sees too much, and I enjoy spying, not being bloody spied upon. So I spit at him every time I see him."

"I'm surprised Mr Frisk keeps you here if you treat his grandson like that."

"He daren't get rid of me. Gubbo and me, we do the fishing, and he needs the money. He won't get anybody else to work for him in this god-forsaken hole. Besides..." and he dropped his voice to a stage whisper, "...I know things about him."

"What sort of things?"

"That'd be telling, and once I'd told I'd have less power. And you haven't arrested me, so I don't have to say a thing."

Magnus looked at him sharply. "You've had dealings with the police before, haven't you?"

"Course I have, they were always picking on me. But I'm careful now, 'cause I've got Gubbo to look after. He can be a naughty boy, can Gubbo, but I sort him out right enough."

"By calling him a loony, as you did earlier?" asked Magnus. "Or is that mark on his wrist the result of you sorting him out?"

Olof Petter squawked with delight. "It is, it is," he said excitedly. "I tie him to a tree by one wrist, then put his food down in front of him just out of his reach. And Gubbo loves his food, he's desperate for it, and you should see him yank against the rope, and beg and cry, but I won't push the food closer until he's agreed he's sorry and that he'll be a good boy again. Oh, you really should see it, it works a treat, and you can have the idea for free to use it on your prisoners. They'll soon talk then."

Magnus stood up, allowing his feeling of distaste to take him over. "How can you be certain Gubbo saw nothing last night?"

"He was here with me, we were playing charades. He likes that, and he's very good at it."

"How can he guess if he can't speak?"

Olof Petter glanced at him sardonically. "He writes it."

Magnus felt a fool. "He can read and write?"

Olof Petter nodded, and Magnus could tell that despite his careful lack of expression he was laughing at him. "He's as good at it as I am. I hope you didn't think he was an idiot."

"So he could have written a statement? Why didn't you tell me that?" Although he tried to control it, the exasperation showed in Magnus' voice and he knew it would please Olof Petter even more.

"You didn't ask," he replied, opening his eyes wide in innocent perplexity. "But I tell you what I'll do. You bring me a list of questions and I'll get him to write the answers, then sign it Gubbo. He wouldn't do it for anybody else, he'd get in a state, probably tear the paper up, but I know how to coax him, I'm the only one who can. But the answers'll be the same as I told you 'cause he's always with me, gets upset if I'm away from him. That's why I wait till he's asleep before I creep around outside."

"I can always bring a social worker with me, then you won't be needed. It might be an opportunity to get Gubbo's needs properly assessed as well."

Magnus had spoken out of irritation, and he was unprepared for Olof Petter's extreme reaction.

"I'd kill anyone who tried to take him from me," he hissed, stepping towards Magnus so threateningly that he tensed himself for any necessary defence. "Gubbo's suffered enough from experts, and now he's found me he's happy at last. Whatever it looks like to you, I help him working on the boat, which he enjoys, and keep him away from hospitals which terrify him. Don't you dare interfere with that."

Magnus stepped cautiously away from him to give Olof Petter the chance to calm himself. "You really do care about him, don't you?" he said in some perplexity.

Olof Petter nodded, unable to speak but looking surlily ashamed of his outburst.

"I'll think about giving you the questions, and letting you get the answers from him," conceded Magnus, "but only on condition you consider very carefully the way you treat him. It may be that you do look after him in your own way, but if I have cause to believe you're abusing him in any way I'll inform the authorities and they'll act as they think fit. And how does he know he's terrified of hospitals if he can't remember anything?"

"It's what happened before the accident he can't remember. He remembers everything that's happened since, that's why he'll be able to write down answers to your questions if I ask him nicely. He's never at his best with people in authority like you."

Magnus turned away, walking back towards his car, and as he went he heard the laughter, Gubbo and Olof Petter enjoying a joke at his expense. He felt depressed, knowing he'd not handled things as well as he should have done, and the day's work was far from over. He'd be at it long into the night preparing all the statements, and he didn't feel at this stage he needed anything more from Gubbo, though he accepted that failing to produce the questions and hand them to Olof Petter would be something of a defeat for him. He should never have got himself into such a ridiculous position, and it irritated him. Olof Petter's bitterness had given him potentially useful information, and he should have listened and learnt, and not reacted. He looked about, wishing he could see Hanna, but nobody seemed to be around. Though he'd found out much about the little community, he'd discovered very little about the murder. He knew the dissatisfaction with himself stemmed principally from the guilty awareness that he'd failed to keep the professional distance from Hanna he had achieved with all the others. It was the first time he'd been so very much in charge, and though he'd always longed for the responsibility he was discovering the dangers of having no one else close at hand to supervise him. In the Östersund force he'd been part of a team, and though often forced to work alone because of the vast area they had to cover he'd always remained aware of the reins ready to hold him in check if he went wrong. But here Amrén had loosened them to such an extent he was free to make mistakes unless he stopped himself – and he was finding that harder than he'd expected. He would have to compose the statements very carefully, rigidly excluding from Hanna's anything which might make it read more favourably than her actual words allowed. Nor must he leave her out when he asked Amrén to run a number of confidential checks.

DAY 2

CHAPTER 8

Doctor Burman rang him early to confirm death had been caused by a single stab wound occurring between midnight and the very early hours of the day he was found.

"It looks as though he was knifed while he was stooping, so one can presume he was taken completely by surprise. I've bagged up the clothes and shoes, so they can be delivered to Hillevi Zander if that's what you want. Have you spoken to her yet?"

"No," said Magnus. "Maybe I should collect the stuff from you and drive up to see her. That'll give me an opportunity to talk to her face to face."

"Brave man," commented Burman with a laugh. "But you're quite right, if you can get her interested she'll do the job. The autopsy didn't tell me much, but the teeth had been expensively treated, and he had several small scars, quite old, knife cuts by the look of them."

"Did that bring any special sort of man to your mind, given the quality of the clothes and shoes?"

"Rich, international, but a bit of a thug in his youth."

"You still don't think he's Swedish?"

"I'm sure he isn't. Any reports of missing persons who might fit his description?"

"I haven't been in touch with Inspector Amrén yet, I'll ring him next. According to their statements nobody at Frisks seem to have seen him before, so let's hope somebody docs miss him and then alerts us."

"I'd be a bit cautious about those statements. Have you talked to anybody outside Frisks?"

"Not yet."

"Well, try Scholander who runs the *surströmming* factory, I know him, he's a sound man, won't mislead you, and as he's dealt with Frisks for years he'll know quite a lot about the family."

"You obviously think the people at Frisks might deliberately mislead me." Magnus was sure there was no change in his voice, though he did feel a twinge of resentment at Burman's certainty.

"I'm suggesting nothing," replied Burman stiffly, "but I cannot be unaware of rumours. I was simply trying to be helpful."

He rang off abruptly and Magnus knew he had needlessly annoyed someone he ought to have kept firmly on his side. He considered ringing back and apologising, but didn't know what to say in his own excuse. Instead he rang Amrén.

"Nothing from Missing Persons, but I'm circulating those photos you took of the body to other forces, and you can show them around in your area, so something's bound to come up sooner or later. Did Axel find anything? And what about the statements?"

Magnus briefed him, and then asked tentatively if confidential checks could be run on all those at Frisks.

"That's a matter for the prosecutor, but I'm sure he won't agree to a blanket search. Do you really believe the answer's there?"

"It's no more than a feeling, but I'm sure I'm not being told the whole truth."

"Are there any you feel are especially in the frame?"

"Olof Petter has a violent streak and admitted he'd been involved with the police, though not recently. August Frisk's the sort of man who feels he's above the law, and he's certainly hiding something, though it may be nothing to do with the killing."

"Anyone else?"

"Gubbo's got me curious. I fell for a scene that on reflection was too much like something out of a Steinbeck novel, and now I'm wondering whether he's as empty-headed as he and Olof-Petter wanted me to believe. I'd be interested to know what sort of accident he was involved in, what's actually wrong with him, and particularly how much his brain was affected, if at all. Olof-Petter said he met him in a place called Gubbo six years ago, and the only Gubbo I know is in Dalarna, near Ludvika, not near the sea at all."

"There's another place of that name in Halland, which sounds more likely. As for digging into medical records, they're highly confidential and Vessberg won't allow that; and with only a nickname we wouldn't get far anyway. But you could ask August about his real name, and anything he knows about the accident, and meanwhile I'll have a chat to a colleague in Halmstad who might remember the accident. Is that all?"

Magnus swallowed. "Hanna Frisk, the daughter-in-law. It's a long shot, but I've picked up things about her past and she might have needed to close someone's mouth to prevent the truth coming out. I know this is all largely supposition, but I'm struggling, really out of my depth at the moment, and I desperately need any clue I can get."

"All right, I'm not promising anything, you know this sort of check is all tied up with civil liberties, and that makes all prosecutors nervous, but I'll do what I can."

Magnus had not had very much sleep, and he was increasingly unhappy with himself. But he gathered up the statements he'd laboriously put together and took them across to Frisks, becoming tense as he knocked on the door of the main house. But it was August who opened it. He signed his statement, scarcely glancing at it, and of the others it was only Elin who checked every word. He gave Olof Petter a brief list of questions which was returned to him shortly afterwards with some scrawled answers, all matching Olof Petter's statement. Hanna and Jon, according to August, were out shopping, so Magnus said he'd come another time to get her signature. August offered to pass the statement on to her when she got back and bring it over to him, but Magnus quickly pointed out that each statement was confidential and so he was required to deal on a person to person basis.

"I saw you talking to Jon," said August. "Did he make a statement too?"

"It wasn't an official conversation, just a chat which he initiated, so it doesn't need recording. But I did want to ask you about Gubbo. You're his employer, and I'd like to know some details, especially his real name. I'm assuming you do keep records?"

August gave him a tight smile. "You know damned well I don't keep employment records. He and Olof Petter help out with the fishing, and I give them somewhere to live and pay some of their expenses."

Magnus sighed. "Black labour, undeclared earnings, you really will be in trouble."

August shrugged. "I doubt it. I've got an ace up my sleeve if any nosy taxman comes round, but I'm not going to tell you what it is. As for Gubbo's real name, I'm afraid I've no idea. I believe he was in a boat accident, engine exploded or something like that. He drifted in here some years ago with Olof Petter who seems to have appointed himself his carer."

"Pretty unorthodox for a carer."

"Frisks has always been open to the needy, and whatever you may think of Olof Petter, he's nearly as needy as Gubbo."

"But more dangerous?"

August considered this. "Probably. But in certain special circumstances most people are dangerous."

"Has he got a police record?"

"That's a matter for you. I know you'll be running us all through the police computer, whatever human rights you infringe. Interesting, really, when you consider it; you criticise me for breaking society's rules, but you lot do it too."

Magnus saw Henning beckoning excitedly and took the opportunity to walk away without having to acknowledge August's thrust.

"Come and see the goats," shouted Henning, and Magnus didn't have the heart to disappoint him, though he pointed out it would have to be a quick visit on this occasion. They climbed up through the trees behind the house, moving gradually away from the sea, and eventually coming out into a large clearing with a barn, a hay store, a tool shed and a new milking parlour with a cheese and yoghurt preparation annexe. Ingegerd was busy there, and smiled a greeting, and he saw that Elin was helping too.

"I should be making my jewellery," she said grumpily, "but Ingegerd needs my help more and more now she's getting old."

Outside, the goats were contentedly cropping the grass and Magnus felt he was back on his father's Jämtland farm. He hadn't come across this particular breed before; they were smaller, with pale pink nostrils, short alert ears, and the snowy white hair was less coarse than usual. At first he was disappointed that all the wildness seemed to have been bred out of them, making them little more than pets; but when he stared into the yellow eyes he was relieved to see some vestiges of ancient freedom, a retained pride which kept them from servility, as though the present partnership was freely entered into, and might yet be broken if the conditions were not maintained. An hour passed in earnest talk with Henning, discussion of comparative breeds, haymaking techniques and the relative merits of different winter feeds. When Magnus finally said he had to go, Henning insisted on accompanying him, taking the opportunity to light a cigarette. He led him down a slightly different way, passing a neat little graveyard where he buried the goats which had died. Each grave bore a wooden cross carved with the goat's name, and Magnus noticed that one of the graves was very fresh.

"Bad luck losing one in the summer," he commented. "Lynx don't usually come so close to farms until snow's on the ground and they're desperate with hunger, but I suppose it might have been a bear. Or was it some sickness?"

To his embarrassment Henning's eyes filled with tears. "It was Lina, my best goat," he said plaintively. "It was so unfair, there was no need for it, no need at all." He hurried on down the path, blowing his nose loudly, and by the time Magnus caught up with him they were not far from his car.

"I'll leave you here," Henning said. He reached out suddenly and gripped Magnus by the arm. "You know farms, you're a countryman like us. So you must see we have to fight for survival even if we don't like it." He was looking pleadingly at Magnus, willing him to understand. "It's worth it, you do think so, don't you? And you'll do all you can to help?"

Magnus, unsure what was expected of him, told him he thought farms like his should always be part of the Swedish countryside, and thanked him for letting him see it. He'd forgotten to raise his voice and wondered if the old man heard him, for he shook his head philosophically and set off up the slope again. Magnus hurried to his car and went to pick up the bundles from Doctor Burman. But it was Mrs Burman who handed them to him, saying her husband was visiting a neighbour, and so Magnus had no opportunity to make his apology. Then he drove out of the High Coast across the new 1,800 metre bridge which had opened up the previously isolated area to tourism. He admired the views along the wide river below him but obstinately clung to his belief that the billion kronor cost would have been better used improving police resources. Swinging right he headed for Kramfors, wrinkling his nose as the wind brought him the faint stench from the distant Väja wood pulp factory, and finally pulling up in front of a hideous modern house behind Kramfors station. For reasons which seemed to have nothing to do with artistic merit, the architect had designed a concrete box with matching concrete tiles and all of it had attracted layers of grime. To offset the pervading dirty grey somebody, presumably the occupant, had painted the front door shocking pink, which succeeded in drawing even more attention to the soiled aspect of the house. Straightening his uniform, Magnus pressed the bell but didn't hear it ring, and so shortly afterwards he gave a policeman's authoritative rap upon the door.

It opened so quickly he realised the infuriated elderly Barbie doll who now confronted him had been standing right behind it.

"Fuck off," she bellowed. She was a formidable size, reminding him of a padded ice hockey player, though no ice hockey player he'd ever known would have been seen alive or dead in such a freakish frilly pink outfit. It was as if she'd taken a conscious decision to match her house, but she'd have been unattractive in any circumstances, and the little-girl clothes and bizarre make-up rendered her grotesque. Yet despite the unwiped nose, the chewing gum peeping from between the rubbery lips, there was such a sharp astuteness in the green eyes that Magnus guessed she was deliberately caricaturing herself and her house. He found that brave and amusing, and he smiled at her.

The door slammed explosively in his face, and when it opened again to his insistent knock he saw the kitchen waste bucket in her hand.

"You think I'm funny, do you?" she snarled, and this time he caught the whisky smell. "Well, now you can learn to mind your manners." The bucket swung back ready for a forward sweep straight into his face, but Magnus did not budge.

"I was laughing at the cleverness of the pink door," he explained swiftly. "You've made architecture imitate life."

The bucket remained poised, but it did not swing forward. "Explain that," she said interestedly.

"In the ugliness of life there is always a bright spot?"

"Utter tosh," she said briskly, "but not bad for a policeman. Who are you, and what do you want?"

He saw she was balding, her legs were painfully swollen, and he thought how merciless age could be. "Magnus Trygg, on temporary duty in the High Coast, and I need your help."

She peered closely at him, the chewing gum protruding aggressively. "Why are you that colour?"

"I'm half Thai."

"Mother or father?"

"Mother."

She considered him as if he were an interesting specimen. "A Thai and Swedish mix, I've not seen it before. Why do you need my help?"

"A man's been murdered, stabbed. He may not be Swedish, nobody seems to know who he is, and I've brought his clothes and shoes along in case you can find something."

"Who told you about me?"

"Inspector Amrén, Sundsvall police."

"He's all right, used me in an odd reindeer dribble case. Now if you'd said Axel Burman, you'd have got my rubbish all over you. You'd better come in."

He followed her into the dingy interior which smelled of cat. There were dirty plates and glasses all over the table as if she only used the dish washer when nothing clean was left. She swept the crockery up to one corner and told him to put the bags on the cleared space. Praying she was not going to open them there and contaminate any evidence, he sat down on the chair she indicated and watched her settle her bulk into a rocking chair opposite him. The pink dress rode up one bare thigh and as soon as she saw his glance she shook an admonitory finger at him.

"Stop peeking, you naughty boy. I know what your sort wants, but you won't get it that easily, not at least until I know you better." She cackled at his embarrassment, then suddenly became businesslike. "Tell me the facts. Try to be brief, but rigidly accurate, no generalisations at all. If you don't know something, say so. And you can call me Hillevi."

She listened to him in silence, seeming totally absorbed. When he'd finished she sat for a while in thought, her eyes closed. He watched her, trying to imagine what it must be like to be born so ugly, especially for a girl, visualising the torment at school and the rejections of the teen-age years.

"What are you thinking about?" Hillevi shot at him, her strange and rather wonderful green eyes fixed on him.

"About you," he answered honestly.

"And wondering what my story is, and was I always like this, and how did I end up here? Well, you'll just have to wonder because I don't discuss myself." She held out a hand glittering with rings. "Pull me out of the dammed chair and follow me with those bags."

It took some strength to get her out, and he thought of the struggle it must be when she was on her own. She led the way through the house, and to his astonishment she opened the door to an immaculate laboratory built on at the back.

"Put the bags down by the door. I don't want you to go in because I try to keep it as sterile as possible and heaven knows what you're carrying on that uniform." She chortled at his surprised look. "There's more to me than meets the eye, which is pretty lucky really. And this is where I work if I'm sufficiently interested, and as I find your case intriguing I'll see what I can find. Don't flatter yourself I'm doing it just because you're a sexy young buck, though of course that does make it nicer for me; and whatever you may be thinking about the whisky I haven't lost any of my skill. Now go away. I need a shower, some black coffee and complete peace and quiet when I'm working, and a young Thai mooning over me is a distraction. Come and see me the same time tomorrow and I may have something for you."

On the way back Magnus stopped at a kiosk for a grilled hot dog with mustard and ketchup, and thinking of Hillevi he ordered a black coffee too. He wasn't at all sure what to make of her, and he could understand Burman's violent reaction when he'd mentioned her name. But, however odd she might be, he felt more confident about the case now she was prepared to help him.

CHAPTER 9

"I've found out a few things for you," said Amrén, his voice on the phone sounding quietly satisfied. "Nothing on August Frisk, but Olof Petter has quite a record, mostly petty but there's some drug dealing and one bodily harm."

"Recent?"

"The last one was seven years ago."

"And he's been looking after Gubbo for six years, so maybe his claim to be a reformed character is correct."

"Maybe. But my contact in Halmstad remembers something about a maritime accident and is digging out the details; and he's pretty certain there were substantial compensation payments, so Olof Petter's interest in Gubbo may be more complicated. As soon as I hear more I'll let you know. Did August know his real name?"

"No. It seems he doesn't keep employment records. But he did say he thought Gubbo had been in some boat disaster, engine explosion perhaps. Anything on the dead man?"

"Nothing. But Frisk's daughter-in-law, Hanna, does have a record, though it's ten years old. She was picked up for soliciting in Stockholm, aged sixteen, then a year later warned for falsifying her date of birth when registering in a brothel there."

"Which year was that?"

"1994."

"The year before she married Daniel Frisk."

"The best news of all is that you may not have to worry about any of that, because Paulus seems to have done a runner. According to the Sami liaison officer I spoke to it's rumoured he's conveniently gone to visit his Russian Sami relatives on the White Sea south of Murmansk. I'll contact the Russian police and say we want to question him, but nothing'll happen, it never does. But if you can't find anything more substantial, and we don't know who the victim is, you can at least wrap the case up neatly, marking the file 'pending further developments'. I know the prosecutor would be content with that."

"Yes," said Magnus uncertainly.

"You don't think it is Paulus, do you?"

"I don't know," answered Magnus. "It just seems too easy, and it conveniently depends on August Frisk's testimony. Nobody else saw Paulus that evening, and the fact he's headed for the White Sea may simply be because he's heard we're looking for him. He probably owes money all over the place, and he's said to be argumentative when he's been drinking, but it doesn't make him a murderer."

"Yet the victim was killed with a Sami knife, and that's another thing I wanted to talk to you about. I think you should show the knife to Finn Jonsson here in Sundsvall. He's the biggest collector of Sami artefacts in Sweden, and he ought to be able to tell you straight away whether the knife might have belonged to someone like Paulus – apparently the decoration varies according to the region. Drive in this evening when you've finished, you'll easily do it in under two hours, and I'll take you to his house and introduce you. Try to make it about six-thirty."

He rang off before Magnus could say he'd planned to drive home that evening to see Sonja and the children, and this abrupt change of plan forced him to confront the source of all his recent uncertainty and unease. His marriage was in trouble, and he'd been banking on this surprise visit to Sonja to bring them close again.

Moodily he made himself a coffee, and began to pace about his office. All around him were excuses to put off any self-examination, not just the murder, but all the more minor matters it had compelled him to put on hold. There'd been a break-in at a restaurant and alcohol had been taken; a wallet had been handed in containing over a thousand kronor, but no identification; a shop had been reported for selling banned Dutch tequila flavoured ice pops. Most bizarre of all was a request for help passed on to him from Euro Parking Collection.

It followed the refusal of a High Coast resident to pay a fine for a parking offence in England involving a snowmobile he insisted had never been taken out of Sweden, and which he was accused of parking in an area where no snow had fallen for several years. Normally he enjoyed the minutiae of police life, and in this particular case he would have found it challenging, and amusing, to translate the accused's obscene and detailed statement of what EPC could do with their claim into diplomatic language. But this was the crux of his problem. He loved his job, he loved his wife and he loved his children; and at the moment he simply didn't have the time to do justice to them all; and when it came to a choice it might just be true that he usually put his job before his family.

As soon as he'd allowed himself to think it, he knew it was always true. He could have spoken immediately, before Amrén rang off, but he hadn't done so. He wanted to meet Finn Jonsson, wanted to solve this case, and he wanted it more than sorting out his marital difficulties. He felt ashamed and helpless, caught up in something seemingly beyond him. He'd never heard his parents quarrel, didn't believe they ever had. He'd been brought up in a very simple household, where the roles of father and mother were distinct and neither ever seemed to cross the boundary. His father farmed and earned the money, and took all the decisions relating to those matters. His mother ruled the household, and he'd never known his father intrude upon her territory. It dawned on him now that his father, in sending for a Thai wife, had brought about exactly the sort of household he'd wanted. But both had been happy, he was sure of that, and he'd been happy too, secure in a circle of affection where parents loved each other and both loved him, and he returned that love to them. Looking back it seemed unreal, idyllic, but it had been true. And he'd assumed his marriage would be the same; and when he fell in love with Sonja, a fellow student, it seemed natural to marry her soon after he'd settled into his job, have children, and live the same contented life as his parents.

It had begun so well. Working in the Jämtland police he was close to home, and emotionally close to Sonja. The arrival of Angelica and Johan seemed to strengthen the bond; and Sonja, working as a nursery-school teacher, still remained interested in all he did, and he always looked forward to returning home. When he'd been shot Sonja looked after him so devotedly it hadn't occurred to him to think how she felt about it, so nearly losing her husband and her children's father. Did she begin to turn against his job then, just as he began to feel the necessity of moving to a different force? They'd never spoken about it; and with the greater insight he seemed to have acquired recently he realised that though he and Sonja talked about the family, and the excitements and problems of his work, he never discussed his deeper feelings with her. He tried to be the loving, ever-optimistic husband and father, the perfect hard-working family man. So he never voiced his concern that his constable's pay would soon be insufficient for their needs, or explained that promotion would prevent the financial problems threatening their security. Certainly he never admitted his Thai blood made him socially a little uncertain, and that was why his family needed to be the secure unit in which he could be perfectly at ease. To become an inspector would demonstrate he was as good, or even slightly better, than those who were wholly Swedish; and he realised now he did want such a public accolade. So when Amrén offered him the chance to move, to get on the ladder to certain promotion, it seemed so obviously right he accepted without consulting Sonja. Just as, he now realised, his father had bought new beasts without discussion with his mother. Faced with the consequences of his rashness he excused himself by saying the decision had had to be made at once. But he knew he could have waited a day, just as he could have postponed this evening's meeting with Finn Jonsson; and guilt is never a helpful presence in a confrontation.

He could still hardly bear to think about the row. Hurtful things were said, terribly hurtful things; and as he remembered so clearly what Sonja said, but much less clearly what he himself replied, he still felt aggrieved.

He'd hurried home that evening, bursting with his news, and blurted it out as soon as he was through the door, before he even hugged her. "What do you think, I've got an immediate temporary transfer to the High Coast, so I'll be working under Amrén at last instead of Hermansson. You know how difficult that's been, and I'll never get promotion while he's my immediate superior."

"Five hours there and back is rather a long journey each day," Sonja said quietly, and too late he recognised the looming problem.

"There's living accommodation attached to the office, and I'll be able to stay over if I have to," he answered defensively.

Sonja looked at him in a way she'd never done before, a cold, scornful glance. "Don't tell me you'll be back every free moment you have, because I know you too well by now. You don't take free time; you work all the hours there are. Be honest for once," she continued scathingly as she turned away and headed for the kitchen. "You'll be away five, probably six days each week. Work always comes before us, but at least until now you've been back at night. Now you'll be an absentee father."

"That's unfair," he said, raising his voice because she started to bang the cupboard doors and clatter saucepans. "I'll be back whenever I possibly can, and it's only temporary, until they get a permanent replacement."

"And then you'll be back working for Hermansson again, so what have you actually gained?" Sonja threw at him, as if she knew there was more to come.

"That's the best part of it," he retorted, "I won't ever be working under him again," and then his heart sank as he saw the deepening gulf in front of him.

Sonja stopped what she was doing, folded her arms, and stood waiting for him to continue. There was no mercy in her look and he was frightened. "Amrén's offered me a permanent job."

"With the Sundsvall police?"

"Yes."

"And you've accepted?"

"Well, I indicated, I suppose I said I would be interested, yes. I had to give an answer straightaway."

"Without consulting me, or the children?"

"I thought you'd be pleased," he said desperately, and that was when, for the first time since he'd known her, she completely lost her temper. She shrieked at him that she'd never leave a house she loved so much and had made into a home for all of them, never move to a town, never change Angelica's school just when she'd settled, never give up her job, never move away from all her friends. She deliberately smashed the plate she'd picked up, began to sob, but nothing stopped her outpouring of fury.

"Did you even think about me at all? Did you consider the children? No, you just thought about yourself and your precious promotion so you can feel big and swagger about while the rest of your family has to bear the cost. Well, you can stuff your promotion because I won't move and nor will the children."

He stood there appalled, and frightened, hearing things about himself he never knew she thought, cruel sneering comments deliberately designed to hurt. And then he got angry too, reminding her of things he'd done for her, defending himself, proclaiming loudly that he loved her; and she threw it in his face just as both children came rushing from their rooms, screaming and begging them to stop.

They patched it up, but it was a temporary truce. The next day he left for the High Coast where living and sleeping alone allowed him time to brood on all the things she'd said, going over and over them in his mind until he almost convinced himself she must have become totally dissatisfied with the marriage. But he didn't quite convince himself, aware, in his calmer moments, how selfishly he'd behaved, and beginning to understand the panic she would have felt at suddenly discovering he was planning to move them all to Sundsvall. She was a country girl, she liked their present simple life, enjoyed the support of all her friends around her, had made the house so perfect, adored her job and it was true that Angelica and Johan were contentedly settled. He had, in one sense, only thought of his career and his promotion; but it wasn't quite that simple Before he'd left she'd thrown down a challenge. If he went to

Sundsvall he would go alone. Magnus found it hard to understand how she could so lightly contemplate the virtual ending of their marriage; and a stubborn streak in him made him reluctant to beg. So, weakly, he'd decided to let time heal the breach and soothe their pain, and when there was a proper opportunity, he would, of course, apologise.

It was in such a state of emotional uncertainty he met Hanna and was thrown off balance by his reaction to her. He'd never been unfaithful to Sonja, had never wanted to be, had never even thought of it. But what was far worse than being so disconcerted was the reality of the excitement he'd experienced, then, and ever since. Something new had come into his life, something he found very hard to control.

He wrenched his thoughts back to the information Amrén had given him. It didn't dismay him that Hanna had once been on the game; if anything, it intrigued him. He was not surprised Olof Petter had a violent record, or that money might be involved in his relationship with Gubbo. But it all brought the Frisks community into sharper focus, made sense of some of the titbits of bitter gossip he'd heard, that Hanna was a tart, Olof Petter evil through and through, August a once regular user of a Stockholm brothel. There was something there at Frisks, an untruth, a secret, a festering itch, and he was sure the murder was in some way linked to it. He simply could not believe the solution lay with Paulus of Jokkmokk, though he realised it might end up as the only possible answer. But, deep down, he felt there was more to find at Frisks. He'd always trusted his instinct, and usually he'd been right to do so; but now even his instinct might have been infected by Hanna who had become his own festering itch, and who might be the unadmitted cause of his wish to concentrate the investigation on Frisks and nowhere else.

He took a deep breath. He was beginning to hate himself, to distrust his motives, and he needed to confront his weakness and overcome it. That meant confronting Hanna, seeing her alone, away from the settlement, and destroying the demons that were putting his marriage at risk and making his position as the investigating policeman impossible. As soon as he took the decision and reached out for the phone, he felt the aching surge of excitement, the knowledge, deep, deep down, that he who had been strong, and proud of it, longed to fail the coming test.

It was Hanna who answered, and he explained he needed to visit her so she could sign her statement.

"Come anytime," she answered cheerfully. "I'm around all day, and I'll be glad to see you."

"Certain matters have come to light," said Magnus, keeping his voice official. "I would need a little time to discuss them with you on your own."

There was a pause.

"Are you an early riser?" Hanna asked him.

"Yes."

"There's a steep track through the forest which starts some distance behind the left hand corner of the house. The blueberries are ripe now, so I'll be walking up that path at six-thirty tomorrow morning to pick some for a pie. I'd be glad of some help, and we can have our discussion as we work. How about that?"

She seemed completely uninterested in what the discussion might be about, and utterly relaxed about meeting him in the woods. He said he would be there and she rang off.

To stop himself dreaming he followed up Doctor Burman's suggestion, and rang Scholander, arranging to meet him in half an hour.

The *surströmming* factory was not at all what he expected. It was modern and clean, neatly laid out with gardens and a fountain, and even when he went inside there was no vestige of the pungent rotting-flesh odour of the fermented herring, a stench his father had taught him to overcome with such success he was now strangely addicted to the taste and had become an aficionado of northern Sweden's most renowned and unusual delicacy. Scholander wheeled himself out to meet him in the corridor, a fair-skinned balding man with the rubicund face of a jovial and well-fed medieval friar.

"Do you like *surströmming*?" he asked eagerly as he shook hands and spun his wheelchair to lead the way into his spacious office.

"I love it." It was an instant answer, and Scholander laughed delightedly.

"Then I shall reserve two tins of our Prima Ultra for you, and I can guarantee you'll never have tasted anything as wonderful before. It's going to be an especially good vintage this year. Of course I shall have to charge you something, otherwise I might be accused of bribing the police." He laughed again, a deep, contented and infectious laugh. "Now sit yourself down and tell me what I can do for you."

Magnus pulled out the frail looking stainless-steel chair from under the desk and sat down warily. "It's about the body found at Frisks. Have you heard about that?"

Scholander nodded vigorously. "News and gossip travel fast in a small place like this."

Magnus took out a photograph and showed it to him. "Have you ever seen him before?"

Scholander studied the body with interest, then shook his head. "He's not from round here, though we're so flooded with visitors at this time of the year that normally it wouldn't mean much; new people are coming and going all the time. But this man would have stood out from the crowd and I'd certainly have remembered him if I'd seen him."

"You know August Frisk?"

"Who doesn't? The Frisks must be the oldest surviving family here. It's a tragedy."

"A tragedy?"

"One must, I suppose, admire his refusal to change, his determination to keep Frisks as it was in his grandfather's day. But it's doomed to failure, and he knows it as well as everybody else. Flexibility is the keynote now."

"He used to sell you herring?"

"Still does. But whereas he used to have a fleet of boats and supply me with most of what I required, now he has just one, he's almost cut off from the sea and he provides me with a mere fraction of the eighty tons I produce." He gestured to the window. "Look out there."

Magnus walked across and looked down in amazement at a huge man-made salt lake containing innumerable barrels of the prepared herring. "They have to stay there for months, in water which is kept at a constant fifteen degrees," explained Scholander, rolling up beside him. "That way the herring ferments slowly, which improves the flavour. There's a lactic acid enzyme in the backbone which creates the reaction, but to induce it the salt level and temperature must be right."

"How did it all start?"

"We don't know exactly, but the fisher-folk of Gävle were certainly coming north up here in the fifteenth century. It's likely they discovered that fermenting preserved the herring and enabled them to take it home and eat it over the winter. Food preservation was big business when the only alternative was starvation. The earliest documents show they were granted the legal right to fish these coasts in 1557, but it must have started long before that."

"Gävle's quite a way south. Coming up here must have been a major expedition for them."

"Nearly two hundred miles by boat, and the fishermen didn't only bring supplies with them, they brought children, servants, linen and even livestock, usually pigs and goats. Probably a few adventurous wives, too, and when they got here they built summer-only villages to house them all. Fishing was a major industry then, thanks to the Catholic church."

"What did the church have to do with it?"

"Religious fasting rules were very strict and frequently permitted only fish."

"But what did they keep the fish in? They didn't have cans back then."

"No, it was wooden kegs until the 1890's when the first tins of fermented herring were manufactured here on the High Coast. We've been the centre for it ever since."

"And what do you think of the new filleted fermented herring they're beginning to sell in some places?"

"I think it stinks," replied Scholander, and though it must have been a joke he'd made countless times before he still laughed so infectiously that Magnus was carried away as well, and had to wipe his eyes before he could ask how he knew when the herring was ready to be taken from the salt pool.

"By the smell when you open the barrel," said Scholander, still chuckling. "But we taste as well, one of the few things which hasn't been modernised. Five years ago I completely rebuilt this factory, and I improve it every year. In the old days we used to help catch the fish ourselves, and we washed and prepared them all by hand. Now we buy the fish in, we use machinery for everything else, and we're not only surviving, we're doing very well. It's progress, and that's what August has turned his back on."

"Is he a friend?"

Scholander shook his head. "August's a loner, a law unto himself. I've worked closely with him, I admire his dogged spirit, but I can see he's losing the battle, and it upsets me."

"How does he keep going?"

"He has to rely on whatever comes to hand. He sells the fish he still catches, cuts and markets his timber and does a bit of summer farming, mainly goats. He rents his winter pasturage to the Sami, and has to do anything else that'll earn him money – as long as it isn't tourism."

"What sort of things?"

Scholander looked awkward. "I really don't know, I've probably said too much."

"Things against the law?"

"He's not a criminal, that's for sure. Upright in his way. But in recent years he's developed a contempt for what he sees as government interference, petty bureaucracy, regulation of any kind. There was a sort of change in him after he lost his son, an inner anger, an intolerance of new ways, perhaps even a resentful belief that people were trying to do him down and he had to fight his corner. I doubt if a modern young man like you can understand what a son meant to him. It was the most important thing in his life, the continuation of the family name, the continuation of the land itself, the whole future of Frisks."

"And he drowned?"

"Boating accident," said Scholander briefly, perhaps, Magnus thought, too briefly. "It was tragic for August."

On the way out he added Magnus' name to a list of preferential customers, but refused to take more than ten kronor. "The *premiär* is the 24th August, so I'll have these delivered to you a day or two before. And if you enjoy it as much as I'm sure you will, you'll come back and buy from me again, so it's good business for me. You may even be eating a piece of a herring caught by August."

Magnus touched the wheelchair. "How did it happen?" he asked.

"My wife and I were on holiday, five years ago, one of those Estonia/Poland tours, Tallinn to Gdansk, but we only got as far as Lithuania. While we were sightseeing in Vilnius we were knocked down by a speeding driver. I was the lucky one; my wife didn't survive."

"Was the driver apprehended?"

Scholander shook his head. "Never," he answered, "even though bystanders had taken the number of the car. I've always assumed he must have been a man with influence or power, and the police couldn't touch him. There's still a lot of corruption there."

"How does one ever come to terms with something like that?"

Scholander shrugged. "At first I was filled with all the fury and frustration you'd expect, but it's over now. Life must go on."

Magnus drove slowly back to his office. He could understand why Burman had wanted him to talk to Scholander. It was clear he knew more about Frisks, and August in particular, than he'd been prepared to reveal, and it lent strength to Burman's contention that he should not rely too much on statements emanating from there. But it was not *evidence*, and until he got a proper lead it just added to the background information he was accumulating. He thought about the contrast between Scholander and August Frisk, the one welcoming change, the other rejecting it; and he looked with new eyes at the land around him. He'd never before considered the tragedy the coastal rise could cause, had never understood that the UNESCO decision in 2000 to add the High Coast to its list of World Heritage Sites had been the death knell to a far older way of life. Looked at in that way the yachtsmen, the campers, the hikers and the sea-food gourmets could be seen as invaders, the model fishing boats on sale everywhere, in bottles and on stands, as memorials to what had once been a proud way of life. In the tiny wooden seamen's chapels they had, for centuries, hung model ships from the ceiling to commemorate a loss at sea; now similar models were sold to commemorate a day-trip to the seaside, and the chapels were full of briefly clad sun-worshippers gawping at the quaint sixteenth century paintings of Christ fishing with his disciples, Jonah and his whale, and then making a video-recording of them so they could remind themselves of what it was they'd seen. Momentarily he understood the venom which must fill August. But Magnus was a modern man, enjoying the fruits of progress, and overall he felt sad for him, and wondered into what dark areas his refusal to conform had led him. Had Daniel, his son, shared his views on progress, or had there been a tension there? There was so much he did not know.

CHAPTER 10

Magnus drove into the Norrmalm open-air car park still feeling frustrated with the case. But as soon as he spotted the figure standing quietly under the trees just beyond the vehicles his uncertainties evaporated. Amrén had had that effect on him since the first time he'd met him, and now he could not help smiling at the way he appeared to be concentrating on the bridge which crossed the stream there, though Magnus was sure he was perfectly aware of his arrival. The Selånger had recently been dredged, cleaned and widened, attracting some venturesome boats. These provided colour and interest to the throng of shoppers passing over the bridge towards the main street and the central square where the big stores were to be found. Some small boats had simply moored up to the bank and their occupants waved to any on the bridge who showed curiosity about them. It was a cheerful, bustling scene, but it seemed to Magnus that Amrén was not actually staring at the shoppers, the boats, their crews or even the bridge. He was watching over the town itself, conscious that he would shortly be responsible for its safety and preparing for the moment when he would need to sense any looming trouble and stifle it before it was able to manifest itself in any conscious action.

Magnus loved the confidence that seemed to bubble up in Amrén and overflow onto his subordinates. It was what had convinced him that he wanted to work with him, just as he knew it was Sonja who enabled him to cope so apparently easily with family and social life. Although Amrén looked more like a banker than a law-enforcer, his homely figure and pink soft-skinned face giving no hint of toughness, and his eager little walk more like that of a boy who'd saved his pocket money and was impatient to reach the shops than that of a man about to become Chief of Police, he never seemed to feel any need to change himself.

Yet Sonja resented Amrén and was forcing Magnus to choose between the two people he needed most in his life.

"You act as though you're married to him, not to me," she'd flung at him during their quarrel, and he'd been tongue-tied, unable to explain what he felt about Amrén. He dared not say that he needed him as he needed her; and it seemed boastful to remind her that Amrén believed he was an able officer who deserved promotion. Nor could he bring himself to say that the first time he'd looked into his eyes he'd been struck by the sharp intelligence they revealed, the natural authority, the utter confidence in his own individuality; and that his reputation as a fearless officer, shrewd, reliable, honest, was, to his mind, confirmed by the fact that Amrén himself never referred to anything in his past. Still less could he admit that Amrén, always ready to listen and give praise where it was due, drew from Magnus an undeviating loyalty he could not easily give to others. Least of all could he tell her that Amrén was the only Swede he could remember since his father who had not seen him as half-Thai but just as someone he wanted to work with him. For such explanations would mean admitting a fluttering self-doubt and a need for approval that he was ashamed to confess. But keeping silent had put him in the position where, if he joined Amrén's force in Sundsvall, neither Sonja nor the children would be with him.

As usual the two men shook hands formally without exchanging pleasantries and set off to the impressive house where Finn Jonsson lived. As such a well-known collector, Magnus had assumed he occupied the whole house, but in fact everything was in the first floor apartment. Amrén rang the bell and the door was opened almost instantly by a diminutive but sprightly man who smiled up at him and then turned his shy gaze on Magnus. He had a high-domed balding head, a sensitive mouth which seemed to tremble with an excitement he could barely contain, and a puckered elderly face which contrasted oddly with the youthful eagerness of his expression.

Amrén introduced them and then tactfully withdrew, leaving it all to Magnus. As soon as Finn had closed and carefully secured the door he motioned Magnus to go ahead of him; and, astonished, he found himself entering a Sami wonderland. It did not seem a home where someone lived at all, much more a vivid overflowing museum treasury of every kind of Lappish art.

"So many of my best pieces are in the current exhibition in Japan," Finn said apologetically, handing him a lavish catalogue. Excitedly he lent towards him and turned the pages for Magnus, showing him miniature reindeer so realistic they seemed about to walk off the page, a finely wrought sledge to carry a tiny baby, highly decorated skin clothing, a Shaman's drum, and then several paintings. "All of those are by Nils Nilsson-Skum, the central figure in Sami art," he explained, "so insurance has been a nightmare. He was an extraordinary man, wrote, sculpted, crafted, drew and painted with an authenticity and feeling unmatched at that time."

"I know nothing about Sami art," Magnus confessed. "When was 'that time'?"

"He was born in 1872 when Lapps, as they were called then, were still considered by most people to be mere savages; but his best work was produced in the early nineteen hundreds when more discerning collectors were becoming interested in such art. I've got one of the knives he made, somewhere here, but he wasn't a knife specialist like Jan Pålsson-Fankki. I'd show you some of his if they weren't on loan to the Jamtli Museum in Östersund, but I have got a surprisingly good one I discovered last year by his cousin Pava Katarinasson Fankki who was virtually unknown until then."

Quick and agile in his movements, he began to open cupboards, drawers and wooden chests, all bulging with horn spoons, carved needle cases, inlaid wood scoops, woven baskets, broad fabric belts intricately decorated in silver wire, extraordinary hats, wooden powder flasks and numerous knives of all sizes from the almost-miniature to heavy-bladed short machetes. "But perhaps you saw my Pålsson-Fankki knives in the museum when you were with the police in Östersund?" He cocked his head to one side, looking up interrogatively, shrewd eyes fixed on him.

Magnus shook his head. "I wasn't at all interested in Sami art until I was moved to the High Coast recently and discovered some Sami overwinter their herds there."

Finn stopped his search for a moment and nodded. "It was once an important Sami area, and there are still a few interesting remains of their occupation." He shifted a number of bear and wolf spears which were stacked in a corner with some decorated skis and sledge driving sticks. "There were settlements of non-migratory Sami there as well, living off the fishing." He moved a bag made from the skin of a black-throated diver, and held up the knife hidden under it. ''Here it is at last.'' He peered at it critically, then sighed. ''It's not the signed one I wanted to show you, but it's by Pava and though it's early work, it's very good.'' He passed the knife to Magnus. It was surprisingly slim, almost delicate, with elegant decoration all over the hilt and sheath, and a highly polished leather throat with impressed designs.

''It's not much like the one I brought to show you,'' Magnus said as he handed it back. Finn looked appalled, and then embarrassed. "What on earth am I doing, chattering away like this and trying to find examples to show you? You didn't come to see my collection or learn about Sami art, I remember that now. Ragnar told me you were bringing something for me to see and you wanted my opinion. Whatever can you think of me?"

"I've found it very interesting and I'm ashamed I'm so ignorant about the art," Magnus answered reassuringly. "But I suppose policemen tend to concentrate on what they need to know to help them with an investigation."

Finn laughed. "And collectors tend to concentrate on their own narrow scholarship, which was exactly what I was doing."

He swept some reindeer boots off a chair and waved Magnus to it, pulled up an upturned boat-shaped sledge and sat on it beside him. "Now show me what you've brought and tell me what you need to know."

Magnus took out a plastic box which now contained the evidence bag already punctured in several places by the razor-sharpness of the knife inside it

"I need to know if this is the sort of knife a Sami herdsman would wear. It's evidence, so you mustn't touch it, but I hope you can see it well enough in the bag."

Finn sat for a while staring at it, turning the box this way and that, and once getting up to hold it nearer the light. "Truly amazing," he said finally. "He really is a master; this alone demonstrates how he transformed Sami craftwork into an art form. This must have been one of the last he made before he fell ill. He was only in his early fifties then, but it put a stop to his work and there may never be another like him. Fortunately he'd acquired a handful of disciples, and they're trying, with some success, to emulate the sublime mixture of tradition and modernity that was his particular genius."

"You know who made it?"

"That's like asking me if I recognise a Rembrandt. Esaias Poggats of Kaitum is that special, he really is." Magnus had never heard of him, but Finn's voice was full of awe and he seemed unable to drag his eyes away from the knife. "Examples of his work are in most of the major museums of the world. He really can be justly credited with a renaissance in Sami art."

"Are the knives valuable?"

"I think all Sami work is still undervalued in monetary terms. Whoever bought this probably paid no more than thirty thousand kronor for it, three thousand pounds or its equivalent if it was bought by someone in the English-speaking parts of the world, as so many are."

"Thirty thousand for a knife," exclaimed Magnus incredulously.

"Only thirty thousand for a work of art?" countered Finn.

"Is it likely a Sami herder would have this knife?"

"Impossible." Finn's reply was unhesitating. "If any knife he makes isn't snapped up by a museum it would usually be bought by a serious collector or some rich man wanting to make an investment. A Sami herder wants a knife to use, and usually makes it himself. Rough use of this, or even any use at all, would lower its value. And it's not just about money. Speaking personally, any nicks in the blade, or scratches on the horn, would destroy some of its aesthetic beauty. Have you got the sheath?"

"No."

"Do you know what it would look like?"

"Like the Pava one you showed me?" guessed Magnus. "Horn with a leather throat?"

Finn opened a drawer in his desk and without any searching at all took out a reindeer skin bag from which he carefully extracted a knife. Magnus could see at once it was made by the same hand, but the sheath perfectly completed the graceful curve, the subtle colouring – and there was no leather throat at all.

"It's called a whole-horn knife," said Finn. "It's the hardest sort of knife to make, so only the best attempt it. Usually it's the leather throat which holds the knife firmly in the sheath, but in one of these the horn must be sprung so that it grips the hilt."

"How's that possible?"

"Two matching pieces of horn are hollowed out, then the lower two thirds are glued strongly together. The top third is left free, the edges not quite touching, and, if they've been properly shaped, when the knife is pushed in the two sides open sufficiently to let the hilt enter, then close to hold it tightly." He handed Magnus the knife. "Draw it slowly," he said, "and you'll see how it works."

Magnus tried it, and was astonished how easily it could be drawn yet how firmly it was held when in the sheath. "It's so simple," he said admiringly, "but it's perfect."

"Only the finest makers can do it as well as that, but this one shows ability artistically as well as mechanically. Look at the gradation of colour in the horn, there's no obvious difference between the hilt and the sheath, and that provides the unity that makes it so perfect."

"I thought they bleached the antler so it was always white?"

"It used to be the custom, but the new makers leave the horn with its natural surface, marks and all, and the best know how to select the finest antlers. That's how they get this wonderfully deep patina, the texture and natural colouring. Here it's like a northern sky reflected in a lake, but in another knife it might suggest other images. That's why matching the horn is so vital and, of course, so difficult. I had to wait two years before this knife was ready for me."

"Is ordering direct from the maker the only way somebody could get one?"

"No, a number were always marketed through Wennberg's, the main Sami art outlet in Stockholm and Kiruna. It has its own website, so it sells worldwide, especially to America."

"It's bound to keep records then, and I ought to have a good chance of finding out the name and address of the purchaser?"

"If Wennberg's sold it there'll be a record, yes. I suppose you can't tell me where the knife was found and in what context?"

"We're at a very early stage of the investigation so I'm afraid I can't say any more at the moment."

"I only hope it wasn't used in any violent way. The Sami have been in Sweden since the ice started to retreat ten thousand years ago and in all that time they've never formed themselves into either small troops or large armies. It's an unconscious pacifism that distinguishes them from almost all other European societies. For what it's worth, my opinion would be that if this case involves any violence the perpetrator would not be Sami."

"I'll bear that in mind," said Magnus, standing up.

Finn took something from his reindeer skin wallet and handed it to him. "Take one of Wennberg's cards. Even if the first purchaser sold the knife on to somebody else it's likely there would be some knowledge of where it ended up. Wennberg is very protective of the important pieces he sells."

Magnus thanked him with real warmth. He'd been struggling through a fog, and Finn Jonnsson had given him his first satisfactory lead.

As he drove home through the late July dusk, already missing the magic of the recent midsummer twilight, he was tempted to make a long detour and go home. Despite the lateness of the hour he would wake Sonja, tell her how sorry he was, confess what a fool he'd been and, if forgiven, spend an hour or so in her arms. But for the first time in their married life he was uncertain of his welcome, remembering her eyes as she'd told him that as far as she and the children were concerned he could stuff the Sundsvall plan. So, weakly, he told himself it might be more sensible to resolve his feelings for Hanna when he saw her tomorrow and then he'd be in a stronger position to sort out his marriage. He felt better for the decision; but he was left with an uncomfortable feeling, too, suspecting himself of not being entirely honest in his thinking. Such an unsuspected ability to delude himself about his real motives nagged at his conscience and for the rest of the drive he felt unsettled.

DAY 3

CHAPTER 11

Magnus parked his car away from the house, aware that everything he was doing proclaimed his sense of guilt. He even seemed to skulk as he walked through the fringe of trees towards the path. It was only 6.15 and he sincerely hoped Olof Petter was back in bed after his nightly prowl. The path veered away to the south, winding its way up a higher hill which overlooked a different stretch of the sea. There was a profusion of blueberries, cool and fresh from the night, and he had placed a few in his mouth when the thought came to him of kissing Hanna with blue stained lips and teeth, and he spat them out. It was the second time he had consciously thought of kissing her, and it worried and excited him. He stood still against a tree, staring down at the inlet still obscured by the sea-mist trapped between the ridges on each side, then up at the well-worn path criss-crossed by flattened tree roots, a path which might lead him into the unknown territory of unfaithfulness. Although it was so early he seemed to smell the meadowsweet, and his mind was filled with Hanna's face, looking at him so openly but showing such apparent indifference. He longed for her to become soft and welcome him, to allow him to follow the tattoo on her lower back wherever it might lead him. What he had learnt about her past was probably trivial, a young girl's silliness, and he admired the way she had put it all behind her, become a mother, organised a home. Yet there was a disturbing thrill in thinking about what she had learnt then, what she had done then, and might still do with him. There was a matter he had to raise, more for his own sake than that of the investigation, but he would not allow himself to think of that until the moment he had to ask the question.

He saw her leave the house, a bucket in one hand, a metal picker in the other. She was wearing her hipster jeans, her sleeveless top was brief, the hair still tangled as though she had only recently risen from her bed. He felt like a foolish adolescent again, sick with apprehension, wondering whether she would let him run his fingers through it, tidy and smooth it.

She saw him by the tree and threw the bucket to him, not smiling, but at ease, companionable. "The best ones are higher up," she said, and set off up the path in front of him. He followed, his eyes fixed on the tattoo, seeing the serpent move as she moved. A greater spotted woodpecker scolded him for his thoughts, distancing itself from him in low swooping flight. When they emerged from the forest for a time, climbing up through an open slope, he noticed the sun was warm already, and it made the snarls in her hair more golden. The long grasses, colourfully mingled with a yellow flower he did not recognise, brushed against her legs. He hoped she would rest, throwing herself down in the grass, but she strode indefatigably upwards until, nearer the summit of the hill, they re-entered the forest. It closed about them like a private room, a dense mixture of pine, juniper, birch, alder, mountain ash and sallow. Beneath an ancient Norway spruce, ghostly with hanging-beard lichen, she began to bend to pick the plump fruit from the low bushes, and more of the serpent was revealed.

She looked up at him, catching his gaze fixed on the gap between her top and jeans. "Help me pick, you lazy thing. I didn't bring you with me just to carry the bucket and dream about my unrevealed parts." She smiled as she said it so that he knew she was not offended, did not mind at all, found it entirely natural, expected it, was not concerned; but she was not flattered either. He realised she neither fussed nor flirted, and anything that happened would come about entirely naturally. He did not need to push, pay compliments, declare himself; she knew already, and he could wait for her. He felt a huge relief, and settled down to pick beside her, not hesitating now to make his tongue and teeth as blue as hers already were. Their hands often brushed, their bodies were close, and several times she put an especially large bilberry into his mouth and he felt her fingers touch his lips. Once he took a pine needle from her hair, freeing it gently as he untangled the hair. At first neither of them spoke.

He knew he could kiss her when he wished, but he was in no hurry now. It was as if time had no meaning any longer, it would never run out, there would always be the moment for whatever had to happen between them. Then they began to talk, easily, relaxed, as though there was nothing more beyond the friendship they were forging. She asked him about his wife and family, and he was able to answer honestly and simply, without the anger and the guilt which so warped his own internal deliberations. He told her about their earlier happiness, and the problems so suddenly confronting them.

"Clients always liked to talk," she said, checking the sweeping motion of the picker and gazing at him frankly. "I'm sure you're good enough at your job to have discovered I was a prostitute, then in a brothel, and I imagine that's why you wanted to question me alone, so no one else would hear. That was kind."

"I wanted to be alone with you," said Magnus, knowing he must match her honesty. "I don't really care about your past."

Hanna looked at him seriously, studying him as though there was a decision she could reach only by seeing into him, a decision which concerned her as much as him. Then she put down the picker, stood up and held her hand out. "I'll sign my statement now so you don't have to come another day."

He stood up too, feeling he was about to be dismissed. He handed over the statement and a pen, looking away from her as she read it, then taking it back when she'd nodded and signed.

There was a pause while she seemed to struggle with her thoughts, and then she looked him in the face, her blue eyes clear of any doubts which might have temporarily attacked her. "There are questions you have to ask me about my past. Let's get the police work over, and then we can consider the best way to resolve your other problems."

She gave him the bucket again, took the picker in one hand and reached out the other, taking his and leading him firmly away from the path, up over the mossy ledges of stone where water trickled, and into a tiny secluded hollow, the edges carpeted with pink heather, smooth rock below where lichen shone yellow in the sunshine, forming a witch's circle within which they would be secure. There was a tantalizing scent of wild thyme and the surrounding spruce drooped their branches to give them privacy. In the very centre of the dip, in the sun, within the circle, a rectangular slab of granite formed a seat, and there she settled herself, releasing his hand so he was standing before her.

"Don't sit down until the questions are over," she said. "We have our own particular roles in this investigation, and we mustn't muddle them yet. And, so you don't feel awkward about what you must ask me, I'm assuming you've worked out where my path first crosses August's, and that will have set you wondering."

Magnus nodded, relieved she was making it so easy for him. "After his wife's death I believe August used to visit a Stockholm brothel at regular intervals. Was that where he met you?"

"Yes."

"And did he bring you back from there to Frisks, and that's where you met Daniel?"

"Yes." She held up a warning finger, using his name for the first time. "Please, Magnus, I know what your next question must be, but don't ask it. Instead I'll just tell you the answer, and that way I'll never have to know from the tone of your voice whether you thought it might be possible. I never was with August in the brothel. He was a regular, had been coming for years, and he had his own particular favourites. I was the new girl, and he never looked at me. But because he always stayed the night, and everyone was so accustomed to him, and he listened to the chatter, he soon heard about me, how young I was, an abandoned child, brought up in care, the usual crap. The others thought I could be saved, I'd not been at it long enough to fix me in the rut, so he, soft fool that he is, offered me a job and home at Frisks and I went back with him."

"Do you think he hoped that Daniel...?"

"Oh, yes, August never wastes his time or money. He reckoned Daniel might fall for me, or more probably that I'd seduce him, and then there'd be a marriage, because marrying is what Frisks do, and the next generation of the family would be assured. That's what August really cared about, far more than me, more even than Daniel."

"And the fairy tale came true?"

Hanna looked up, and fleetingly she seemed utterly naked before him and he saw pain and despair. Then it was covered by a smile. "What use are fairy tales if they don't come true?"

"The fairy tale was tragically brief for Daniel."

Hanna sighed. "Poor Daniel. He was a lovely boy, so innocent but so mixed-up. I think I made him happy, too, happier at least than he'd ever been before; but it wasn't something that could last." She stood up and approached Magnus, and put her arms round him, a mother, sensitive to suffering and always ready to soothe it. "And now I seem to have acquired another mixed-up innocent. Have you more questions for me?" He shook his head, feeling her body against his and quite unable to speak, and she went on, "Oh, Magnus, you are such a fool. What shall I do with you?"

She pulled him down beside her, shifting her body onto the heather to get herself comfortable, and he saw the movement of the breasts beneath her top, the slight lowering of the jeans down the tattoo.

"We're quite alone here," she said reassuringly. "There's no one to see us, no one to interrupt us, and whatever you want, I want too. I can give you anything you've ever dreamed of, even those things you've hardly dared to dream about."

Magnus felt himself swell until he thought he would burst, and he turned eagerly towards her.

"You learn about marriage when you're on the game," she continued, regarding him seriously now, and leaning towards him to give him a fleeting kiss. "Many relationships go through difficulties, and from my great experience it's often the sex that's at the root of it. However much a man loves his wife or partner there's sometimes something more he wants from her, something she won't give him because she doesn't fancy it, something perhaps he cannot even suggest, can scarcely even admit it to himself, something he wants to do, or wants her to do to him. At first it doesn't seem to matter, but after a while he thinks about it more and more, it becomes a rankling discontent, the basis of other discontents sprouting from that secret seed. And if you can look honestly into yourself, and see that what I've said fits your present difficulties, then I'll give you what you want. Whatever it is, I've done it when I was a hooker and I'll make it wonderful for you, so wonderful you'll forget your other silly discontents and go back to your Sonja, and you'll be at peace and realise what a lucky man you are to have someone who loves you."

The blood pounded in his head. She was offering him sexual bliss, it was there within his touching distance, he could feel her body beside him, remembered her lips on his, however briefly, and wanted them there again, and it would far exceed anything she'd been able to describe because, to him, she was not a prostitute but someone very special.

He stared at her, yearning for her, but knowing now he couldn't have her, and guessing she'd realised how it would be and had deliberately brought him face to face with it. He felt the excitement drain away, leaving only the bitterness of defeat. "Hanna," he said, cherishing the name when all else seemed destroyed, "if I were to do it, it wouldn't end the way you say. I'd want to stay with you, and not return to Sonja. If you were what you used to be, perhaps it might be different, but I can't think of you as you once were, I can only think of you as the woman you are now."

He took her hand, still staring at her, filling his mind with her, sensing it was a farewell of a kind. "There's probably something wrong with me," he added reluctantly, "but I can't separate sex and love. If I make love to you, whatever special ways we might do it, it will be because I care for you. And if I care for you I'm tied emotionally, and I'll bring misery on Sonja, on Angelica and Johan, and eventually on you and Jon, because I won't be able to bear the guilt of what I've done."

"And what if I care for you?" asked Hanna in a sudden change of mood, and he could see tears starting in her eyes.

"Do you?"

She dashed the tears away and struck at him with her fist. "I wanted you, you fucking idiot. I'm young, I've been a widow far too long, I wanted to give myself, forget I had a child, forget my responsibilities and just for once give myself up to total pleasure."

"But do you care for me?"

She sat up, glaring at him. "Christ, men are fools sometimes. Have you forgotten you're a policeman and I'm a possible witness; a suspect for all I know. If you'd had sex with me, I'd have had you in my power, and the weirder the things you'd done to me the more power I'd have had over you. If I reported you, made an official complaint about what you'd done, cried rape even, you'd have been off this case, disgraced, probably out of the police as well. Do you really think I wouldn't have gone to a doctor to be examined when you'd finished with me? Your semen would be on record, and I could use you or destroy you as I wanted. Is that caring for you?"

She burst into tears, and he put an arm round her. "You wouldn't have done anything like that," he said gently.

"That's easy to say, because you'll never know," she replied, sniffing, wiping her eyes and shrugging off his arm. "So leave me alone, go to your wife tonight, forget the stupid disagreements, make it up with her and keep out of my life."

"Shall I go now?"

"Not until you've helped me fill the bucket. Then you can walk down with me in full view of everybody instead of sneaking guiltily through the trees as you were when you arrived this morning. Now you have nothing to be ashamed about, and only you and I know what a bloody close-run thing it was."

They went on up the path, becoming increasingly selective in their picking so that the upper layers in the bucket looked like a fruiterer's display. It was still and hot, even the aspen leaves were motionless. When they reached the top of the hill Hanna led him out onto some rocks at the forest's edge. Below them the sea lay flat beneath the sun, as steely blue as the blade of a cherished old carving knife.

"Is that where Elin finds her amber?" he asked, pointing down to the narrow pebbled beach which looked so isolated that anything washed up there might lie undiscovered for many years.

"Ask Elin," answered Hanna brusquely, "she doesn't confide in me. But I wanted you to see that headland, because it's the one that forms the far side of our inlet, and it's the explanation for much of August's bitterness."

"Because there's open water on this side?"

"Exactly. Our little harbour will soon be totally blocked, ending the fishing which has been the family's way of life for more than a hundred years. It's breaking August's heart, and yet just the other side there's completely open water, no sign of rising rocks at all. It's so unfair."

Magnus peered carefully at the open inlet below him. "It looks as though there's an old wharf there, and some buildings. Are they still in use?"

Hanna shook her head. "There's been no fishing from there since I've been here, but there are rumours the owner may turn it into a fishing museum, and run day trips from the quay to the nearby islands."

"Can't August buy it, and run his herring fishing from there?"

"He's been trying to for years, but he can't raise the money. Since the High Coast became a major tourist area prices for everything have gone sky-high. He could only raise that sort of sum by selling the land and houses at Frisks, and he won't do that. But it's hard for him to watch Jon growing up and know there'll be no fishing business left for him."

"Do you feel the same?"

"No, but that's no help to August. I know Jon's qualities, and he'll always make his way in life, so I'm not worried by it all. But a mother's love can blind her, I suppose, and August might be partly right."

A picture rose in Magnus' mind of Jon watching him from beneath the tree. "I don't think you're blind," he said. "He's a very special boy."

"And your son, is he special as well?"

Magnus laughed, and realised he no longer felt any lust at all for Hanna. Though he liked her more and more, enjoyed her company, the immediate crisis had passed. "I think Johan's wonderful," he admitted ruefully, "so maybe I'm blind too. But he'll be a better man than me, the full-blown Swede I've always tried to be, but somehow never quite achieved."

They turned for home, Magnus still carrying the bucket which was full to the brim and pleasantly heavy. Now there was no need for it, romantic birdsong burst out all around them, a pied flycatcher provided a celebratory display of aerobatics, feeding on the wing, and they discovered a patch of luscious wild raspberries which they could put into each other's mouths. Then, just before they left the cover of the trees and entered the pasture behind the house, Hanna stopped him.

"Now you're yourself again, I'll show you something. I saw where your eyes went, and I guessed the fascination which seemed to hold you captive." She half turned away from him and pulled down her jeans and polka-dot briefs. The sea-serpent was exposed, his tail not going to any hidden part of her at all but rolled up as he balanced precariously on a skate-board.

"You thought it was up my arse, or tickling my fancy," she said, smiling at him. "But he's just a delusion, as what you saw in me was a delusion. So, please, please, Magnus, think of the serpent in future and remember that things are not always what they seem."

He walked down openly beside her, helped her carry the bucket into the kitchen, and then, reluctantly, he turned to leave.

"You don't have to look so utterly miserable," said Hanna, pretending to be exasperated. "Come here, for heaven's sake." She pulled him to her and kissed him. "Now leave here cheerfully," she ordered, "I'm very fussy who I kiss."

When he had gone she started to pick-over the blueberries, but turned as August came up behind her.

"Well?" he said interrogatively.

"I was right and you were wrong. I gave him his chance, but he wouldn't take it, though he wanted to."

"That's a pity."

"No, August, it's better this way. Even if he'd lost his head this morning he's too honest and decent to have let himself be manipulated for fear of us revealing what he'd done. This way he's grateful, and his gratitude will be worth much more." She reached out and squeezed August's hand reassuringly. "Trust me, August. I know men, and I'm right about him."

August nodded slowly. "Do you like him?"

Hanna looked at him fondly. "I think I was even more tempted than he was, which was not at all what I'd intended. And if he'd been free, and asked me to live with him, I'd have abandoned all of you and done it. So yes, I suppose I like him."

There was such wistfulness in her voice that it was his turn to squeeze her hand, but before he could say anything another voice chimed in.

"Who do you like, mum?" asked Jon, creeping in quietly behind August. "Do you mean the policeman?"

Hanna pulled him to her and hugged him. "Yes, my darling, I do mean the policeman, and his name is Magnus."

"Are you going to marry him?"

"Would you like me to?"

"Yes, I think I would."

"Then you'd have to persuade him to leave his own nice wife, and his little boy and girl, and I don't think that'd be a proper thing to do. Anyway, just because I like him I don't think I really want him here, under my feet the whole time. I've got enough trouble with you and August."

Jon sprang up into her arms and kissed her. "I don't really need anybody else either. You and grandpa are fine, though it'd be nice to have a dad who carried a pistol all the time."

"I've got guns," objected August, "and I've let you fire them."

"But that's just a shotgun and a rifle, grandpa. I'd like to shoot a pistol."

"Be off with you," said Hanna, putting him down and pushing him towards the door, "I've got a bilberry pie to make."

"I'll go and see uncle Henning and the goats," Jon called over his shoulder, and then he ran out of the house.

"I wish it would all be over soon" said Hanna wistfully.

"You're the one who claims to know men," replied August. "Does your policeman seem the sort to miss the trail completely and then give up?"

Hanna shook her head. "No," she said thoughtfully. "He doesn't give anything away, but he's certainly not going to give up, and I don't think he's as interested in Paulus as he might have been. He notices a lot and thinks a lot. He even asked me where Elin got her amber; so he'll be around for a while yet." She brightened as she said it, and added teasingly, "So there is a good side, and I'll try to concentrate on that."

CHAPTER 12

On his return to his office Magnus had to take an immediate decision. Three eighteen year old German hikers had set off the day before to explore the six and a half thousand acre Skuleskog National Park, including its deep ravine. They'd left no indication when they expected to return, nor whether they intended to stay out for the night; but in the early hours of the next morning two of them staggered into the Visitor's Centre in a state of utter exhaustion. They'd got lost, they'd quarrelled with the third member of the group, Christian, over the direction they should go and finally he'd lost patience with them and gone off on his own without a mobile phone. They also admitted they hadn't kept to the marked trails, but thought it would be more fun to explore the wildest reaches. They'd seen no sign of Christian since they'd parted, and the leader of the four man park team which set off immediately to search for him had just rung Magnus to report that they'd had no better luck. Magnus, sighing at the thought of the expense and hoping it could be recovered from the hikers or their government, ordered out the helicopter. It was a no-win situation. If he'd refused, the hiker would probably have been found seriously injured or dead, and there would be an outcry over police lack of concern for tourists; but now he'd said yes Christian would probably be found enjoying a hearty breakfast at his camp fire, requiring no help at all, and the resulting furore would concern a police officer's reckless disregard of financial restraints.

On his answer-phone there was a brusque message from Hillevi telling him she was still working on the clothes and shoes, so not to come until three o'clock. He wrote an up-to-the-minute report and sent it through, cleared as much other business as he could, and then turned his attention to photographing the murder weapon. Putting on latex gloves he took the knife out of the box and damaged bag, laid it on his dark blue mouse-mat, and using his own digital camera took pictures of both sides from every angle, deleting any that were poor and re-taking them. Then he concentrated on close-ups of the decoration and the blade. When he was satisfied, he took out the memory card, downloaded the photos onto the computer and rang Wennberg's in the Old Town of Stockholm, explaining what he wanted. The young girl who answered was alert and sensible, confirming they kept full records of purchases and purchasers. But as the knife expert was currently in Kiruna he should send the photos to that e-mail address, and if it turned out they *had* sold the knife she ought to be able to get him an authoritative reply by the next day.

Magnus lay back in his office chair, stretching his long body and closing his eyes as he reviewed what he'd discovered so far. The murdered man appeared to be a stranger, probably a foreigner. He'd been stabbed with a Sami knife too valuable to be in the possession of Paulus. Nobody had seen Paulus in the vicinity except August, who only thought he had; but, even so, Paulus had done a runner. Anything which might have provided personal details of the dead man had been removed, so presumably the killer didn't want him identified. Nobody at Frisks had seen or heard anything, not even Olof Petter, the only one who did not seem under the thumb of August, and the only one who had a record of violence. Frisks was in terminal decline, and eight years ago August had lost his only son, a son who'd married the prostitute he had provided for him.

Magnus pondered this. Why had August brought back a brothel girl? Why did he imagine his son would be interested in her, and why had Daniel apparently been so smitten he'd married her? Hanna had said she hadn't loved Daniel and he hadn't loved her. It had been a marriage of convenience for both of them, and he could understand the respectability and financial security she had gained. But what had been convenient in the marriage for him? Had it simply been a matter of shyness, the need to have an experienced girl who could show him the way? If so, it had certainly been successful, for he'd got her pregnant. Magnus felt he should have asked Scholander more about

Daniel, who was beginning to intrigue him. In retrospect it seemed to him that August hadn't spoken of him entirely as a loving father should; Hanna hadn't spoken of him as a loving wife should, either; Scholander had been cryptic, and neither his great uncle and aunt, nor Elin, had mentioned him at all.

Magnus looked at his watch, stood up, and went to make himself a coffee. He would have to leave soon, and there was no point in thinking too deeply about Daniel unless some link could be established between Frisks and the dead man.

Just as he was about to leave to see Hillevi, he received a call from Skuleskog, giving him good news. The hiker had been found with a badly broken leg, in an entirely different direction to the route he'd intended to follow. The ranger thanked him, added something exceedingly rude about amateurs, and left Magnus with the superstitious feeling that it might be an omen. The day, which had almost begun so disastrously for him in the forest, would now be lucky for him. It would take an hour to drive to Kramfors, and he might be two hours there. By the time he drove back his office would be officially closed; but if, instead, he drove in the opposite direction, home to Sonja and the children, his luck might hold and give him the chance to restore his marriage to normality, to feel clean again. Impulsively he decided he'd do it, and hurried excitedly to his car, smothering the knowledge he was following Hanna's advice and that far from banishing her from his thoughts he had only adjusted how he thought about her.

Hillevi let him in. She'd been eating, and the evidence was clear not only on her lips and beaded cardigan but also in the colour of the chewing gum which protruded from the corner of her mouth and emphasised her words as soon as she began to speak.

"Have you learnt anything more about your corpse?" she asked, notifying him that garlic had been a lunch ingredient.

"Nothing," said Magnus. "Nobody knows him, nobody seems to have seen him. He certainly isn't local."

Hillevi settled her bulk comfortably into her chair, then looked up at him archly. "He came in by boat the day before he was killed, from Poland, I think."

Magnus stared at her in amazement. "How do you know that?"

"What did Burman say about his shoes?"

"They were Italian, and very expensive."

Hillevi snorted, the gum almost exploding from her mouth and partially adhering to her chin. "How typical," she sneered, pushing the gum back and wiping her hand on her magenta blouse. "He's such a dandy himself he can't see beyond the quality and the price. If he'd looked at the soles instead of the polished bits he'd have seen that although he was a city man who normally walked on pavements, he'd recently been in wilder places unsuited to such fine footwear. There are grains of sand deeply embedded in the maker's name shield so ostentatiously stamped into the heel, and on top of the sand minute particles of a fragile seaweed found only on the rocks of the High Coast. I've been collecting specimens of sand from around the Baltic since I started in this sort of work more years ago than I'm going to admit to a randy young sod like you - it might turn you off." She fluttered her eyelids coyly at Magnus, reached out for a bottle of Tällberg's Festive Aquavit and took a long gulp. She offered him the bottle but Magnus shook his head.

"You need to loosen up," she grumbled, "or you'll become a joyless bureaucrat like some of your colleagues, or a self-regarding prig like Burman. Where was I?"

"Sand," answered Magnus, trying to look more relaxed.

"Yes, I checked it against the hundreds of samples I have, and the type in his shoe, very pale and fine, comes from the Vistula Spit, a sand bar running along the Polish coast east of Gdansk. It's so fine it doesn't stay long in the crevices of a shoe when you're walking about. But it would stay there if you stepped from the sand into a boat, remained seated for most of the voyage, and then got out onto a rock covered in wet seaweed which would adhere to the shoe and seal in the sand. If you're stabbed shortly afterwards, and haven't done too much walking in between, both sand and seaweed will still be there – and it was."

Magnus was excited and showed it, reaching for the bottle, toasting her with it and pretending to take a swallow. "What you've done is absolutely incredible," he said admiringly. "A little bit of sand and seaweed shows where he came from, how he travelled, and where he disembarked."

"My dear young boy, it tells us more than that. If he didn't walk very far, then he was killed near where he landed. And you must ask yourself this – if a man was coming by boat to the High Coast, what would he normally get out onto?"

"A wooden jetty, I suppose. Every harbour has one."

"So why do you think a visitor who pays a large sum of money for his shoes, and is obviously proud of his expensive clothes, would get out of a boat onto a wet seaweed-covered rock?"

"Because he wanted to land secretly, away from any place where others might see him?"

"Exactly, like an illegal immigrant, though a man with his money certainly wouldn't be that because he could pay his way into any country."

"But then there would be some sort of official record, and he might not want that."

"Good boy." Hillevi took another swallow from the bottle, and Magnus did not refuse it when she pushed it back towards him, for he was wildly jubilant. There had been a massive leap forward in his knowledge, and it was greater even than Hillevi herself, who did not know the lay-out of Frisks, could possibly know. He grasped the bottle by the neck, hoping his thumb and forefinger were wiping it clean of any adhering chewing gum, then took a gulp. It was smoothly powerful, rich with the flavour of bitter orange, ginger and rosehip; and the heat it engendered ran through him mingling with the warmth of his additional knowledge of a more fundamental reason why a man might be compelled to leave a vessel at a rock and not a jetty.

"I don't know how to thank you," he said earnestly. "Inspector Amrén said you were good, but I'm staggered at what you've been able to tell me from a pair of shoes."

"Dear, dear boy, there's plenty more." She waved him to a dishevelled arm chair, and when he'd sat down, but hadn't let himself sink into it, she eyed him shrewdly. "Going on somewhere after me, are you?"

"I'm going to visit my wife and children. They're in Jämtland while I'm stuck temporarily in the High Coast."

"God in Heaven," exclaimed Hillevi, sounding scandalised. "Children! You hardly look old enough to be out of college. How many have you got?"

"Two. A girl and a boy."

"And you've been missing them, and your wife, and you can't wait to see them, even though you'd be welcome to stay and have fun with me. It's understandable, I suppose, but make sure you remember your wife will have been missing you too, so give her an extra-specially good poke. That's what I always waited for when my husband was away, but he never did it and the marriage fell apart after a year. Sex is an important glue in a marriage, though idiot marriage-guidance counsellors are usually too prissy to tell you that. Of course it's also a great compensation when the marriage is no more."

She winked at him lasciviously, indicating encounters he preferred not to think about, and he attempted to take her back to her forensic skills by asking her what else she'd discovered.

"Sex," she answered dreamily, and Magnus feared the drink had put her onto a single track. "Sex is another thing I found, semen to be precise. Did the great Dr Burman not tell you?"

Magnus shook his head and Hillevi looked maliciously triumphant. "Because he never bothered to look, that's why. He's not interested in sex, finds it rather unpleasant, even rejected me when I offered to help him overcome his distaste for it, and so he doesn't see it unless it's drippingly obvious. But I always test the crotch of trousers and there it was: semen seepage. Not much, I confess, but I don't miss things like that.

So yesterday I went to have a look at the body when Burman wasn't there, and sure enough I found semen on the tip of the penis; and what a whopper he had, too."

"And that means…?" asked Magnus cautiously.

"Oh, darling, you are an innocent. It means he was sexually excited just before he was stabbed."

"Which might be a motive for stabbing him?"

"Jealous husband or lover?" pondered Hillevi doubtfully. "It's possible, I suppose, but he hadn't got his trousers down or there wouldn't be semen inside them, and he hadn't ejaculated later, so he wasn't caught in the act. And I'd have noticed if somebody had tried to pull his trousers up after he was dead, or even put them back on him. Anything like that leaves indications, and there weren't any, at least not the sort consistent with something like that. It's not easy to re-arrange clothing once a person's dead, and after so many years I can read clothes like a favourite book. There was nothing but pine needles and a little earth on the front of his jacket and trousers where he'd fallen when he was stabbed, so I think we can assume he was either standing alone, exciting himself in his thoughts, or he was about to do something to another person, was aroused at the prospect of it, but was killed before he could get started."

"It's odder and odder," Magnus reflected, relaxing now into the chair as he began to treat Hillevi as a clever colleague. "Why should a man cross the sea from another country, land in great secrecy, and then get sexed up in some way that resulted in his death?"

"I can tell you the scientific facts, but I'm no good at speculation. If you've got that gift you'll make a good policeman. But I must remind you there is no evidence that his sexual arousal and his death are necessarily linked, though you may feel there is a presumption of it. At this stage you must keep an open mind, accepting he may have been watching something he could see through a window perhaps, something as simple as a girl undressing; and then he may have been opportunistically killed while his attention was elsewhere, for some reason we know nothing about yet."

"But why did he come to the High Coast? What could he want there?"

Hillevi shrugged. "People travel to other places for many reasons, to meet up with a secret lover, for example, or to exact revenge. Either of those would account for the sort of clandestine visit this seems to have been. But there are so many other possible reasons, and you'll have to think them out. But there is one more thing…" She held up her hand like a conjuror about to produce a rabbit from a hat. "But if you really want it you'll have to work for it."

Magnus smiled at her dramatics, feeling suddenly much more at ease with her. "I'll do anything I can," he replied. "You've helped me so much already, and I'm still going to need all the assistance I can get. I can't do this one on my own."

"Then I want you to tell me all you've discovered about the murder weapon. It's not idle curiosity, it's vitally important."

Magnus told her, and she listened in silence. Then she nodded, as though what she had heard satisfied some theory she'd already formed. "You'll have to trust me for the moment, for I'm not going to tell you any more. You've learnt a great deal from this Finn Jonsson and it was clever of Amrén to put you on to him. But he has one weakness he can't help, poor man. He's not a Sami so he can't answer certain tiny but, to me, vitally important questions about the knife. So I want you to go to Lapland as soon as possible, to Jokkmokk. The Sami People's High School is there, beside the museum. Ask for Olav, the Head Tutor, and tell him I sent you. He's a fine artist, makes wonderful knives himself, and if he knows you're from me he'll be more likely to reveal what are, to the Sami, well-kept secrets of how they do the decoration. He'd never respond over the phone, or by email, not to me or anybody else. It has to be a personal visit, a face to face discussion and even so the shameful history of centuries of ill-treatment by the Swedes makes the Sami reluctant to trust their former oppressors. Politicians everywhere should be more aware of the time it takes to wipe clean the evil done to others. Look at Ireland, look at the Balkans and look at the hatred that's being built up in the

Middle East. Fortunately you look more like a Sami than a Swede, so I've a feeling Olav will open up to you."

Magnus felt his heart sink. Jokkmokk and back would take at least two days, and even if he could get permission to go he didn't know how he could spare the time.

"What do you need to know?"

"First, the exact ingredients used in the making and colouring of the designs on the handle of the murder weapon. You can, of course, promise complete confidentiality. Second, I must know the precise material which would have been used to attach the missing sheath to the belt."

"I'll do my very best," Magnus assured her. "But I'm only a constable, I'll have to get permission."

"Who from?"

"Inspector Amrén."

"You'll get it then. He's not a fool."

"Can you give me any idea why it's so important, so that I can tell him?"

"You naughty boy," shrieked Hillevi delightedly, "trying to find out about your present before it's beneath the Christmas tree. But you won't get round me, however much you roll those lovely eyes. You bring me the information, and then I'll really surprise you."

DAY 4

CHAPTER 13

Magnus got out of his car and ran up the steps to his office. It was still before seven in the morning, but he'd woken so early and so happily beside Sonja he'd decided to slip away before anything could spoil the perfection of their reconciliation. But looking at Sonja's sleeping face, relaxed and at peace now, a wisp of dark hair lying across one cheek, he'd been unable to resist kissing her, and she, still not properly awake, pulled him to her and they made slow and comfortable love in contrast to their hot and urgent coupling a few hours before. Then there had been flashes in his mind of blonde hair, a smaller, tauter body and a tattoo his imagination luridly distorted; but as they reached their mutually ecstatic climax the vision seemed to be obliterated, burnt out for ever, he hoped, in the fire of his rediscovered love for Sonja. And in the morning light, making love again, he did seem free of it, seeing only Sonja, feeling the wonder of her plumpness, inhaling her warm clean smell and wondering how he ever could have strayed, and desperately relieved it had been kept to mental straying only.

Contrary to his expectation he'd felt even more awake when they'd finished, more vigorous, eager to return to work, to follow up all he'd learnt the day before. So he left Sonja sleeping, crept in to Angelica and Johan, kissed them without disturbing them, then set off driving east back to the High Coast, his mind still coming to terms with what had happened the evening before. He'd arrived home still full of tangled guilt and resentment, but as soon as Sonja opened the door, and he saw the surprise and delight in her face, and the two children rushed at him as if they knew at once the tension was over, he felt quite different, conscious only of his own selfish thoughtlessness. He held Sonja close, whispering apologies in her ear and telling her he'd learnt his lesson, and that of course they wouldn't move, he could drive in to Sundsvall every day when he began to work there. But then he heard her hushing him, and saying it was her fault, she'd behaved so stupidly, and while he'd been away she'd driven in to Sundsvall, looking at it with new eyes, and now she was excited at the prospect of a change. She, too, he realized, had recognised the danger threatening their marriage and all they'd built up together, but, unlike him, she'd acted to make the best of a difficult situation. So they went inside, their arms around each other, and ate as a family, and he put the children to bed, and read to them, and then he and Sonja talked and talked. He, trying to match her flexibility, suggested that if they did decide to move it needn't to be to Sundsvall itself, but to the surrounding countryside a few miles north, Bergeforsen or somewhere like that. She jumped at the idea, telling him some friends had spoken highly of the nearby schools there; and as it was so close to Sundsvall there would be plenty of opportunities for her to find interesting work. Each encouraging the other, they became more and more excited, looking at houses for sale in the local paper, discussing changes to curtains and some of the older furniture; and gradually the excitement over all that might be before them became a different excitement, for each other, and he'd carried her to the bedroom.

Hanna and Hillevi were both right, he thought, driving through the freshness of the early morning. Hanna had told him to forget his stupid disagreements and make it up with Sonja, Hillevi had provided somewhat more down-to-earth advice; and poking his wife certainly seemed to have reassured her, demonstrating at least that he still couldn't keep his hands off her. He smiled, reflecting on the oddness that such a delightful act should, at times of crisis, assume an importance out of all proportion to the crudity of Hillevi's descriptive phrase. He wondered if Sonja sensed he'd hurried home because he'd begun to feel attraction in another direction, and needed her to keep him from temptation. She often showed uncanny perception where he and the children were concerned, knowing when something was wrong, and what it was, before there'd been any outward indication; but whatever she'd perceived on this occasion he knew she would keep it buried inside, and he felt thankful for her generous loyalty. From now on Hanna must be just another woman in his investigation, as she always should have been; and the only source of slight discomfort was the knowledge she'd subtly saved him from himself when she'd played the forest tart, and gratitude might tempt him to see her in a more favourable light than any future evidence might warrant. But on reaching Nordingrå and entering his office, all such considerations evaporated. A fax was waiting for him, giving him the name of the probable murderer.

It was from Wennberg's, a copy of the mailing details of the man who had purchased the knife. He was Konstantin Savchenko, a Russian from Kaliningrad.

Magnus sat down, his mind racing. It all made sense. Hillevi had told him the victim came from Poland, and now he knew the killer was a Russian. It might, therefore, be a political assassination, or a revenge killing rooted in the past when Poland was under Russian control. That would mean it was nothing to do with Sweden, nothing to do with Frisks; it would explain why no one there had seen the murdered man, and no one else had recognised him. He'd been fleeing Poland, knowing someone was after him, and that was why he'd landed so secretly. But Savchenko must have been waiting for him, killed him, and then probably went back to Russia. Such a scenario would mean the case was solved; and what a relief that would be. He would no longer have to risk his re-established happiness by seeing Hanna again and he would not have to dig among the secrets at Frisks that might reveal things about her he didn't want to know.

His euphoria lasted for many seconds before his common sense compelled him to put an end to it. It was a wonderful dream, but it didn't fit the facts. A terrified man, aware he might be killed at any moment, doesn't become sexually excited. And why would a Pole on the run come to such an out of the way place as the High Coast, and how did he know about the entrance to Frisks? Why didn't he run aground on the rock? And what had happened to his boat?

Despite the early hour he rang Amrén and found he was already at his desk. Excitedly he briefed him on his approach to Wennberg's and on Hillevi's discoveries, then dropped his bombshell, telling him the murderer's name and giving him his address. "She's a miracle, that Hillevi," he said. "I seemed to be getting nowhere, and suddenly, thanks to her, a pattern's started to emerge. The victim came to Frisks by boat from somewhere near Gdansk, got out onto that rock, which implies he'd either been there before or knew someone at Frisks, came ashore, got sexually excited and was then killed. Now Wennberg's has given us the jigsaw's missing piece, that the murderer was a Russian named Konstantin Savchenko." He paused, and then asked diffidently, "Do you think there's any chance it could be political?"

"Frisks is an odd place for political assassination," Amrén said cautiously. "You've done good work, very good work, and Hillevi as well, of course. But although we think we know the name of the murderer we still don't know who the victim is, why he was killed or what happened to his boat. If Savchenko was waiting for him at Frisks it implies he was already in Sweden so I'll get hold of Immigration as well as pursuing broader enquiries to try to trace him. I'll also contact the coastguards in case they have anything on a strange vessel in the High Coast area. Meanwhile I think you should go to Jokkmokk to get the information Hillevi needs. I've known her for many years, and when she wants something as urgently as that it's usually a crucial piece of evidence. Apart from anything else, it's to do with the murder weapon, so we must follow it up. Even if we know the murderer, and apprehend him, we still have to build a case against him."

"I'll find out about the trains, and go today," said Magnus. "Jokkmokk must be seven hundred kilometres, so I'm afraid I'll be away two days at least. Can you cover me for so long?"

"No," answered Amrén dryly. "That's why I'm going to call in a favour from the top man at Midlanda, and get him to put you on this morning's flight to Kiruna. It leaves at 11.10, and don't wear uniform or the other passengers will suspect a terrorist threat against the plane and panic. If you don't hear from me in the next half hour it'll mean it's fixed. You can claim a hire car on expenses, so organise one for Kiruna, something modest, not the top of the range. You'll have to move fast while you're there because I can only spare you for a day so you'll have to catch the evening flight back. As well as following up on Savchenko I'm going to send photos of the dead man to a colleague in Gdansk. If, as it seems, the victim came from the Vistula Spit near there, he may be able to get information on him. We've worked together before, and he'll help me if he can. By tomorrow, with any luck, we may know the name of the victim as well as that of the murderer."

Magnus tried to clear his desk as much as possible, then changed out of his uniform, locked his pistol into the safe, and put the box containing the knife in a sports bag together with a spare notebook and camera. Hearing nothing further from Amrén, he drove down to Midlanda airport relieved it was north of Sundsvall as he'd cut the timing rather fine. While he was waiting to board he rang the museum and made an appointment with the Head Tutor, Olav, for half-past four that afternoon.

By the time he'd picked up his hire car at Kiruna he needed to drive quite fast but found he was constantly slowing down to admire the strange beauty of his new surroundings. He was inside the Arctic Circle, above the tree line, and he revelled in the wild bareness, the great outcrops of rock, the distant mountains forming the border with Norway, the immense arch of the sky above, the sense of his own irrelevance in the vast indifferent emptiness where the power of nature so greatly exceeded the puniness of humans. Often herds of reindeer compelled him to go even slower as they roamed beside the road and sometimes on it, and as, in Lapland, they had right of way, any accident would cost him a lot of money. But it was not that threat which made him drive so carefully, but more his fascination with the creatures themselves. At this stage of the year both males and females bore massive horned weaponry which ought to have been daunting. Yet they moved along the road with such a comical wobbling gait, like elderly but intrepid shoppers at country market stalls, that it was hard to feel any fear of them at all and he just loved them for themselves

At the Ajtte museum his identity was checked, and then he was led through into the school and along to a small workshop. Racks of tools ran round the walls, chisels, files, saws, punches, clamps of all sizes,, electric drills, sanders and strange instruments presumably for leather-working. The room was dominated by a work-bench, and behind it sat a figure of total concentration, knees primly covered with a large leather apron, head and shoulders bent over a brightly-lit magnifier, hands holding a piece of horn upon which he was carving an intricate design. He had his back to Magnus, but he must have sensed his presence for he put down the short-bladed knife he had been using, placed the horn carefully on the bench vice, drew off the leather apron and rose to his considerable height, turning to face him. Magnus was surprised by his appearance, and instantly ashamed he should be so. He did not know exactly how he had expected a Sami knife-maker to look, but it was definitely not the gravely courteous man extending his hand to him who reminded him of a criminology lecturer he had greatly admired during his police training. Behind the round spectacles intelligent eyes regarded him with gentle curiosity, and Magnus took care not to crush the long sensitive fingers in his own usually firm grip. But the fragility was deceptive, the hand calloused and steely strong.

"I am Olav," he said formally, brushing his left hand through his thinning hair in an effort to tidy it, then pointing Magnus to the seat he'd just vacated and perching himself on the bench opposite him. For a moment both of them were silent, weighing each other up; then Magnus, realising Olav had said all he felt was necessary at that stage, briefly explained about the knife and its importance as evidence, though not mentioning that it was a murder case. He told him he'd been sent by Hillevi Zander and then produced the knife itself which he'd placed in a fresh bag. Olav took it reverently in his hands, silently staring at it for some minutes

"We may never see anything like this again," he said sadly, and Magnus saw there were tears in his eyes. "Esse's a very special friend, he worked here for many years to pass on his knowledge to the young, and when he became ill he persuaded me to take his place as Head Tutor. We all learnt from him, but nobody will ever equal him." He held up the knife again. "Such restraint, but perfect in every way. Look at the colour of the horn, so fine it can only have been taken from a reindeer bull slaughtered in the autumn. See the forging of the blade, the finest steel; and the deceptive simplicity of the decoration, which was so typical of him. Very few have ever been able to achieve such time-consuming precision. Of course all its qualities would strike you even more if the sheath were here. That's not been found?"

Magnus shook his head.

"How terrible that such a work of art should be involved in a police investigation. I hope that, as evidence, it will not be shown to the press?"

Magnus appreciated his tactful way of asking about its involvement in a crime, but he was as reticent as he'd been with Hillevi.

"It's too early to say. It will depend very much on how the case develops. But I do have two specific questions for you. You mentioned the sheath, which we haven't found, but we need to know how it would have been attached to a belt."

"By a loop of the finest quality reindeer hide."

"He never used any other leather?"

Olav looked solemn. "A true Sami maker only uses reindeer hide for a suspension loop, and reindeer sinew for any stitching."

"And would the sheath have been decorated too, like the grip?"

"Yes."

"And can you tell me how the decoration was done, what ingredients were used to colour it?"

Olav gave him a melancholy smile. "Hillevi is asking these questions, of course. She always wants to know everything. But these are not matters we usually discuss. Each maker has his own techniques, but it is not for others to know."

He sat very still, staring at Magnus, almost as though he were a piece of antler and he was trying to fathom its qualities and how best to shape it.

"Is it absolutely necessary that you know? Is it just Hillevi's curiosity, or can you assure me it will really help the police enquiry."

Magnus looked straight back at him. "Hillevi wouldn't tell me why she needs this information, but she's helped us so much already I trust what she says, and she believes it's necessary to know. I can give you my personal assurance that any information you give us will treated as confidential."

Olav nodded slowly. "Then I will trust you." He reached over and took the piece of horn from the vice. "All makers cut the design into the horn, as here, though the depth and delicacy of the cutting varies according to the ability of the artist, as does the style of ornamentation itself. But each artist makes up his own mixture to put into the tiny grooves, to colour them, to make the whole design stand out. Many ingredients are common to us all, but there is always some personal variation."

"Do you know what would have been used here?"

"Oh yes, Esse and I hid nothing from each other. He never used black lead, for example, nor did he use the more usual ground birch bark Instead he insisted on alder bark, taking it from a dry tree, scraping away the grey surface and then carefully rubbing off the brown inner bark with medium fine sandpaper and letting the powder fall into his collecting bowl. Then he would add a little soot and cocoa powder, blending it carefully to get the precise shade he required, mix it with warmed linseed oil and heat it gently until it achieved the correct viscosity. Only then would he apply it. And if all that sounds easy, you should have seen the care he took, the concentration on the exactness of the blend, the selection of the moment when it was sufficiently viscid, because then you would have known, as I knew, that you'd never get it quite as perfect as he did."

He stood up, went over to a cupboard, and came back with a knife, and what looked like a bottle and a scoop, both of wood inlaid with decorated horn. "I cannot match his technique," he said, "but these are examples with similar design work to his."

The knife took his attention first, much shorter than the one he had brought with him, with silver set between the matched pieces of horn of the handle, the sheath-tip turned back almost at right angles.

"Traditional Northern Sami knives have sharply angled sheaths like this," Olav explained. "Southern Sami sheaths are straighter, and they have their own forms of decoration. We keep very much to our individual traditions."

"What about the scoop and the bottle?"

"It's not a scoop, it's a milk pail. You place it beneath the female reindeer and milk her into it. And it's not a bottle, it's a salt container. Although Esse showed us the possibilities of new art forms, our subjects are still mostly from the time we all followed the reindeer on the annual migration. Everything then had to be practical, strong and easy to carry and we accept those challenges even now."

Magnus carefully studied the designs, but he was quite unable to see the minutely carved groves which had been filled and polished to satin smoothness; and with his new eyes he understood he was looking at the very highest quality work.

"Are there any women knife makers?" he asked as he handed the pieces back.

"Not knives," answered Olav. "Tradition again, I suppose, so men make knives. But there are many fine Sami women artists, especially in tree-root basketry, embroidery using pewter thread, weaving, and of course painting and poetry as well."

As soon as Magnus had finished his notes, promising to destroy them once he'd shown them to Hillevi, he stood and shook his hand, thanking him for his trust. Olav showed him out, back into the museum shop, and Magnus, diffidently, said he'd been so impressed by what he'd learned he'd like to purchase three small examples of Sami art as presents for his wife and two children. Understandingly Olav offered to point out the best within his price range, and Magnus left with a miniature knife for Johan; a tiny horn ptarmigan, the local mountain grouse, for Angelica; and for Sonja a higher quality and considerably more expensive birch wood box inlaid with decorated horn which he thought she might be able to use as a jewellery box.

He just made the late evening flight back to Midlanda, and having written names on his gift wrapped purchases he took a circular route back, driving through the midnight gloom round by his house. He let himself in as soundlessly as possible, put the presents on the table at the bottom of the stairs, then crept out and drove down to the High Coast feeling pleased with himself even though he would get only a few hours sleep.

CHAPTER 14

August could not sleep. At first he lay in bed shifting irritably from side to side, then rolling onto his back, but it was no use. Memories flooded through him, mixed with concerns and fears, and, unable to settle, he was driven to find some relief in pacing about his bedroom. Finally, despairing of sleep and anxious the creaking of the floorboards should not disturb Hanna and Jon, he got dressed and quietly let himself out through the front door. It was as dark as it ever got at this time of the year, a dim and gently comforting twilight. He made his way down through the trees until he could see the water. There was no wind and the night was warm. He stopped by an old pine tree whose trunk had split at chest height into two curving horns which formed a rounded window where he could lean his elbows on the sill and stare out across the sea. He'd stood there on the afternoon a neighbour's ship had come in close, the owner shouting and gesticulating wildly. He, realising it could only mean that Daniel's missing boat had been found, had caught his breath and felt the fear strike him in the midriff like a painful punch. He'd discovered the note by then, and knew what to expect. With an effort he'd controlled himself, strode purposefully to the beach, waded out and flung himself aboard, his face showing no emotion as he was told one of their fishing vessels had been discovered tilted at an angle on a rocky projection off the tiny uninhabited seabird sanctuary of Gnäggen. No body had been found on board and so they'd come for August, believing he would wish to lead the search.

No one seemed to doubt it had been a tragic mishap, and August never, then or since, let out a word about the note. Thoughtful as ever, Daniel had killed himself and made it seem an accident. They spread out cautiously along the shore where the body, thrown off the boat by the impact with the rock, would probably have been washed up. Thousands of screaming razor bills and guillemots mobbed them from their colonies on the cliffs as if they were mourners, wild with grief even before the corpse had been discovered. And after a fruitless hour, turning a corner at the islet's end, the father recognised the clothes, the special way his son sprawled on the stones, apparently asleep, and steeled himself to go up close, knowing the birds might well have taken the eyes and perhaps the facial flesh as well.

But the birds had respected Daniel and he looked serene in death, his troubles now all over. August hugged him to his breast and kissed the damp cold skin. There was none of the anguish and the horror he'd seen the last time he'd looked into his son's living face, none of the fury that had succeeded those emotions as the feelings both had suppressed so long erupted in a final frenzy of mutual blame. After years in denial he didn't doubt now he'd driven Daniel to his death, but it had never been his intention. In the midst of all the anger he'd gained an understanding of his son that had not been there before. The more they'd bellowed at each other, the bitterer the words, the more he'd felt, deep down, below the fury, that they might have reached a turning point, the long years of incomprehension finally over and a new start possible. In time, he'd told himself so often afterwards, he could have come to love him, to pour out on him the reservoir of affection walled up within him, never used.

But Daniel, to the very last, saw matters from a different point of view, clearly believing the only possible new beginning had to be an end. Then, when he was just a memory which could be smoothed and re-shaped by grief, it might be possible for his father to release that long awaited love. It was probable, he hoped, that Daniel went calmly to his death, believing it would resolve the problems which had dogged his life, that now at last his father would be able to think of him with a tenderness unfelt while he had lived.

Hanna took his death more philosophically than he did. She saw the note before it was destroyed, and understood that death had been his earnest wish, felt glad he was at last at peace. Perhaps, thought August, she wouldn't allow herself to be upset because of what she hoped she had inside her. So, gradually, life seemed to resume its usual rhythm, though August knew it was only on the surface, for him at least. With Daniel's death something died in him as well, and though he would fight for the unborn child as hard as he'd always fought to preserve Frisks for his son, he no longer cared about the means he used.

He walked down to the shore and stooped to pluck some northern rock-cress, placing it on the little cairn of stones raised in private memory of his son; and staring down at it he knew, within himself, conscience and self-awareness were turning to self-disgust. But his task was nearly done. If only the policeman would go away, admit defeat and stop his probing, Jon would have an inheritance he could be proud of. It was almost within his grasp, and if only Arvid had still been the local policeman he would have recognised he would get no further in the investigation and would have wrapped it up, naming the missing Paulus as the likely perpetrator. But Magnus seemed unable to back off. He wanted to know who Gubbo was, he wasn't put off by Olof Petter's sudden rages, he'd ingratiated himself with Henning and Ingegerd, and even Elin blushed when he was spoken of. Jon seemed to see him as a father figure, and Hanna was playing a dangerous game relying on his gratitude. She should have seduced him when she'd had the chance, it was what he had expected. But she'd surprised him, disappointed him, and he was worried she might be cutting her own path instead of following his.

He knew Magnus had talked to Scholander, and he'd certainly pick up hints and innuendo from everyone to whom he spoke. Behind the Thai features, so alien in these surroundings, he'd be putting together the pieces he'd collected. Perhaps he already knew about their visitor? If not, it wouldn't be long before he did.

DAY 5

CHAPTER 15

When there was no response to the bell Magnus was worried Hillevi might still be in bed at nine o'clock, but just as he was about to ring again she opened the door and he hardly recognised her. She was in white overalls, her hair was pulled back from her face, she wore no make-up and her green eyes were brighter and more alert than he'd ever seen them.

"I've been in my laboratory double-checking the results," she explained briskly. "Come in."

Outside the laboratory door she pointed to a second pair of spotless overalls and Magnus climbed into them. "Put on the over-shoes, then pull the hood up and make sure it covers all your hair," she said, adjusting her own and checking him critically before leading the way into the lab. She eased herself onto a stool by the work surface, telling him to sit down opposite her, and then pushed towards him a pen, a piece of paper and an envelope. Holding her finger in front of her lips to warn him against any questions, she switched on a recorder incorporated into the bench and spoke clearly and carefully.

"I am asking Officer Trygg to write down for me the information he has obtained in Jokkmokk. First, the material which would be used to attach the sheath of the murder weapon HC 409 to a belt. Second, the ingredients which would have been used by this particular knife-maker to highlight the designs on the hilt, and the currently missing sheath which would have matched it."

She paused, nodded to Magnus, and he wrote the details on the paper.

"I am now asking him to sign the paper as a true record of what he has learnt, to add the date and time, to place the paper inside the white envelope, seal it and hand it to me, confirming in speech what he has done."

Magnus did what she instructed, held out the envelope, and said, "I. Officer Trygg, hand to Doctor Zander the details I have just written down, sealed in the white envelope."

Hillevi took the envelope, opened a drawer, took out another envelope, and said, "I, in turn, hand him a blue envelope containing the laboratory results of my analyses HC 409/7 and HC 409/8, and ask him to open it and comment upon the contents."

Magnus slipped his finger into the envelope and tore it open. Then he unfolded the paper. It recorded, in handsome old-fashioned writing, that fragments of reindeer hide had been found on the victim's belt, and that on the trousers, just below the same section of the belt, there were minute particles of soot, cocoa powder, and powdered alder bark, all once soaked in linseed oil.

Magnus stared at the paper, astounded at the accuracy of her analysis but appalled by the implications. Then Hillevi's imperious signal forced him to speak. "I, Officer Trygg, have read what is written here, and confirm it is identical to the facts I learnt in Jokkmokk."

Hillevi could not keep the look of triumph from her face. She ripped open the white envelope, confirmed what he had said, then switched off the recorder.

Magnus stared at her. "It was his own knife," he said dully. "He was stabbed with his own knife."

Hillevi nodded. "I thought it might surprise you, but you seem disappointed, too."

"I got the name and address of the purchaser of the knife from Wennberg's yesterday. I thought I'd found the murderer."

"And of course you had to show off your triumph, so you told Amrén, and now you feel a complete fool?"

"That's exactly how I feel," admitted Magnus, sighing. "I'll have to ring him straight away. Thank God I didn't say anything to anybody else."

"Too impulsive," said Hillevi, not unkindly. "But it's often better than being over-cautious."

"And you've proved you must be the best forensic scientist in the world. I just don't know how you could have found such tiny indications, or analysed them so accurately."

"I accept your praise of my analytic skills, but I'm impulsive too, and I guessed such an expensive knife would probably be his, it seemed to match his extravagant clothes and shoes, so I was looking for indications on the belt and just below it. There's something else, too. Whoever stabbed him didn't want it known it was the victim's own knife. So he removed the sheath by cutting through the reindeer hide suspension loop. I found tiny pieces of cut hide trapped between the belt and the trousers, and they could only have got there when the severed loop was pulled free."

"Why not undo the belt and slide it off?"

"He was afraid of leaving fingerprints, which shows he hadn't got gloves and so it probably wasn't premeditated."

"I'd better search for the sheath."

"I'm sure Amrén will be delighted to supply you with enough men to scour the forests, the bottom of the Gulf of Bothnia, and then dig up the beaches." The sarcasm hurt, but Magnus knew she was right. There were just too many hiding places. "Always use your brain rather than muscle," Hillevi went on. "Ask yourself why anyone would want to hide the fact it was his own knife."

Magnus frowned, thought for a moment, then looked at her. "I'm a fool," he said. "To put suspicion on somebody else. Sami knife, so Sami herder Paulus."

"It seems likely," said Hillevi drily. "Once you're pretty certain who really did it, then it may be worth searching their house and so on just in case you're lucky enough to find the sheath. But think it all out first, particularly the motive. That's the most interesting bit, because you have to know your suspects very well indeed, understand how they tick, and there's nothing more fascinating than human beings."

"Before you showed me the owner of the knife was the victim, not the murderer, I'd been trying to convince myself it might be a political killing, a Russian killing a Pole. But now it's almost certainly a Swede killing a Russian who'd travelled to Poland and crossed the Baltic from there."

"Which part of Russia did he come from?"

"Some place I'd never heard of, Kaliningrad. But more of the Polish background may fall into place soon. Inspector Amrén is in touch with the Polish police, though thanks to my rashness he still thinks he's asking about the murderer, not the victim. I really must contact him straight away and set the record straight. But I'll always be grateful to you, I'd have got nowhere without you."

"If you want to demonstrate your gratitude my bed is always open to you," said Hillevi as they left the laboratory and took off their overalls. "But you look so different to the last time I saw you, so sleek and satisfied, I suspect you followed my advice about your wife and so have lost your reprehensible but flattering lust for me."

Magnus was about to protest he'd never thought of her like that, but stopped himself just in time. "I did follow your advice," he said, "and, as always, it was good advice. But now I've got to continue to keep my marriage together, so I'm going to have to control myself."

"That's too bad," grumbled Hillevi. "But you know where I live, so I'm sure we'll meet again, professionally if not romantically. And if I may give you one more piece of advice, for Christ's sake look at a map so you at least know where Kaliningrad is."

As soon as he was in his car Magnus contacted Amrén. "I've made a blunder," he confessed. "Hillevi's used the information I got from Jokkmokk to prove the murdered man was stabbed with his own knife. So Konstantin Savchenko isn't the murderer as I thought, he's the victim. I'm sorry if I've made it awkward for you with the Polish police or anybody else."

"That's all right. Immigration knew nothing, the coastguards had no record of a strange craft. As for the Polish end, Jurek Bojanowski was pretty certain he recognised the photo of the dead man as some Russian Mafia hood, and thought he'd heard the name Savchenko in a similar context, so he won't be at all surprised they're the same person. He has a lot of dealings with people like that, which is why I thought he might be able to help. So where do you think the new information leaves us? With August Frisk?"

"It seems that way. He was the only one to claim he'd seen Paulus, and so put suspicion onto him." Magnus explained about the evidence Hillevi had for the removal of the sheath.

"But we haven't got the smell of a case against him," said Amrén firmly. "He only said he was pretty certain he saw Paulus, there's nothing to link him to Savchenko, no motive, and no one at Frisk's is breaking ranks. I've got a little more information for you about Gubbo. His real name is Ove Hallman, the only survivor from the fishing vessel *Solsken* which sank when the engine caught fire, the fuel tanks exploded and the boat sank. He was found tangled in rope attached to some floating debris. He'd lost his memory and his power of speech, but I don't know about brain damage. As I'd expected, the Prosecutor has ruled out any check on his medical records."

"Gubbo's background doesn't seem so important now, after all the other things we've discovered. What do you think we ought to do next?

"I doubt if we'll make any progress until we find out why Savchenko went to Frisk's, and then everything may start to unravel nicely. That means you've got to go to Poland, to Gdansk. Jurek wants to see one of us, he's got some crazy plan to get more information but he needs a Swedish policeman with him. To be precise he wanted me, but when I explained I couldn't get away, and that I hadn't even seen Savchenko's body, he agreed it should be you. Vessberg has accepted it as well. He's been impressed with your investigation so far, not least because nothing yet has required him to become personally involved."

Magnus suspected Amrén had deliberately arranged to let him stay in the front line, and he was excited. "When do you want me to go?"

"There's an early evening flight from Stockholm, so I'm afraid it's back to Midlanda to catch the afternoon plane. I'll get the bookings made for you, and I'll meet you there half an hour beforehand so I can give you something for Jurek. He said you should take your warrant card and badge, but you shouldn't wear uniform."

"Did he give a reason?"

"Jurek's not much good on reasons," Amrén answered awkwardly. "He's unorthodox, you could certainly say that, and policing in that part of Poland is a great deal rougher than it is here. It's probably got something to do with keeping you safe. He may want to take you over the Russian border, and they don't like foreign policemen there. But he's a good man, and you'll be safe with him. Just do what he tells you, keep your thoughts to yourself whatever you may feel inside, and take care; the border areas can be pretty dangerous. I'll have your office phone switched through to this station so nobody can complain about your absence." There was a pause, and then Amrén added wistfully, "Report to me as soon as you get back – I can hardly wait to hear what Jurek gets you into."

CHAPTER 16

Bojanowski met him at Rebiechowo airport, fourteen kilometres west of Gdansk. He was a big man, as tall as Magnus, though considerably older and bulkier; but there was still a lot more muscle than fat. His close cropped hair scarcely revealed the grey, but it was there in his heavy moustache, and there were dark pouches under his eyes as though he did not often sleep. Unexpectedly Magnus was overcome with diffidence. This was Amrén's friend, a close companion from a past Magnus knew next to nothing about, a man who had wanted Amrén to come to him and who had been lumbered instead with a very junior unknown quantity. It made him awkward and he did not know what to say or what language to say it in.

"Forget my rank and call me Jurek," the man said brusquely in English, staring at Magnus and sizing him up with deep-set hard brown eyes. They shook hands, each feeling out the strength in the other's fingers, and then Magnus gave him the package Amrén had entrusted to him. Jurek gave a huge grin, ripped it open and extracted a tube of old-fashioned northern Swedish cheese-butter and a soft dark loaf of sweet bread. "*Messmör* and *limpa*," he exclaimed ecstatically, and as they walked towards the car he tore off a hunk of bread, squeezed the spread liberally over it and stuffed it into his mouth. "RaRa never forgets," he said when he had swallowed it. "My favourite Swedish food, and you cannot get it here in Poland."

To his surprise Magnus noticed Jurek was not driving him into the city, but east along the coast, and the thought suddenly came to him that he was probably covering in reverse the journey Scholander would have completed with his wife if that unexplained accident in Lithuania hadn't brought it to such a tragic end.

"I have a summer house at Krynica Morska," explained Jurek. "There are things to make clear to you, some necessary items to pick up, and then we start from there. You don't need sleep?"

"I had a sleep on the aeroplane," lied Magnus.

Jurek nodded in satisfaction. "I require little sleep myself. RaRa said you spoke English so I hope it's all right if we use it. My Swedish is not so good, though fortunately I could understand enough of the extremely rude version of one of your hymns RaRa sang to keep me alive during a dangerous mission I may tell you about later. Of course you Lutherans lack the respect for religion we Catholics have, and though it was funny I was also outraged enough to refuse to die until I'd told him what a profane shit he was." He put his foot down and the BMW surged forward, holding the corners as though there was glue on the tyres. Magnus, exhilarated by the speed, thought what a contrast it was to Amrén's habitual caution and he wondered whether the two of them had got on so well together because of their differences.

"The last ferry goes at twenty-three hundred," explained Jurek, "and we won't make it unless I speed up a little."

At Przejazdowo he swung off the E77 and headed north. Escaping death by a hair's breadth as they passed through Sobieszewo they finally screeched to a halt at the edge of the Vistula just as the ferry had left. Jurek leaped out of the car bellowing "Policja" at the top of his considerable voice, and waving his badge. The ferry reversed direction and Jurek got back into the car and drove on, showing no gratitude at all but lowering his window and snarling some Polish at the crewman which sounded extremely rude, though to Magnus all Polish sounded rude. He got out of the car and stared with interest at the water pouring so forcibly into the same sea which fringed the High Coast.

"That is Stegna over there," said Jurek, coming to stand beside him and pointing west. "And beyond it is the Vistula Spit which you'll know quite well by tomorrow. It used to have gaps in it for ships to go through, so the whole area was one huge harbour, but they've silted up now. Instead we have the Vistula Lagoon, only five metres deep, but with a lot of fish. In the winter we hold the international ice-boat competitions there, but most of my time is spent catching the smugglers. Having only one official entrance into the lagoon has certainly made that easier."

Magnus nodded, his mind full of questions which, unwilling to show his ignorance, he did not ask, hoping the answers would be made clear soon enough.

"As far as conversation goes, you could be descended from one of the Teutonic Knights who had strongholds all along this Prussian coast," complained Jurek. "They were sworn to poverty, chastity and silence and I only refer to the latter, of course. Though in fact the Knights *were* allowed to speak in combat, so perhaps you're the same and I'll have to wait to get to know you until we're face to face with the Russians. Come to think of it, I don't think the Knights bothered very much about chastity and poverty in battle either, probably raping and looting as much as all the others. But they were bloody good soldiers and that gives me some hope for you."

Magnus laughed, beginning to relax. "I'm not usually so quiet. I think I'm still a bit bewildered about why I'm here and what I've got to do. I'll probably talk too much once I've got my thoughts in order."

Once they were off the ferry they drove through Stegna and then beside the forested embankments of the seaside sand dunes. "Nazi concentration camp," commented Jurek as they passed a sign to Sztutowo. "It was the first to be set up in Poland, and the last to be liberated. Perfect site, sea in the north, Vistula in the west, fens in the south and east, so escape was assumed to be impossible. There was no need for watchtowers and dogs, but as Germans tend to be over-zealous they had them too. Eighty five thousand of our people died there, including many of my family. My father's brother, a giant man with red hair and a temper to match, did actually manage to escape and to get through the fens, the only man ever to do so. It was a great satisfaction to him, even though fever killed him two weeks later."

Magnus looked at him with interest. "In Sweden we can't talk as easily as you do about the Second World War. Even though there aren't many left who were adult at the time, it's still a difficult subject to discuss frankly. We have a hang-over of guilt about our neutrality and the fact that some Swedes secretly admired the Nazis."

Jurek shrugged. "Many Poles were pleased to help wipe out Jews, but our temperament is not given to guilt like your gloomy Nordic conscience. We find sin and goodness a lot less clear than you do. It was Russians who liberated the camp, so they were the good guys; but then they enslaved the whole country instead. How do you weigh those two things in the balance? I grew up under communism, I know of their atrocities; but my father was freed by Russians just as the Germans were about to shoot him. Maybe you need to accept that things happen, good and bad, and you just have to get on with your life. "

"So you've forgiven us for attacking you in the seventeenth century?"

Jurek grunted. "We refer to it as The Deluge, and it's not a compliment. You invaded this area, took over most of our country and forced our nobility to swear allegiance to your King Charles X; so it's certainly not something we've forgiven you for. We may not be good at guilt, but we are very good at hating."

At the small village of Katy Rybackie Jurek stopped the car on a rise and got out, motioning Magnus to follow him. He climbed through the tall pines, slipping occasionally in the sand, and then, on the top, he pointed. Stretching out in the evening light, like a finger laid along the coastal sea, Magnus saw a narrow high-ridged strip of sand disappearing into the distance, majestic white dunes dividing the calm water of the lagoon from the choppy waves of the Baltic Sea. It was like an attenuated desert, as rippled as a child's dreams of the Sahara, the dunes of classic parabolic form with knife-edge crests where the wind curled the sand onto the downward slope.

"The Vistula Spit which becomes the Curonian Spit," explained Jurek. "If you want facts and figures it was formed more than five thousand years ago, it's the biggest drifting sand dune in Europe and it provides the Baltic's only ice-free winter port. In places it's no more than five hundred metres wide and seems a lot less than that as you'll see when we drive along it, parallel to the coast, to my house. Later, it'll be our way in to the part of Russia which is of interest to us both, Kaliningrad. It's where your dead body lived and worked before he was conveniently killed." He pointed across the immense lagoon which the extended dune enclosed, and Magnus could just make out towers against the night sky. "That's Frombork cathedral," announced Jurek in the mockingly sepulchral tone Magnus now realised he reserved for his grim brand of humour, "and it brings us back to the matter of why we can't forgive you Swedes. Copernicus lived in the city, and when your hated King looted it he took all his astronomical texts and instruments. You've never given them back to us."

"I'm surprised you can put up with me," said Magnus, smiling.

Jurek clapped him on the shoulder. "RaRa vouched for you," he said, and they walked companionably back to the car. They drove slowly through the pine woods which covered whole areas of the Spit, and Magnus asked if it was their roots which prevented the sea washing the whole frail structure into the lagoon.

Jurek nodded. "The Russians didn't understand that at first," he said. "When, in 1757, their army besieged Kaliningrad, they chopped down all the trees along the dunes to build hundreds of flat boats to get their soldiers in close. They took the city all right, but in the years afterwards the wind whipped up the sand dunes and they began to move, swallowing up many of the neighbouring Lithuanian fishing villages."

It was nearly ten o'clock when they reached Krynica Morska, and Jurek parked beside a small half-timbered house at the edge of what seemed to be a largish resort facing the lagoon.

"Nice place," said Magnus, looking round approvingly at the orderly houses.

"Kaiser Wilhelm and his family liked it, so it became the fashion," commented Jurek wryly. "It was still Prussian territory then. But before that it had a different purpose. It was where they put their mad people and maybe that's rather suitable considering what the two of us are going to attempt."

They walked up to the projecting porch supported on carved wooden posts, and when Jurek had unlocked the stoutly-made door Magnus was ushered into a comfortably shabby room with a variety of well-worn bits of furniture. It smelt unaired, and Magnus guessed he had little enough time to make use of such a summer-only residence. Jurek poured two glasses of vodka and handed one to him. "You'll need it," he said, "and if you don't have that little smell of vodka on your breath you certainly won't fit in where we're going."

He unlocked a steel safe and threw a short-barrelled revolver and a cut-away belt holster to him. "Put it on under your jacket. You don't have to use it, unless everything becomes a balls-up, but it's a necessary part of the picture I have painted of you. To them you are the tough Swedish cop who killed Konstantin Savchenko."

Magnus, stunned, took a gulp of vodka before he replied. Then he said firmly, "I think it's time for an explanation."

Jurek jerked his thumb at a map pinned to the wall. "What do you know about Kaliningrad?"

"Nothing," admitted Magnus, moving nearer to the map and remembering he'd failed to follow Hillevi's parting advice to find out exactly where it was. "Was it named after somebody special?"

"Mikhail Kalinin, president of the Supreme Soviet during the second World War and known in his homeland as the Kind Grandfather. In Poland we have less flattering titles for him because he ordered the 1940 Katyn massacre by Soviet forces, the deliberate mass execution of the Polish officer class, fifteen thousand of them."

Magnus heard the bitter repugnance in Jurek's voice, saw the bleakness of his expression and shivered as he remembered his comment that the Poles were very good at hating

"That sounds like something so bad it's almost impossible to move on from?"

"It's certainly one of the things that brings us closer to your Swedish problem, the inability to have totally honest attitudes to certain events. I, for one, can't forgive that massacre. But as for Kaliningrad itself, it's a very special place. Russia needed an ice-free port on the Baltic and so took Königsberg, the capital of East Prussia. But when the Soviet Union broke up, Kaliningrad, as they'd renamed it, became completely isolated from Mother Russia, a tiny bit of territory with sea on one side, Poland on another, and Lithuania on the other two. The Russian fleet is rotting there, and it's become a sort of Mafia hell-hole, controlled by gangsters who make a good living from smuggling. By boat they have easy access to Estonia, Latvia, Finland, Sweden, Germany and Denmark; cross-border they can get into Lithuania and Poland, though that doesn't stop them using the sea routes as well."

"We'd discovered Savchenko lived in Kaliningrad," said Magnus, "but because I'd never checked it I had no idea it was so separated from Russia proper. Is there anything to link him to organised crime there?"

"No proof, just the fact that he *did* live there. But I knew I'd seen his face before, and as I spend a lot of time among criminal records there was good chance that's where I'd come across him. So I followed it up and asked a few questions among some contacts I've established in Kaliningrad."

"And...?" asked Magnus.

"Not very much, so far. They're a secretive lot anyway, but they're also very afraid. The big boys are not nice people, and they have unpleasant ways with informers or any who stop co-operating with them. It's always a death sentence, but usually carried out very slowly. So I've taken a little gamble and set up a midnight meeting in Kaliningrad with one of the bosses, and, if he thinks it's worth it, he may give us information."

"Why should it be worth anything at all?"

"There are three main groupings, and I'm hoping Savchenko belonged to one of the rival families, not his. That way he'll be pleased to hear you killed him, especially if you can convince him he's really dead."

Magnus stared at him. "You're taking me to the meeting, telling them I'm the killer, and you don't even know whether he's one of their own men?"

"I told you it was a gamble," Jurek replied imperturbably.

"And if it turns out Savchenko *did* work for him, what then?"

"He'll feel threatened, it'll turn nasty, and I'll probably have to kill him," answered Jurek with a delighted grin. "I would enjoy that, it would solve many problems for Poland, and you would have to help me shoot our way out. Are you a good shot?"

"I'm a police marksman," admitted Magnus. He took another gulp of vodka. "But it's not the usual way I…"

"It'll never happen," Jurek reassured him cheerfully. "But you need to look tough, and act tough if necessary, it's the only thing they respect."

"And it's necessary they believe I killed him?"

Jurek nodded. "It's no good going to people like this with crap about law and order, murder investigations, identity checks and getting evidence. They do not understand such things. But reporting the death of a rival whose crime network they can take over, that *will* interest them; and in return you may get information to help you nail the real killer."

"When do we leave?"

"As soon as we've eaten. Just over half the Spit is Polish, then it becomes Russian, so I've made arrangements."

Jurek fried sausage, cabbage and egg, and they ate it with hunks of bread. He washed it down with more vodka which he drank like water and with as little apparent effect. Magnus opted for real water. "If I need to shoot I want to be clear enough in my head to avoid hitting you by mistake," he explained.

Jurek looked at him curiously. "It must be the Thai blood," he grunted, "but I don't hate you as much as most Swedes."

"What about Inspector Amrén?"

"He saved my life when we were working together once, threw himself at the gunman as he was shooting me and spoilt his aim; so he's an honorary Pole. The gunman still hit me, but missed any vital bits and I was able to kill him before I fell down."

"Was that when he sang the hymn?"

Jurek nodded. "I was losing a lot of blood, and RaRa was afraid I'd die if I lost consciousness, so he prevented it by making up silly versions of hymns he knew. He's a very bad singer, but what I understood of it made me laugh, especially the bawdy bits, and so I stayed awake until the ambulance came. RaRa's as tough as hell in a fight, absolutely fearless, and you're lucky to have him as boss. He's got no time for fools, and he spoke well of you, said you were shot recently doing something bloody silly but a bit brave because it may have saved somebody else from getting the bullet. I think that gives me confidence in you, though I'm not quite certain yet. Perhaps you'd like to tell me about it?"

Magnus shook his head. "If I told you the truth you'd lose what little confidence you do have in me. Apart from anything else, I hadn't told anyone where I was or what I was going to do, so I was way out of line. And I'd better confess that, apart from interesting remarks about my colour, the words most often used about me in reports are 'rash' and 'obstinate'."

"Your colour doesn't worry me, nor does your stubborn streak; but where we're going is no place for rashness."

Magnus smiled. "Then I'll make a special effort," he promised.

They drove slowly through the dark twilight, the Spit seeming narrower now, especially as Jurek did not put his lights on. Twenty minutes later, just before they came to Nowa Karcyma, the last village before the border, Jurek parked the car off the track, in a clump of pines. When Magnus got out he could hear the sea lapping close by. The crisp air was invigorating, and the moon glittered coldly on the water, decorating the surface with dancing silver flecks. A grass-filled fold ran down to a miniature bay, and he slithered a few paces towards it, finding beneath his shoe a tiny piece of amber which he kept as a memento, and picking up a handful of the sand to let it stream comfortingly through his fingers. Just as Hillevi had said, it was extraordinarily pale and very fine.

"Come and bloody help," hissed Jurek, and Magnus hurried back to him. He had taken a small dark grey inflatable from the boot and was busy putting air in it. "There's an electric outboard in the back of the car, and a battery. Carry them down to the water and wait for me there."

Magnus stared round him as he took them down but they seemed to be completely alone. When Jurek joined him and handed him the oars he rowed out, trying to keep the flat-bottomed dinghy steady while Jurek attached the motor, and clipped the cables to the battery terminals. Then, without noise, the propeller started to rotate, the boat moved out more steadily and Magnus was able to ship the oars. The shore faded from sight and Jurek increased the speed, the bows rising against the water and the stronger churn of the screw just audible.

"An electric motor is good when you don't want to attract attention," commented Jurek. He swung the boat so that he was steering parallel to the almost luminous white sand of the Spit but far enough out to be virtually invisible from the shore. "We're in Russian waters now, and we ought to see our taxi very soon."

Shortly afterwards a light flickered four times some way in front of them, and Jurek slowed the motor. "They'll throw us a tow-line and take us into the naval harbour, so hang on tight when they go because they're speed-loving maniacs. When we get there, speak as little as possible, leave everything to me, and make no comment if I give you instructions or translate something. That's because I've noticed something about you. You're fucking frightening when you're quiet, a real killer look, but when you smile you look too nice. So stay serious. There'll be time to smile when we're safely back in Poland."

CHAPTER 17

There were two young men in the boat, scarcely more than boys, each wearing Russian sailor's uniform and both giving a nervous smile of welcome. One of them threw Jurek a line, and when he had secured it the Russian outboard shattered the silence of the Spit to which Magnus had become so happily acclimatized. It was, as Jurek had warned, a fast and furious ride, but when they reached the immensity of the naval harbour a sense of tragic awe seemed to overcome them and the engine cut to a funereal slowness, as if they were in church, conscious of their smallness against the towering haunted docks where nothing moved, the silent derricks keeping watch over the ghost fleet of rusting warships and unused submarines rotting in their berths.

"This is Baltisjk," said Jurek quietly. "It used to be the stronghold of the Soviet Baltic fleet, and what a force it was, too. Though Kaliningrad is eight hundred kilometres from Russia proper it had 250,000 military personnel in those days, and a small but thriving economy based on amber. Now there are just a few thousand sailors, bored out of their minds, mostly forgotten, frequently unpaid and so doing things for criminal gangs to get some money – which is exactly what these two do."

"What about the amber?"

"Ninety percent of the world's deposits are here, and there were two very big mines. Now both are nearly at a standstill because two-thirds of the production goes out of the back door. A lot is smuggled into Poland, though now it's with other things that are not nearly so harmless. It's why I have great interest in what's going on here, because it affects what happens on my patch. We can't stop it, but we can make deals to control it."

A very large car was waiting for them at the dockside. Another two men, professionally dour, older than the sailors and more expensively dressed, opened the doors for them, and soon they had left the docks behind. But as Magnus peered through the car window at the fields picked out in the headlights, the sight did nothing to lift his spirits. It was as if some latter-day Jason had sown his twentieth-century dragon's teeth in them, and instead of fighting warriors there had sprung up from the ground a mighty crop of tanks and armoured personnel carriers. There were thousands of them, seeming to stretch as far as the eye could see, a vast steel Cold War harvest, full of vicious potential but petrified, surplus to reduced requirements, parked in their orderly rows as if awaiting the order that would bring them back to life. Though an abundant crop, it was infertile, capable of nothing now but filling space, and left to moulder beneath torn remnants of the camouflage netting, their days of Moscow martial music over, no more salutes, the glory of the Labour Day cavalcades never to return. The only music now was the sea breeze singing to them, the only spit and polish the rain and snow which washed them and the only new insignia the weeds and thistles sprouting through their tracks. Magnus could not decide whether he was seeing a monument to peace, or a memorial to the folly of the superpower arms-race.

Gradually, as the steel gave way to the concrete tentacles of Kaliningrad itself, the nightmare he was driving through shifted to a new dimension, a surreal vision, an urban ugliness which seemed to make no sense, becoming more irrational as they neared the centre. It was as if the Soviet planners had not planned at all, nor cared how anything would look, nor even whether parts would ever become a whole. Buildings, whether necessary or not, had simply been erected on the rubble of the older city their army had destroyed, often left unfinished, some not properly joined to others in the row. Several had been left marooned, islands rising from the wasteland when streets, which should have serviced them, inexplicably went off elsewhere. Along the length of the central thoroughfare there were incomplete bridges, designed as flyovers but never connected, standing as purposeless arches straddling the traffic like the arms of blinded Cyclops reaching down for escaping captives on the track below but impotent to grasp them.

"It's worse even than it looks," Jurek murmured. "The average inhabitant must survive on less than seven fifty Swedish kronor a month, so it's no surprise there's so much crime. As for the AIDS epidemic, you really wouldn't want to know."

In the very centre, glowering over the river, a grotesque building dominated the city. "That's The Hall of the Soviets, but it's usually called The Monster," said Jurek. "It was built on the site of the old Königsberg fortress which was knocked down in the sixties after it was denounced as a monument to Fascism. The Monster was intended to be a monument to Communism instead, but just as it was finished the Soviet Union collapsed so it's never been used."

The man beside the driver turned round, grinning and pointing to the building; then he added something in Russian.

"He says the walls and floors have been stripped of everything that was saleable," translated Jurek. Then he added quietly, "He probably organised it himself."

Magnus stared at the bare concrete walls already beginning to crumble and he shivered, wishing he was back in the duller security of Sweden. Then the car crossed the River Pregola and he caught a soothing glimpse of the re-built cathedral with its fine spire on a fretted base. They turned onto a smaller road and into a quieter, leafier district where the brutalist communist architecture gave way to grander, pre-war German houses which had survived the Allied bombing. The driver and the guard visibly relaxed, chatting to each other in low tones for several minutes until roadworks forced them into a slow-moving queue and they swore. But there was no real passion in the cursing, and Magnus assumed it was an automatic reaction to a common occurrence. He noticed a sand-lorry swing in behind them, and then they reached the place where two men, working under lights, were excavating a hole in the road. A ramp extended over the top, and each car had to drive onto it in low gear and then wait until the traffic bar automatically rose to let it through. As soon as they halted on top of it Magnus, watching in the mirror, saw the driver of the lorry behind them climb down from his cab and get into conversation with the two workers who'd come out from under the ramp, propping pick and shovel against the side of it. Together they walked towards an all-night café some distance from where they'd been working. Their own driver sounded his horn peremptorily because the barrier had not gone up yet, but it only speeded the men into the building. Their haste seemed somehow unnatural, too precipitate, and Magnus, sensing an awful danger and feeling the hairs rise on the back of his neck, turned frantically to Jurek. But Jurek had already acted. His pistol was out, jammed into the driver's plump neck as he snarled something desperate in Russian. The car leaped forward, smashing through the barrier, accelerating down the other side of the ramp, tyres screeching as they hit the road at speed. An explosion underneath the ramp hurled them so forcefully on their way the driver almost lost control, and pieces of flying wood and rubble spattered the bullet-proof windows. The three men ran out from the sheltering café, firing their automatic pistols as they came, but the guard beside the driver had taken his Kalashnikov from the cradle beside his leg, and in what was clearly a practised routine leaped from the car as the driver suddenly slowed, slammed the door behind him and opened fire, bringing down two of them with his first burst. The driver left him where he was, speeding away through the winding streets, and although Jurek had thrust his heavy-calibre automatic back into his under-arm holster, the driver seemed just as frightened by the furious words that poured from Jurek's mouth.

"Someone must've talked," he muttered to Magnus, swearing bitterly. "Savchenko's friends obviously knew we were coming, knew you'd killed him, and this was their revenge. These brainless baboons were meant to be looking after us and they should've had their eyes open."

"How did you know what was going to happen?"

"Just in time I remembered the same trick was used a few years ago in a political assassination. Pretend you're road workers, put a bomb under the ramp, make the car stop on top of it, then detonate. If they hadn't been so fucking useless, so frightened of being hurt in the blast, they'd have got us. I was slow to spot the trap, and that's a worry. It seems I'm getting old."

"At least it shows Savchenko didn't belong to the group we're going to see," said Magnus, desperately trying to control a tremble of reaction.

"Yes, it's good, but I trust nothing here. Christ, I need a drink, I'm shaking like a belly-dancer." He glanced at Magnus. "You stayed loose. You used to being blown up?"

Magnus shook his head, finally letting the tremors run through him and wiping his face with his handkerchief. "I'm not brave," he answered, "I'm just frightened of looking like a coward."

Jurek nodded. "There'll probably be more to come, but it won't be so crude. Our hosts may want to check you're as tough as a policeman ought to be."

They drew up outside the gates of an unlovely but imposing house. Three alert men, also armed with Kalashnikovs, checked the car. The gates opened electronically and then closed behind them, and in the brief time it took the car to swing round the gravel drive and park in front of the house Magnus saw five other armed guards among the decorative shrubs.

They were taken in through a front door which was so thick Magnus assumed it had a steel core, then up a fine curving staircase to a lavishly furnished room with an ornate bar at the far end. It was only a few minutes before midnight.

"Undo your jacket," hissed Jurek as they went in, and the next moment they were hustled to the bar by four men who had followed them up the stairs, given large vodkas and then waved to a cluster of armchairs where two men in suits were already tranquilly seated. Counting the muscular barman and the guards who had closed the doors but undoubtedly remained outside, Magnus reckoned the human odds at nine to two.

The men in the armchairs were worth considering. Both seemed to be in their thirties or early forties, expensively dressed in what Magnus assumed were Italian suits and handmade shoes. One reminded him of the jovial doctor who had looked after him when he'd had appendicitis as a child. He had the same bushy brows, hairy nostrils and comfortable body, but instead of the twinkling eyes of the doctor he was met by a stare which was curiously dead, devoid of any apparent feeling at all. His neighbour, seemingly a great deal more genial, grinned broadly at them, his flesh almost bursting his jacket, and his eyes lost between fleshy crinkles and high hard cheek bones; but his grin had an expectant hungriness in it, as though he was thinking of fun to come. But Jurek seemed utterly at ease. He took out a photograph of the dead Savchenko and handed it to the two men with a flourish. Then he threw himself back in his chair, relaxing with his vodka, his jacket gaping to show the holstered automatic.

There was silence as the photograph was studied. Then the questioning began, in the course of which Jurek jerked his thumb at Magnus, chuckling as he did so. Two pairs of eyes fixed on him, and he forced himself to remain entirely passive. Then the two men got up and left the room by a side door, and Magnus realised this had merely been a preliminary survey and the matter had now been taken to a higher authority. The atmosphere in the room relaxed, the four men who had followed them up the stairs joined them in the armchairs, jokes were exchanged with Jurek, and a signal was given to the barman to refill their glasses.

"I think they'll test you now," said Jurek out of the corner of his mouth. "Don't be at all forgiving."

The white gloved barman came over with an iced bottle on a silver tray. He bent subserviently to fill Jurek's glass, then came over to Magnus and did the same, spilling some over his shoe. Magnus did nothing, and the barman, smiling contemptuously, began to walk away. Magnus swung his long legs, catching him as he moved, one wrapping round the front of his legs, the other striking him resoundingly on the buttocks and pitching him onto the floor with the spilling bottle and the tray. He sprang up, glaring at Magnus who saw Jurek's right hand glide towards his holster. But Magnus was flooded with a sickly-sweet feeling he experienced in extremes of danger, the adrenalin pumping, the absolute certainty he could reach the barman before he could draw a weapon, the knowledge there would be violence, that he would be inflicting it and there was no need to feel bad about it because it was being forced on him, and he needn't necessarily curb the level of it because his opponent was bringing it on himself.

"Any barman can make a mistake," he said quietly in English, "but you shouldn't have left the vodka on my shoe. That's why I had to wipe it on your arse."

Jurek repeated it in Russian and there was a roar of appreciative laughter. The barman's hand was under his jacket and he'd been hesitating, noting the strange eagerness in his opponent's eyes, the physical readiness, the mental longing. But the jeering laughter of his own people was more than he could bear and, going beyond his instructions, he made a bad mistake. He snatched out a knife, the blade flicked open and he launched himself at Magnus. But in the fraction of a second it took him to reach the chair, Magnus, realising his life really was in danger, had left it and was now towering over him, his hand grasping the wrist above the knife, twisting it so that the barman was forced to turn too. Then he thumped the hand down onto the bar so that the knife fell harmlessly from his crushed fingers. With the smallest of smiles, Magnus let go of the wrist, stepped back, and as the barman turned to face him he jabbed two stiff fingers straight at his eyes. He flinched back, as Magnus knew he would, and in doing so he exposed his throat. Instantly a brown fist struck his Adam's apple, a solid blow, hard enough to make him choke without inflicting too much damage. As the barman gasped helplessly for breath, Magnus picked him up, sat him on the bar, gripped his ankles, then neatly flipped him over in a backward somersault so that he fell down onto the floor the other side.

"Sleeping like a baby," he announced as he leant over and glanced down at the body prone on the polished wood boards.

Jurek again translated and Magnus returned to his chair with a round of applause which made him feel self-conscious. Many raised their glasses to him, Jurek did the same with an ironic smile; and Magnus was very glad of a gulp of vodka to help him return to normal. Then the side door opened and the two men emerged, standing smartly on either side to flank a third. The room fell silent and everybody stood.

He came forward slowly, disappointing in appearance, more like a lawyer than a fictional Godfather, small, balding, his spectacles on the end of his nose. But there was an air of authority about him which showed he knew his power and would never be afraid to use it. He walked over to Magnus, stopped in front of him and beckoned him to follow. At once his revolver was removed by one of the henchmen, while the other, seeing that Jurek was intending to follow too, stepped in front of him and shook his head decisively. Magnus braced himself and walked through the side door into a book-lined study, dominated by a fine Georgian walnut desk. Though the ornate gilded table lamps were dimmed two of the pictures on the walls looked familiar, and he wondered whether the insurers of an Oslo museum were already in negotiation for their return. He was ushered to a plain high-backed chair placed ready for him; and when his host sat down behind the desk he suddenly seemed much taller, able to look down at the man before him.

A door closed softly behind Magnus, leaving the two of them alone.

"I am Piatnitsky," the Russian said, speaking softly in English. He looked at Magnus thoughtfully, his weary eyes, dispirited by the long experience of gazing at the basest human emotions, still seemed to reach into his most secret recesses, scanning them placidly, beyond surprise now at any wickedness he might discover. Magnus felt they quickly unearthed the selfishness of his ambition, the Thai uncertainties beneath the Swedish confidence, the sexual desire for Hanna that had grown into an allegiance threatening to affect his actions as a policeman.

"I do not care to help the police of any land," Piatnitsky went on finally, lingering over the English words as though he was withdrawing them carefully from a largely unused memory-vault. "Nor do I think I have been told all the truth. Your Polish colleague is a pragmatist who considers that what is needful is more important than what is true. You could have killed the barman but you didn't; and I do not believe it was you who killed Savchenko."

Magnus felt his stomach tense with fear, as much for the failure of his mission as for the possibility of personal danger. He leant forward, feeling a response was needed and it would have to be a lie, but a lifted hand stopped him.

"In normal circumstances I would not have helped you much," the tired voice went on, becoming even fainter, "even though the news of Savchenko's death in Sweden is helpful and deserves a small gift, whoever it was who killed him. But I understand Savchenko's three brothers, now all deceased, made an attempt to kill you as you came to see me, and that is an insult to a guest requiring a rather greater recompense. The man who betrayed me, and you, by gossiping when he'd drunk too much, will never drink again, and eventually will die of lack of liquid. Your colleague will receive some information you both may need, and I will give you a few reassurances now, though please do not interrupt me with any questions for I must concentrate upon my English words."

Piatnitsky took a silk handkerchief from his breast pocket and coughed, and Magnus felt suddenly certain that cancer of the throat would be his likely cause of death rather than anything more violent.

"Savchenko was a knife-man. He was not one of mine, though from time to time I used him. He was a small fish who dreamed of being bigger in the Baltic Sea. If he had not been killed in Sweden I would have had, eventually, to order his elimination; for he was not a clever man and did not understand cooperation. So there will be, on this occasion, no retribution for his death. Those in Sweden involved in it will not be harmed, and though most of his networks will now pass into my hands, I have no further interest in Sweden except with certain individuals in the sale of arms who seem to need cooperation from me and who are far beyond the reach of policemen. So anything Savchenko set up there will exist no longer. It is my apology for your discomfiture when you were on your way to see me. Please give this to your colleague."

Magnus took the sealed envelope held out to him, scarcely able to free his mind of the horror of what might have happened to those at Frisks if fortune had not so favoured him on this occasion. He had a vision of a mutilated Hanna bleeding to death in the room where she had given him coffee, and he struggled to eradicate it.

"Thank you," he said to Piatnitsky, whose finger was already moving towards a button on his desk. But the finger stopped before it reached its destination.

"Did you kill Savchenko?"

"No," Magnus replied, certain the moment had come when he must speak the truth. "But the information you've given me will enable me to discover who did."

Piatnitsky, whose eyes had never left his face, nodded slowly. "There is a bigger picture, of course, and without that you would have left with less. What was your immediate impression of the docks and the city?"

"It was squalid," Magnus answered honestly. "I've never before seen an area in such a run-down state."

Piatnitsky coughed again, controlling it behind his hand. "You're seeing it at its lowest ebb; but the tide will soon turn. It is finally recognised the decay has gone too far. Moscow has recognised it, the EU has recognised it. Georgy Boos has been appointed as the new regional Governor and his ambitious plans have received encouragement. It is even rumoured he plans to make Kaliningrad the Hong Kong of the Baltic, and that certainly demonstrates his optimism. We are already designated a Special Economic Zone and there will be very attractive tax advantages to lure investors. Kia has assembled its first car here and soon there will be a BMW assembly plant. Large scale furniture manufacture is planned, with cross border customs duty waived in certain circumstances; and the possibilities of Baltic fishing are being seriously considered, as well as oil extraction. I happen to know that the EU is interested in funding certain improvements, too, possibly as a sign of goodwill as

Moscow prepares to offer them a gas pipeline which will be run under the Baltic. The sums involved are not inconsiderable. Brussels has set aside fifty million euros for grants to Kaliningrad and its bureaucrats are researching seventeen possible projects which, if realised, would receive a further sixteen million. There is even talk of building a high-speed train link to mainland Russia, cutting through Lithuania, though personally I do not believe it will ever come to fruition."

"You are remarkably well informed," said Magnus, genuinely surprised at his knowledge.

"I need to be. These are huge changes, so we will have to change too if we are to take advantage of them. We must become legitimate, suspending our involvement in crime and moving into businesses like construction where for several years at least there will be vast profits to be made."

"Surely it will be for many years, not just a few."

"Eventually President Putin will realise the danger of building up the economy of Kaliningrad so much that the people here begin to feel closer to the EU than to Mother Russia. But for the moment he is influenced by his wife, Lyudmila, who grew up in Kaliningrad, and so takes a special interest in these developments. While that lasts we would wish to be involved in how the EU grants are distributed and ensure we have controlling interests in the fortunate companies who will receive them. In those circumstances it makes no sense for us to be implicated in activities that inevitably may irritate EU members like Poland and Sweden. That is the larger picture of which I spoke, from which you too have benefited."

Piatnitsky paused, studying Magnus carefully again.

"From your point of view you came at an opportune moment. But I want you to remember everything I have told you and take back to your government my assurance that we no longer pose any threat to them."

Magnus looked embarrassed. "I'm just a junior officer, the smallest cog in the police machine. I have no influence at all."

"Small cogs are not negligible, especially when they are honest. On your return you will make a full report to your superior and I know it is not in your nature to hide anything. It may surprise you to know that I am in touch with people in the highest echelons of the Swedish police, and Amrén is spoken of as a rising star. I have it on good authority that in the next few years he may well be promoted to a very senior post within the police. Tell him what you have heard from me and I do not doubt he will remember it at the proper time."

His finger touched the button, the door near Magnus opened, and he was led out into the brightness and the bustle of the bar, scarcely noticing when the revolver was replaced in his holster.

Jurek looked relieved at his safe return, though he hid it at once by tossing off his vodka. Wordlessly Magnus handed him the envelope. Then they were both led from the room, down the stairs, and into a waiting car.

"Say nothing yet," Jurek grunted as he brushed against him getting in, and Magnus, feeling the beginning of a reaction as the adrenalin drained away, happily sat silent as they were safely conveyed back to the docks in the middle of a three-car convoy. The same two sailors towed them to the Polish part of the Vistula Spit, and neither Jurek nor Magnus spoke until the inflatable was safely drawn up on the sand, the oars shipped and the electric motor disconnected. Then Jurek tore open the envelope and read the contents.

"Good news?" asked Magnus.

"Very good news," Jurek said, walking a few paces up the sand and throwing himself down with a sigh of contentment. "I've been given leads on several of Savchenko's operations in Poland, especially Gdansk, so later this morning we'll be making arrests and shutting down a number of activities. How about you? Was Piatnitsky in a giving mood?"

Magnus unclipped the holstered revolver and handed it back. "I got assurances there'd be no reprisals for Savchenko's death, and whatever it was he set up in Sweden will be terminated."

Jurek grunted with satisfaction. "That's a lot. I hope you feel this little adventure we took together was worthwhile."

Magnus nodded slowly, hardly able to believe it had gone so well, that he was safe in Poland, and that all at Frisks were safe from any retribution except what the completion of his case would bring down upon them.

"I can't thank you enough," he said inadequately.

"Thank your own coolness and courage. They liked the way you handled the barman. You even managed to surprise me."

"Anything else I need to know?"

"While you were with Piatnitsky there was a lot of talk in the bar about Savchenko. It seems he was a small-time hit-man specialising in the knife for both persuasive torture and executions. Then he got ambition, started to muscle in on tiny and often not very criminal activities, taking them over and making them into something much more profitable, usually involving prostitution or drugs. In a few years he acquired a minor network, mostly into Poland and Lithuania; but recently there was talk of a new strand going into Sweden."

"What sort of strand?"

"Nothing was said about that, but it shouldn't be difficult to work it out yourself now you've seen the set-up."

Magnus thought for a while, digging his fingers into the fine white sand. "I would guess it started as a small smuggling operation, mostly amber, with the usual drink and cigarettes as well. Then Savchenko takes it over and sees it as an opportunity to try to get a drug foothold in Sweden. He goes up to the High Coast to do some persuading, and he's so cocky or distrustful he doesn't even bother to take anybody with him, just his trusty knife. But it's not enough and he gets himself killed with it. Yes, it certainly explains a lot of things."

"Do you know who did it?"

"Not yet. But I've been told a lot of lies, and thanks to this new information I'll be able to nail some of them at least. That'll put the pressure on to such an extent I'm pretty sure somebody will crack."

"I'll drop you off at the airport," said Jurek, getting up. "You'll have a bit of time to wait for the morning plane, but I have things to do." They loaded the boat and motor, and then Jurek held his hand out. "I can tell you now I was upset when RaRa would not come. I'd face anything with him beside me, but I was less happy doing it with somebody I did not know. But I was wrong. You're good, Magnus, and when you're an Inspector, as RaRa says you will be, you can call on me anytime. There are often links between Polish criminals and those in Sweden."

Magnus gripped Jurek's hand. "Why do you call Amrén RaRa?" he asked, unable to curb his curiosity.

"His name is Ragnar, and if you ever see him do his fan dance you'll understand the nickname," answered Jurek, grinning as if at a fond memory. "And I hope you get to work with him, he's the best there is. Say hello to him from me."

They got into the car and drove along the Spit, and as the sun began to rise the dunes flushed pink, then flamed a fiery red which gradually lightened so that for a time they were passing through a golden desert before the sand turned white again.

DAY 6

CHAPTER 18

Magnus got back to Midlanda by early-afternoon, and was touched that Amrén was at the airport to meet him.

"How did you get on with Jurek?" he asked eagerly as they settled themselves in the empty upstairs bar; and once Magnus had reassured him on that point he insisted on hearing every detail. He listened nostalgically to the journey along the coast, Jurek's furious recalling of the ferry, the visit to his summer house.

"I remember it so well," Amrén murmured. "It's extraordinary, it seems like yesterday. What happened then?"

Magnus told him about the boat trip, the decay so visible in Kaliningrad and then the attempt to blow them up. He played down the trouble with the barman, but gave a detailed report of his meeting with Piatnitsky.

"Did Jurek mention me at all?" Amrén asked awkwardly.

"Often," answered Magnus with a smile. "He's never forgotten how you saved his life by singing hymns, and I got the feeling the time you were with him was one of the best in his life."

Magnus expected him to look pleased, but instead he seemed curiously anxious.

"Did he give a lot of detail about those times? He can go a bit over the top when he's got some vodka inside him."

Magnus concluded it would not be tactful to mention the fan dance and his nickname RaRa, so he shook his head, deciding at the same moment not to report all that Piatnitsky had confided to him at the end of their interview. He'd probably been trying to use him to unsettle the Swedish police by starting a witch-hunt among the senior ranks; and Amrén would rightly resent the implication that if he suddenly rose higher in the force he would be prepared to return favours.

"Then it's time to stop reminiscing and get down to business," Amrén said briskly. "Where does all this leave us with our murder case? Does it put the finger on August?"

"It certainly puts him at the centre of everything, and shows he's been lying in his teeth. It's pretty clear now he was already involved in some sort of smuggling racket, probably small-time, maybe with others at Frisks as well. Then Savchenko takes it over, arrives by boat, lands on the rock, probably starts doing a bit of unpleasant persuading with his knife and ends up with it in his back."

"I'm certain August's the one to go for, and we probably have enough to pull him in for questioning. It would provide us with something to give the press who are just beginning to wake up to this case, but will it get us a confession to the murder?"

"He's stubborn, not at all easy to crack, and he might just clam up on us."

"Then I'm wondering whether we shouldn't move more cautiously, forget about the murder, go for the smuggling and see what falls out of the tree. What do you think?"

"I'm sure that's right," replied Magnus, relieved. "If we take him in we'll just raise the alarm, and, as others at Frisks are probably involved, incriminating evidence may be destroyed before we can make a proper search of the whole area. Some of them might even make a run for it. Have we got the resources for a major raid and search which might take days?"

"Not unless we involve another force, and that would delay everything. But if August's the key, as we both agree he is, we must make absolutely sure we don't let him slip through our fingers."

"He's not a professional criminal," Magnus said, trying to reassure himself as well as Amrén. "In most ways he's a reasonable man, and I'm pretty sure he'd never contemplate leaving Frisks, whatever the reason. Frisks is his life. I believe that once he's been told all we've discovered he'll probably admit what's been going on, and still hold the community together."

"Let's agree on a layered approach, then. You can go in, today, and shake the tree. Only show your hand a little bit at a time, in the hope of getting a confession to the minor strands before we move on to the major charge. Never force the pace, only go as far as it leads you, and then come back to me. That may be the moment for Vessberg to take charge. And one piece of advice for you: always keep something back. There have been a lot of lies, and often the only way you can finally recognise the truth is because you know more than they do."

Magnus was so relieved he would still be at the centre of the investigation, at least for a time, he agreed at once, and drove back to the High Coast. But he sensed he'd embroiled himself in a process full of possible pitfalls. Though he knew some things and supposed others, there was much he only guessed. But it was a game he preferred to play at Frisks, now, rather than after an arrest in the presence of the prosecutor and, almost certainly, August's lawyer as well. This way August would just be continuing to help him with his enquiries, an entirely voluntary procedure which was likely to develop into a duel of wits between the two of them.

After he'd changed into his uniform he decided to make another effort to find out more about Gubbo and phoned Lars, a colleague in the Östersund force who had a particular fascination with boats. As soon as he mentioned the sinking of the *Solsken* he had his full attention, and after a five minute delay while Lars visited certain obscure technical data sites on his computer, Magnus had succeeded in converting one at least of his guesses into a fact.

August seemed surprised to see him. "I thought you'd quite given up on us," he said pleasantly.

"I've had a lot on my plate," said Magnus, looking harassed. "But if you've got the time I'd like you to row me out to the rock which is causing you so much grief." He saw August's attention sharpen, and he added quickly, "I see there's a boat tied up at the quay, and it wouldn't take long."

Their eyes met, Magnus ready to insist, August prepared to refuse.

"It'll just be the two of us," said Magnus, and August caught his meaning and nodded slowly. Without speaking they walked down to the wood jetty and Magnus untied the painter while August slipped the oars into the rowlocks. He rowed strongly, as though the physical exercise was helping to calm an inner turmoil, and as they approached the tiny island he jerked his head at the water. "If you look down you can see how near the bastard is to blocking us in and ruining our lives," he said angrily, and seeing the breadth of rock beneath the surface Magnus was astonished August still managed to get his fishing boat past it and out to sea.

Below the fishing hut a ring had been hammered into the rock, and as they glided in Magnus stepped out and tied up. August shipped his oars and then joined him on the highest point of the rock, each staring out at the grey Baltic, more threatening now beneath a sunless sky.

"A lot of facts have come to light," said Magnus quietly. "You don't have to make any comment, though I hope you will. I need your help, and it may aid you if you feel able to tell the truth now."

He hoped August would not bluster, and he didn't; and that made Magnus feel more certain. "We know who the dead man is," he went on slowly. "We know where he came from, and we know why he came." He was watching August's face, feeling a mixture of sympathy and curiosity. It might have been a carved ship's figurehead for all the change of expression, but then he turned away and went down lower on the rock, looking into the water as if he were resigned to what might come.

"He was Konstantin Savchenko," continued Magnus, "a Russian criminal from Kaliningrad. I've just come from there, and the Polish police are working with us too. Savchenko was taking over existing smuggling networks, many very small and fairly innocent, some of them Polish based, and at least one of them here on the High Coast. He was trying to force them to upgrade into drugs and prostitution, and he wasn't squeamish about the methods of persuasion he used. He had a reputation as an enforcer, a long record of torture and execution."

August remained silent.

"What do you keep in this fishing hut?" asked Magnus interestedly, looking at the heavy padlock which secured it. It was a large windowless structure, the thick hand-sawn timbers tarred at the back where it was battered by the Baltic storms but elsewhere washed with the traditional preservative of soft soap and linseed oil coloured with the red copper-rich waste from the Falun mines. The black roof was of corrugated iron, and the hand-made door was painted sea blue.

"Nets mostly, and spare parts. Lots of junk."

"May I see?"

"I haven't got the key."

Magnus went down to stand beside him. "I'm investigating a murder, August. You've already lied when you denied ever seeing this man or knowing who he was, and that alone puts you in the frame. There are considerable doubts, too, that Paulus was here that day, and you're the only one who claims to have seen him. So please, now, tell me the truth. We know too much, and each time you lie you make it harder for yourself, and for all the others who live at Frisks."

August turned to look at him, searching his face for reassurance. "I don't want anybody else blamed for what I did. Can you guarantee that?"

"You know I can't, not until I know the facts. But I can assure you I'll act only upon the evidence. You ought to trust me, August, because you know I've taken a risk in not arresting you and putting in a search team. But I wanted you to have the chance to tell me things from your own point of view."

Magnus hoped he would be forgiven for this small distortion of the truth. At least it seemed to work, for August walked stolidly to the door, took a key from a zipped pocket let into his leather belt, and undid the padlock.

"I'll take the key, please," said Magnus, holding out his hand.

"Don't you trust me?"

"You might be tempted to lock me in," Magnus answered, adding with a smile, "I'm frightened of enclosed spaces."

He took the key, stood aside for August to go in first, then followed him. There were nets everywhere, floats, coiled rope, spars, engine parts, grease and fuel. But there were other boxes, too, stacked behind the nets. Magnus shook one and heard the clink of bottles. He opened his knife, slit the box top, and pulled out a bottle of malt whisky.

"Smuggled contraband," he said. "Is it all whisky?"

"The boxes behind contain cartons of cigarettes."

"And the smaller ones, over there?"

"Amber."

"Anything else?"

"No."

Magnus went outside, and when August had followed him he padlocked the door again and pocketed the key. "I'll seal it off with tape later, but this is now a police-only area."

He knelt at the water's edge where the seaweed clung to the rock. "This is where Savchenko landed, wasn't it? The seaweed was on his shoes."

August gave him a bleak smile. "It's my bad luck to have got a temporary replacement policeman who checks such details. But I don't deny it. He did land here, from his own high-speed motor cruiser, and I met him as had been arranged. It was typical of his contempt for us Swedish country bumpkins that he came by himself. Then I rowed him to the jetty and we went up to my house. I ought to have killed him then, I could see what he was like, but I was curious to know exactly what he wanted."

"Where's his cruiser?"

"I took it out to sea and sank it after he was dead. That was early in the morning, before I phoned you. Lovely little vessel it was too, complete with a mahogany bar and a lot of mirrors."

"How did you get back?"

"I put an outboard on this dinghy, towed it out, sat in it to watch his boat go down, then returned. In these waters you don't have to be far out to find some deep spots away from fishing areas."

Magnus went up to the hut and sat down on the step, and August sat beside him, each relaxing in the sun and avoiding the other's eyes.

"When did it all start? The smuggling, I mean."

"After Daniel's death. I was a little crazy at that time, blaming myself and desperate to make up for it by saving Frisks for the new life inside Hanna. I knew of others who did a little smuggling on the side, and for a long time I'd known a Pole who wanted to set something up with me." He laughed bitterly. "I'd met him all those years ago when I'd lost my wife and started visiting a brothel every so often. Not much of a transgression, you'd think, but it seems God's always on the watch and from it sprang the sins for which he's punishing me now. Anyway, I'd met this Pole there and we got talking, as lonely men will do, and he told me how the smuggling worked, how easy it all was, and profitable too. He'd come fishing northwards, bringing the goods, and we could meet, apparently by chance, as I fished southwards. I'd take delivery at the agreed rate, sell it on and make a profit. But I never took it up until I felt so desperate."

He pointed to the opposite shore line. "There's clear water on the other side of that, and if I had the money I could buy the land and jetties there, build up a fleet again, become the family we used to be. Then, when Jon grows up, he can hold his head high, inheriting a fishing business no longer dirtied by smuggling."

"But you were prepared to dirty yourself for him?"

"I'd do anything for him."

"Even murder?"

"If it was necessary, yes, I would. I don't care about myself, Magnus, not with my wife Amanda dead, and Daniel too. My life's a mess, and Jon's all that matters now."

"How did you dispose of the contraband?"

"I won't tell you that. This conversation is about you and me, and nobody else comes into it."

"Yet Uncle Henning is a smoker, so he'll know lots of other smokers who'd like to save some money on their cigarettes. And Olof Petter will know the drinkers, and your cousin Elin, who makes jewellery, will have contacts in the trade who'd welcome the highest quality Baltic amber from the Kaliningrad mines. You can't pick it up on the Swedish beaches, and I saw Elin was wearing amber when I talked to her."

"And so was Hanna, but I notice you conveniently leave her out," commented August sardonically. "You're stuck on her, aren't you?"

"Is she involved?"

"I'll tell you nothing, not about her, not about anybody else."

"But they've all got something to hide, because they all lied when they denied ever seeing Savchenko. I'm sure he worked on all of you, to force you to move to much more criminal smuggling, and much more profitable too."

"If you pursue this line, asking me about others, you'll have to arrest me, and I'll have a lawyer with me. And I tell you here and now, I won't ever involve anybody else. You can have me, if you really think it's worth it, but you won't get anybody else."

Magnus accepted he'd pushed him as far as he would go and lifted his hands, surrendering. "Fair enough," he said. "I admire your loyalty, it's what I expected, so let's leave it there and talk of other things. Have you raised the money you need to buy clear water?"

August spat bitterly. "Eight years of petty smuggling, all Jon's lifetime, and the money never piled up faster than the increase in price of what I wanted. It kept us from going to the wall, so Jon's inheritance, the land and houses, is still intact; but no, I've failed to get the open water and this cursed rock has won."

"But you could have had it if you'd accepted Savchenko's offer," said Magnus softly. "You must have been very tempted."

"I can fight temptation if I have to, and I discovered there are some things I wouldn't do, not even for Jon."

"So you turned him down?"

"Yes."

"I don't expect he was pleased, and I've heard about his methods of persuasion. Is that why he died?"

August glared at him. "He was the foulest man I'd ever met, pure evil. I'm glad he's dead, I wanted him dead, and I wish he'd died more slowly." He shuddered at some memory, and then he added slowly, "It was the happiest moment in all our lives when we knew he'd never breathe again."

CHAPTER 19

Magnus sensed they'd reached the climax of their talk, a moment so sensitive he was frightened to ask another question yet. He let the silence close around them, hoping August would feel compelled to break it, to continue with the story. He'd noticed it before, in police interviews, if they'd been carefully handled, that there seemed to come a time when it was no longer adversarial, when the roles of accuser and accused changed into the teller of the story and his audience, as though there was a need to tell it, to make sense of it, to free oneself from haunting memories, to justify oneself perhaps, or simply find a sort of peace by ending all prevarication and being done with it.

"He didn't threaten me," August said at last. "He didn't need to, and he knew it. He just laughed and went to see the others, and eventually they came and begged me to agree.They were shit scared, I'd never seen them like it before. Some were trembling, others crying. He was a clever, cruel persuader."

"What had he done to them?"

August looked away. "Ask them if you must, but I won't talk about it, it sickens me."

"So you gave in?"

"I'm a stubborn fool, so even then I played for time. I told him I was pretty well convinced, would think about the implications overnight, and tell him in the morning."

"By which time he was conveniently dead."

"Miracles do happen."

"Why didn't you ring the police when all these threats were made?"

"And admit the smuggling, put us all in jail or face some crippling fines, destroy all my plans for Jon? No, that wasn't the way."

"But killing him was ?"

"As it happened, yes, and I won't deny I always had it in mind. But at first I didn't believe we'd succeed, not with any certainty of getting away with it. We're mostly old, Olof Petter's unreliable, Gubbo's no use at all in things like that, and Savchenko was immensely strong and used to violence. He guessed we might try something, was almost daring us to do it, but he knew we were too cowed. We were being betrayed by our own guilt and gutlessness."

"You said you phoned me the moment you found the body. That wasn't true."

"I lied. I needed time to think, to get rid of his boat, to talk to the others, to prepare a story."

"You falsely implicated Paulus."

"I only said I was almost certain I'd seen him. He was a deceitful trickster with plenty on his conscience so I knew he'd go to earth the moment he heard the police wanted to talk to him. It was a delaying tactic, and many policemen would have taken the chance it offered to close the case."

"And when you talked to the others that morning you didn't need to ask who'd done it?"

"I was just thankful he was dead, and so was everyone else. There's nothing more to say."

The sun had clouded over and a wind was getting up. Magnus had become so involved in the story he was almost surprised to find he was still on the rocky islet. He stood up and stretched. "I'll need to question them all again, and it'll be harder for them this time. They all lied and gave false statements."

"Of course they did," said August angrily, rising too and massaging his buttocks. "This man was a monster, he deserved to die. They were all terrified by his threats, why do you have to hound them, put them under even greater pressure? You should be grateful he's dead. He wasn't just operating here, he had a network, and now it's all been ended. For God's sake, Magnus, leave it there."

"I can't," answered Magnus. "There's been a murder, and it's my job to bring the killer before a court which can decide whether it was justifiable homicide or not."

He went over to the dinghy, untied it from the ring, and August rowed him over the short distance to the shore where he moored it to a narrow upright rock set up in the shingle for just that purpose.

"You've seen us all, you've had a chance to get to know us and discover we're not bad people," said August, and he was pleading now. "Some are old, Gubbo's not in his senses, Olof Petter looks after him and Hanna's got a young child. You'll tear everything apart if you start leaning on them, they can't take any more."

"There'll be no need for it if the killer confesses."

August stared at him placidly, but he shook his head. "I'm not ready to say anything about that, not yet anyway."

"Then I'm sorry," replied Magnus, "but I'm bound by my duty as a policeman, and this investigation will proceed as every murder enquiry must. We'll walk up now and I want you to get them all together, in your house, so I can speak to them."

"Including Jon?"

Magnus shook his head. "No, he's a minor."

August looked troubled. "He's taking this harder than you might think, and I don't want him to be alone while we're all questioned and he's left to imagine the worst, or listen at the door and misunderstand. Get a policewoman to look after him."

"I can't do that, not at such short notice."

"What are you going to do at this meeting?"

"Issue a formal warning that none of you are to leave the area, to go near the rock, the hut or to interfere with anything which might be considered evidence; and that all of you must hold yourselves ready to be re-interviewed against your earlier statements in the light of the new information which has been discovered. I shall also try to find out what threats Savchenko used."

"Then you don't need me at the meeting, because I've told you all I can, and I accept the formal warnings here and now. So let me stay with Jon. He's only eight, he's sensitive and if you compel him to stay alone, without his mother or me, I shall hold you personally responsible for anything that happens to him."

It immediately occurred to Magnus he would have a much better chance of getting further information from the others if August was not present, but he was still reluctant.

"I suppose it would be possible," he said. "I would rather you were present, but in the circumstances…"

"Thank you," said August. "I'll go and find him."

When the others were all gathered in August's living room, Magnus faced them with a certainty he did not feel. Information had poured in on him in the last few days and he had not had time to ponder quietly as he liked to do, to assess it all carefully and logically so he was absolutely confident of the gaps he needed still to fill, and the weapons he could best use to squeeze the necessary information out. He was conscious, too, he was going beyond what had been agreed with Amrén, that he was just to rattle August, and at this stage he should hand over to the prosecutor. But he was convinced he must confront them with what he had found in the hut, and what August had conceded, while he still retained the element of surprise. After shocking them with that, the restrictions he was imposing, and the accusation they had knowingly attempted to impede the course of justice, he ought to be able to use his wits to pick up any signs of weakness and encourage further revelations. He wished he had paid more attention during his training to the tedious lectures on the Swedish legal code, for without research and advice he was not absolutely certain what restrictions of their personal liberty he, as a police officer, could enforce; but since they were unlikely to know either he decided that utter confidence and the weight of his official position would be the best way forward. So he stood before them as they sat around in chairs, imposing upon them the powerful paraphernalia of uniform, belt, handcuffs, baton and pistol.

"I have summoned you here because I've searched the fishing hut and found the remaining stock of illegally imported whiskey, cigarettes and amber. I have already spoken to August

Frisk and he has admitted involvement in smuggling. As charges may be preferred against you, too, you are required not to leave the area for any reason without seeking prior permission from me, or from police headquarters in Sundsvall. The rocky island and the fishing hut on it are now police investigation areas and you may not go there." He paused to let this sink in, noticing immediately that Henning looked stricken and Ingegerd had put a comforting arm around him. Elin had gone pale, and would not meet his eye, but Olof Petter had thrown his legs across the arm of the chair and was openly contemptuous. Gubbo looked faintly bewildered and Hanna was watching him with an expression containing a baffling mixture of admiration and sympathetic concern, the look of a mother regarding a wayward child.

"There is proof, too, the murdered man came here by boat specifically to discuss changes in the smuggling operation. August has given me the details of what he wanted and what the murdered man, Konstantin Savchenko, went on to discuss individually with you. In view of your statements, in which you all denied knowing him, or ever having seen him, there must be a presumption you were attempting to impede the course of justice, for which the penalties are severe. We shall, therefore, over the next few days, require you to attend a police station where you will be taken through your statements in case you should wish to amend them." He was startled to hear his reference to himself as 'we', but was conscious he was working in such isolation he needed to ally himself to the wider force; and once started on it he could not stop. "We, in co-operation with the Polish police, and making use of intelligence from Kaliningrad, in Russia, have accumulated a great deal of information. As a consequence you are all advised to reflect very carefully upon the assertions you have already made. If they are not absolutely true, or matters of importance have been omitted, then in your own best interests you should volunteer to alter them."

Henning will break first, he thought, and he was not mistaken.

"We didn't do it out of greed," he called despairingly, getting to his feet and gripping the chair in front of him with trembling hands. "Ingegerd and I are too old to move, we love it here, it's our home. I'd rather die than be without my goats, stuck in some Old People's Home."

He began to sob noisily, and Ingegerd took his hands in hers and gently eased him down into his chair again. "August borrowed heavily on the property," she explained. "All that mattered to him was keeping Frisks for Jon, and that was why he urged us all to sell the goods he gave to us. We knew they were smuggled in, we knew it was wrong, but we did it more for ourselves than him. Jon's young, he can make his own way, but Henning's too old to change, and so am I. We want to die here, where we belong, with the family, not among strangers." There were nods from the others, and even Magnus found himself caught up in her obvious distress. "We want some dignity at our end, which probably isn't far away. So, yes, we did wrong, it's true. Henning knew many who smoked, and all of them were glad to get a bargain. August was making money, paying off his debts, and we were content until that awful man arrived."

"He tried to persuade you to market something else?"

Ingegerd nodded. "Cocaine," she said. "Not us especially, we knew nothing of things like that, but he wanted all of us to tell August that he must agree."

"What did he do?" Magnus asked, raising his voice, and he looked at Henning.

Henning shuddered, and shook his head.

"I see it's very painful for you," said Magnus, "but I need to know." He paused, and suddenly realized he probably did know. "Would you rather I had the body of the goat exhumed, and then examined?"

"You leave Lina where she is," Henning shouted angrily. "She deserves to rest in peace after all he did to her. He got hold of her and held her between his knees, moving his knife over her as if he was trying to decide where to cut. I was begging him to let her go, but I could see he was enjoying it, and the more I begged the more he liked it. When I was nearly mad with fear, he used the knife to put her eyes out, and then he cut her throat. Only a savage would treat a goat like that, and I should have killed him, I wanted to, I wish I had." His anger left him as suddenly as it had come, and he huddled against his wife.

"Thank you," said Magnus. "I need to understand what he was like, and why you all acted as you did, and what you've told me helps." He swung his eyes to Hanna, hoping she would back him up by speaking and so turn the trickle of admissions into a spate.

"He threatened to hurt Jon," she answered simply.

Out of the corner of his eye he noticed Elin's nod, as though she too had now made up her mind.

"Elin?" he said gently.

"He was a vicious bastard," she burst out bitterly, "but he was very cunning. He looked into all of us and saw what we loved most, the weak spot where we were so very vulnerable. Goats with Henning, the child with Hanna, they were obvious enough; but I don't know how he knew what it was with me, for I like nothing living. Perhaps he'd seen me finger it, for I know I do that sometimes, drawing strength from the only achievement in my life." She glared round defiantly. "You all think I make jewellery just for money, but it's not like that. I'm passionate about it, it's the one thing that can satisfy the yearning inside me, to be an artist."

Magnus watched her with interest. He had categorised her simply as a bitter spinster, but now he was touched by her pathetic plea for understanding and realised he should have looked beneath the surface. There's nothing as fascinating as people, Hillevi had said, and once again she was proved right.

"Please tell me what he did."

"He prowled about my room until he found the place where I keep the most special pieces of jewellery I've made, the ones I'd never sell because, to me, they prove my talent. He laid them out on the table and I thought at first he was admiring them. But then, keeping his eyes fixed on me so he could watch my reaction, he picked up the nearest piece in his huge hands and slowly closed his fingers, crumpling up and destroying, as though it was a worthless bauble, what meant most to me in my life."

"And you gave in to him," jeered Olof Petter, "just as I did when he tied Gubbo's wrist to a table leg and threatened to cut his fingers off one by one. We're weak and useless, all of us, and now we're doing it again. This policeman doesn't know who killed him, can't you get that through your heads. But August's cut a deal with him, why else do you think he isn't here? He's selling us down the river, shooting his mouth off about all of us in return for favoured treatment. That's how the policeman knows so much. And he's not interested in all our troubles, he doesn't give a fuck, he just wants to trick us into saying something that'll lead him to the killer. But we all wanted to kill him, all would've done if we'd had the chance, and I say we should keep our gobs shut because whoever did it is a hero who deserves our thanks, not betrayal."

"Did he actually cut Gubbo with the knife?" asked Magnus, trying to control his annoyance at the interruption, but when Olof Petter shook his head he decided to play a last card. "I call him Gubbo, but I should refer to him by his real name, Ove Hallman, the sailor who was so injured when the *Solsken* sank he received a million *kronor* in compensation."

There was uproar. Everybody seemed to talk at once, but it was Elin's screech which could be heard above the others. "You filthy little creep, I knew you didn't care a shit for him and now I know why you put on this pretence. You're only interested in his money, and I bet you've stolen most of it already."

"Shut your face, you stupid bitch," bellowed Olof Petter, suddenly crimson with fury. "You're just jealous because I'm more interested in looking after Gubbo than fucking you."

Magnus wondered whether he should intervene, but Elin was capable of looking after herself. In three strides she'd reached Olof Petter and she gave him a resounding slap across the face. Olof Petter cowered as she raised her hand again, but Gubbo was too quick for her. He scooped her up and carried her to the settee, depositing her gently but emphatically upon it. Then he hurried back to Olof Petter and threw his arms protectively around him with such genuine affection that all tongues were stilled.

"What did happen to the money?" asked Magnus quietly. "Perhaps this is the moment to put the record straight."

Olof Petter rubbed his cheek, glowering at Elin. "Gubbo and I could have you thrown off this land if we wanted to be nasty," he snarled. "Gubbo owns a lot of it, and he and I work together as if we were one person." He paused, letting his words sink in, puffing himself up and looking round triumphantly. "I'll tell you something else for free, too. August always claims he's got no money, but maybe he's got more than you think, because Gubbo also gave him some towards the future purchase of the other side of the headland, and soon the fishing will be safe for Gubbo and me. Because that's what we want, a place to be and something to do, and that's why Gubbo, who's not half the fool you think, invested all his money here, in Frisks. We're not hired hands at all, that was a joke between us. We're part owners of this place."

"I think you should all go to your own houses now," said Magnus quickly and loudly before he was engulfed by questions hurled at Olof Petter; for all eyes were fixed on him, mouths gaped, and even Hanna looked astonished at what he'd revealed. "On the table by the door I've placed cards with my telephone number and that of Inspector Amrén in Sundsvall, who is in charge of the case with Prosecutor Vessberg. If any of you should want to see me personally, the location of my office is on the map on the reverse of the card. That's all I have to say for the moment."

To his relief they all gradually dispersed, talking, questioning, forming groups, some taking cards; and finally he was left alone. His satisfaction at having shaken the tree so very vigorously was tinged with uneasiness. He'd been putting pressure on a fragile group, and the consequences were hard to predict. He gathered up the remaining cards and went out into the hall, but as he opened the front door Hanna called to him, her voice sharp with urgency.

"Where's August, Magnus?"

"With Jon. He didn't want him to be alone, that's why he wasn't here."

"He's not with Jon, and never has been. Jon's outside in his tree house and he says August went down to the jetty as soon as everybody came in here."

Then Hanna seized his arm, pointing through the open door to the water below. A fishing boat, 'Frisks 3' proudly painted on the bow, was moving at increasing speed along the channel, towards the rock and the open sea beyond.

CHAPTER 20

Once Magnus had revealed he was aware of the dead man's identity, and asked him to open the fishing hut, August knew what he must do. Perhaps it had always been inevitable, and though it had happened more quickly than he'd expected he was not entirely unprepared. The special moment when he'd finally accepted he was, by himself, powerless to prevent a landlocked Frisks had started him down a road which could have only one possible end; and Daniel's suicide, and then the birth of Hanna's child, pushed him even further down it. The advent of Savchenko, and his death, were simply warnings that the end was close; and long before that he'd ceased to care about himself or the means he used to realise his dream for Jon. He'd put his scruples aside, aware he was endangering himself but perfectly prepared to shoulder the guilt when the day of reckoning arrived. And as he left Magnus to his meeting, and pretended he was going to look for Jon, he knew it *had* arrived.

He penned a note to Hanna, another to Magnus, left them on his bedroom table and hurried down the pathway to the jetty and to the vessel tied up there. It was a traditional northern single-masted fishing boat, wooden, clinker-built, the keel reinforced with steel which made it sturdier than ever. It was his last remaining boat and it had always been his favourite because it was named after him, the third of the Frisks. There was no time for regret, he had to act fast. He filled the fuel tank to the top, loaded some cans of petrol from the store, started the engine, cast off, moved out to the centre of the channel and got up speed. He smiled at the irony that he would die as Daniel had, in a daylight boating accident. Then he'd despised his son's weakness, but now he admired his strength, praying his own determination would match it. He'd always acknowledged, to himself at least, that he must die for driving Daniel to his death. There was no way back from killing your son, though it took longer than he'd expected to provide Jon with the future Daniel hadn't waited for. He'd became a smuggler and, despite some debts, the money mounted up. Then Olof Petter arrived with Gubbo, and secretly they invested in his enterprise, for their own security more than Jon's. Secret negotiations began to buy the land and open water beyond their boundary, but just as he thought he'd achieved his great ambition the price went up again. At that moment, as if at the Devil's bidding, Savchenko materialised, offering him riches which would make it all possible again, at the cost of sinking even lower into degradation and tainting himself beyond redemption. At first he refused. But Savchenko knew his man, setting to work to terrify the others into begging August to say the yes he found so tempting. And finally he did tell them he would say yes, though he gave no answer yet to Savchenko. Probably, at the last moment, he would have done; but Savchenko yielded to an impulse to increase the pressure on him while at the same time satisfying himself, twisting the knife a little more and ending with it in his back. After that it took the several days of the investigation to resolve the difficulties over the price of the open water; but now it had been achieved and, with Jon's future guaranteed, he could put an end to any further police investigation by dying, as he'd always planned to do.

He'd often wondered about Daniel's marriage to Hanna. When he first saw her in the brothel he sensed his son might be attracted to her even though he'd shown no interest in other girls; and it would be more likely to occur if she was around him all the time as part of Frisks. So he offered her a place with them, certain he could rely upon her to use her natural wiles on the only young man in the community and hopeful she would soon make Daniel mad for her. He didn't care much whether there was a wedding, as long as there were children, or even a single child. He noticed them drawing gradually closer, deep in conversation, laughing together, and even though he didn't catch them in a sexual clinch he saw them holding hands and hugging. Cautiously he began to hope, though he still thought it would take time. He was surprised therefore, but overjoyed, when Hanna told him Daniel did want to marry her, and she was minded to accept if August didn't hold her past against her. He quickly reassured her on that, delightedly gave his blessing to them both and planned to hold a celebration; but Daniel and Hanna came to him shortly afterwards to say they'd just been married in a civil ceremony. Daniel was as awkward and reserved as he always had been, but August didn't care. The deed was done, and he could leave the rest to clever Hanna, quite certain she would soon be pregnant.

But it didn't happen, though he was in no doubt they were having sex. Living in the same house, he had been woken at least twice by unmistakable sounds; and Daniel's new-found contentment was equally apparent. For the first time in his life he seemed to have some certainty, as though a load had lifted from him and he was beginning, tentatively, to reach out to his father in a daze of gratitude for the gift provided when he'd brought Hanna home to him. A quiet affection began to flower between them, and August almost believed they might, after all, be able to work together, even though Daniel remained so very private about his inner thoughts.

But Hanna seemed to droop as Daniel throve. It was as though they'd changed roles, and it was Hanna now who seemed unfulfilled, retreating into herself and losing the cheerful openness which previously was so much a part of her. And then one day, some months after the marriage, while Daniel was out fishing in the Baltic, August heard her sobbing in her bedroom, in a paroxysm of grief; and he, fearful there might be something badly wrong with her, knocked on the door and, getting no reply, went in.

She was lying on her bed, the summer duvet all rucked up where she'd thrown herself about as she was crying. She glanced across at him, and he saw desperation in her eyes.

"I can't go on," she muttered, seeming to look beyond him at some imagined image of her husband. "I love him, but I can't go on like this, I'll have to leave him."

Awkwardly he went across to soothe her. "What's wrong?" he asked her gruffly, not wanting to involve himself but hoping she might feel better if she talked.

"There's nothing wrong, not in the sense you mean it. I haven't got a headache, period pains, or anything like that. If only it were so easy, just swallow a pill and it'll be better. But it's all tangled up, and it's me, just me." She hesitated, and then burst out, "I never thought I'd be like this, but I'm as broody as hell, I'm totally desperate for a baby, and it's killing me." She wiped her eyes, sniffed and blew her nose. "Bloody stupid, isn't it? A hooker who wants a baby from a client, that's a first, I'm sure."

He was bewildered, though a premonition, a flutter of something he'd long known but never allowed himself to think about, began to panic him. "Daniel's your husband, not a client," he said gently, as if explaining something to a child. "And you're not a hooker, you're a Frisk. You'll have a baby, of course you will, you've just got to give it time. I had to wait years for Daniel."

She laughed, and it verged on the hysterical. "Yeah, right, but it'll take more than time," she countered, the tears beginning to flow again. "It'll take a fucking miracle to get me pregnant in the parts he puts it."

Immediately she looked appalled, realising what she'd said, and for a moment both were speechless. Then Hanna sprang off the bed and grabbed him fiercely by the arms. "I didn't mean to say it. Forget it, please. It's our problem, Daniel's and mine, and I'd no right to blurt it out. Forget it, please."

"He's gay," said August slowly. "I suppose I've always known."

"Then you've probably always been wrong," retorted Hanna. "It's not as simple as that. Nothing with Daniel ever is. He's never been with a man, I'm certain of that, and I'm not sure that's even what he wants. It may be true he likes me because I haven't got huge boobs like some fertility figure and I wear trousers all the time, but I'm not at all manly. I think it's more to do with the horror he has of childbirth and that part of me that makes me female. He's terrified of it, won't look at it, hardly dares go near it, and he told me at the very beginning, before the marriage, he wouldn't father a child." She clutched August, almost shaking him. "He never misled me, he was always honest. It was me who got it wrong, I didn't think I'd mind not having a baby, and now I do, and the need grows all the time and it's eating up our marriage."

"Could it be something to do with the fact Amanda died giving birth to him?" mused August. "Maybe he's riddled with guilt, believes he killed her, is petrified of pregnancy, will never give you a child in case it kills you too."

"I don't know," Hanna said impatiently. "I'm not a bloody psychiatrist, and I don't much care what made him as he is. I only care about what I'm going to do. I'm very fond of him, I like living with him, I love him for the person he is, he's gentle, warm, affectionate and I like him loving me however he does it. He's even tried to do it ordinarily just to please me, not unprotected of course, but it's no good at all – he's impotent at once. So there we are. I want a baby and I won't get one staying with him."

"Would he mind if you became pregnant with his baby without the need for intercourse?"

"Artificial insemination you mean? I've mentioned that, but he won't discuss it. It may not mean he's totally against it, though he probably is, but he's so full of fear he gets in a state if I raise anything like that. Occasionally I think he'd actually like a baby to be a father to, to bring up and to love, but he won't risk the birth. He doesn't like me even wanting a baby, so we can't discuss it."

She wiped her eyes on his shoulder. "Oh, August, you brought me here, you saved me, what am I going to do?"

"You're an attractive girl," he answered decisively. "Go out, get pregnant, it won't be difficult for you."

"Prostitute myself again?" Hanna shouted angrily, glaring at him. "Go with any man because that's what a hooker does? No, crazy though it seems, Daniel is dear to me, I want his baby, a baby who'll look like him and be a real Frisk."

August felt the old fury rise in him. "Then I'll damned well make him behave like a proper husband, and one way or another he'll give you a baby. He's always defied me, ever since he was a child, but this time I won't let him wriggle out of it. For once in his life he'll bloody well obey."

The rock was getting nearer now, and August adjusted the wheel so the bows were lined up with the fishing hut, and then he lashed it firmly so it could not shift. He crossed to the cans, opened them and poured petrol all over the boat, deliberately soaking his clothes as well. Then he picked up a rag, drenched it too, and took out his lighter. In his mind he heard, for the final time, Daniel's agonised cry of horror and disgust that had haunted him ever since, the cry that proved to be the harbinger of his death. And now August echoed that cry as he lit the rag and threw it into the pool of petrol which had collected in the bows. The roar of the conflagration mingled with it, and with the shriek of metal as the keel rode up the rock, demolishing the hut and tearing the bottom from the boat. Then the flames reached the fuel tank and the faint reverberation of his cry, rebounding from the rocky headland, was snuffed out by the explosion.

CHAPTER 21

The letter, addressed to Magnus, was brief:

'I killed Konstantin Savchenko. I was defending my family and he deserved to die, so I have no regrets. I was responsible for the smuggling and the blame is all mine. Jon inherits everything, and Hanna will look after Frisks until he is of age. You were too clever for me, you found out everything I tried to hide, but with my death your investigation is at an end.'

The writing was firm and clear, and August had signed the note with a steady hand.

Magnus and Hanna had set off running as soon as they'd seen the boat. Magnus still thought in terms of stopping his escape, but Hanna saw more clearly. "He's going too fast," she screamed. "He's going to smash himself up on the rock. We've got to stop him."

The others followed them, streaming down over the Devil's Field, down to the water and along the pebbled shore towards the rock. But they were too late, and Hanna seized Jon who was frenziedly shrieking for his grandpa and held him, pressing his face against her as the boat began to burn, then struck the rock and the explosion rent the air.

Magnus radioed for the ambulance and the coastguard fire ship as he ran, but knew it would be no use. Warily he crept as close as he dared, but the heat was so intense August could not have survived. The boat burned fiercely, the flames fanned by the sea breeze and spreading greedily to the fishing hut and its contents. He managed to free the dinghy tied to the rock, and pull it further away along the inlet so the cascade of sparks could not reach it. All he could do then was wait; and by the time the fire ship arrived the flames were dying down and the crew, warned about the rock, were still able to get in remarkably close to drench the area with sea-water. Shortly afterwards

Magnus rowed the paramedics out to the rock and helped them recover the charred remains which had been August Frisk.

"It's over," said Magnus later to Amrén, ringing him at home from the shore. "August's killed himself, leaving a confession, and I feel terrible about it, almost as though I'd killed him myself. I was beginning to think I was good at my job, but he must have been more vulnerable than I thought and I pushed him too hard."

"I should have foreseen the possibility myself," Amrén admitted. "It's a terrible thing to have happened, but it's no use beating yourself up about it. I'm afraid you'll have to learn to live with a lot worse than that as you climb the promotion ladder. The difference between blame and success is sometimes very small."

"It's made me wonder whether I'm as fitted to be a policeman as I thought."

"You'll go on wondering it time and again; and there's nothing wrong in that as long as you never take the easy way out and just give up. We can't know what's really in people's minds, and we'll probably never know what finally pushed August over the edge. But we did what we thought best, and it may turn out our judgement wasn't so very faulty. Did he confess to the murder and the smuggling?"

"Yes."

"Then you're right, it is over. A tragic end, of course, but a satisfactory one too."

"Is it really worthwhile pursuing the others for whatever they may have done to spread the contraband around? Wouldn't a caution be sufficient?"

"In view of what's just happened, I'm pretty sure Vessberg will take no further action against anybody," answered Amrén soberly. "Thanks to your careful investigations it's wrapped up and put to bed. Frisk obviously thought he'd get away with it, especially after putting the blame on Paulus, and he probably would have done without your perseverance."

"It wasn't me," said Magnus candidly. "It was Hillevi Zander, Finn Jonsson and above all your friend Jurek."

"That's true enough, but it's still the officer in the driving seat who deserves most credit. You put it all together; you challenged August Frisk and pushed him into a confession and his own way out. You've done well, as I knew you would, and you'll be down here in Sundsvall for certain now, as one of my inspectors, with Vessberg's recommendation as well as mine."

Magnus was going to add something about the doubts still washing around inside him, but it didn't seem the appropriate moment; and, since he was aware he had a tendency to err on the side of rashness, it might be better to take more time to think it through, and then sleep on it. So he walked wearily up to his car and drove through the wonder of the summer twilight, so out of keeping with the tragedy he'd just been witnessing, back to his office, for there was nothing more he could do at Frisks. Jon and Hanna needed time to grieve, and all the community had to consider their future now August, hitherto such a dominant force in all their decisions, was no longer there to lead. Would Olof Petter, claiming his rights as part-owner with Gubbo, refuse to cooperate with Hanna, August's designated successor until Jon was of age? How would the older generation of Henning, Ingegerd and Elin take to the leadership of someone who was only a Frisk by marriage and who must, to them, seem very young? And had Hanna herself the strength to bear such a burden of responsibility while managing her own grief and somehow consoling a boy who'd lost so much? He longed to go to her, to give her his support, but knew it was out of the question.

Instead of making himself an evening meal he re-read the letter August had left for Hanna. He'd felt compelled to take it from her once she'd perused it, as it would be needed for the inquest, but he'd promised her a copy.

'Dear Hanna,

You now have the final responsibility for Jon and for Frisks. I know you will not let me down. Daniel's death killed much of me, but Jon's birth gave me new life. I hope he'll never forget me, and you must tell him often how very much I loved him.

In sacred trust,
August

He compared it to his own letter and felt there was a link. Even on the brink of death August was still commanding them. Hanna was reminded she had a sacred trust, the responsibility for Jon and Frisks, and she mustn't let him down. He, in his turn, was told his investigation was at an end. He attempted to put himself into the mind of August, or any man about to die who didn't have much time to write. Surely he wouldn't waste time on farewell platitudes, but concentrate on what was in the forefront of his mind at such a moment, those things which needed to be said, which must be said before he could feel free to end it all. And, as he must have realized such messages would quickly become public property, a man as shrewd as August would have made them seem quite ordinary to disguise what he was really saying. Reading them again, Magnus wondered why, in the note to him, August so stressed the ending of an investigation which, with his confession, was bound to end in any case? And in the other note why did he tell a mother her son was a sacred trust when, in Hanna's case at least, her every action showed it to be part of her very nature? Why tell her she had the responsibility, when, as the widowed parentless mother of an only child who was still a minor, nothing could be more obvious? And why, at such a moment, should he even consider the possibility she might let him down?

He lay back, stretched out his legs, closed his eyes, and thought; and as he considered all he'd learnt about Frisks, from those outside the community as well as inside, and from his own observations, tentative conclusions began to form. The sacred trust must be something more than simply caring for Jon. It was something for which she had the final responsibility, something she might be reluctant to do, something which would let him down if she failed to do it. That was the vital last instruction he was sending, that he was leaving her to do something which she alone could do, and whatever her personal feelings, she must do it. And to keep it a secret which Hanna alone knew, August was reminding him, and, through him, Amrén, that his death was the closure of the case and so no more prying would be necessary. But what, then, did he fear might be discovered? Was it something Hanna knew, but the police didn't? To stretch it a little further, and to personalise it, it might be something he feared Magnus was close to finding out. So he began to concentrate on what he knew about August, what they'd talked about and, perhaps more importantly, what they had not discussed. August loved his grandson, but he seemed even more concerned about his inheritance, the whole survival of Frisks, the maintenance of the fishing by the purchase of the open water just beyond his boundary. He'd lied when he claimed he hadn't saved much money, and even when threatened with a tax investigation he'd never revealed that Gubbo and Olof Petter were anything more than hired hands. Olof Petter, when he'd been crowing over the others at the meeting, had implied that August was close to purchasing the land and open water, and the sacred trust might therefore be the successful negotiation of the purchase. But why should Hanna be opposed to it? He remembered she'd told him she wasn't worried about Jon's future, and unlike August she didn't think the maintenance of the fishing was a necessity. But it *would* be for Olof Petter and Gubbo, and that might lead to dissension and confrontation. He shook his head and went to make a coffee and an open sandwich. Hanna would never be reluctant just because she might face opposition; he was going down the wrong trail.

It was while the coffee pot was heating and he was munching a liver pâté and green pepper sandwich that he allowed himself to consider the other issue. August's suicide had raised two problems in his mind, and he'd preferred to concentrate on one, the letters. But the other was more comprehensive; the more time that passed after the immediate impact of the death, the less he believed August was the killer. He hadn't been at all surprised to discover he'd been involved in smuggling, an activity which seemed to suit his character; but stabbing someone in the back did not. It suggested a cold-blooded premeditation which was foreign to August's temperament. Magnus didn't doubt he'd been capable of killing, but it would have been in the heat of anger, defending someone he loved.

Magnus poured out his coffee, the last thought still in his mind, and it assumed greater importance the more he thought about it, though he was still unable to grasp its precise relevance. August, in his note to Magnus, claimed he'd been defending his family, which was an admirable reason for the killing. But it was no reason at all to kill himself afterwards. Magnus sipped the scalding coffee and tried not to lose his concentration. August was motivated by love, by the need to protect somebody, and the assumption he was encouraging in his note to Magnus was that he'd killed out of love and the need to protect. But there was only one killing he'd undeniably committed, for Magnus had been a witness. He'd killed himself, and if the guilt of the murder hadn't driven him to it, and Magnus was convinced it wasn't that, might he have killed himself to protect someone he loved, taking the blame for the murder so the investigation would be over before the true culprit could be discovered? It didn't seem entirely feasible, for suicide surely required motivation far beyond the normal, but August was a complicated man who might have other demons too, and on this occasion the opportunity for self-sacrifice on behalf of someone he loved might have proved irresistible. Yet something was missing, something he himself had missed, something August had known but he didn't, something Hanna was handling now, reluctantly but in obedience to her father-in-law's last wish.

Suddenly he was utterly exhausted and he could hardly drag himself to bed. August's death, the recovery of his remains, the sight of Jon and Hanna's grief, it all weighed heavily on him, and after fruitless efforts to sleep he rang Sonja and told her all about it. She'd always been a good listener, and by the time he'd poured it out he felt the relief becoming an overwhelming tiredness. He tried to keep his eyes open as she told him about the children, and then reminded him it was her father's sixtieth birthday at the weekend, and they couldn't go to the party without a present. She'd bought her own gift and little things from the children, but she knew her father would be especially pleased if he got one present personally chosen by Magnus.

"Choose something manly and a bit special. I know you'll find exactly the right thing, you're always clever at that."

She made a kissing sound and rang off, leaving Magnus half-asleep yet vaguely conscious she'd said something which was desperately important. He woke once in the night, knowing exactly what it was and determined to write it down. He reached for the short IKEA pencil he kept beside the bed and began to write on the pad, returning to sleep after two words. But when he read them in the morning he understood exactly what 'birthday party' meant, realised what it was he had been missing in the puzzle. And once he'd made three hurried phone calls, he drove at speed to Frisks, praying he would arrive before it was too late.

DAY 7

CHAPTER 22

He had always been a conscientious man. It was in his nature, and he couldn't alter it. But in the car, driving so fast, coming closer and closer to Frisks, he wished he could have been a little less conscious of his duty, at least on this occasion. He'd phoned Amrén to tell him he was on his way to try to rectify his oversight, then rung Scholander to obtain the number required for his all-important third call. But when he rang that number he received the totally unexpected answer which sent him scurrying to his car. Now he would again have to disturb a community he longed to leave in peace, driven to do it because he couldn't avoid the truth that it was not really the community he wanted to spare, but just one person in it. But his inconvenient conscience wouldn't allow him do that. Since August's death, Hanna was the one who had the power to make decisions, and so it would be her, and no one else, he must confront.

To his relief there was no one around when he reached the entrance and he drove up to where the forest was thickest on either side, then parked his car across the track, completely blocking any access or exit. There was still no one in sight as he walked up to August's house, and when the door was opened by Elin, in answer to his knock, it was clear from her expression that his visit was totally unexpected, and unwelcome. Half-heartedly she tried to block his way, peering anxiously over her shoulder at the open living room door, but Magnus walked in past her. As he approached the room he heard Olof Petter say angrily, "Gubbo and I will never agree to that. It goes against everything August wanted."

"That policeman's here again," said Elin piercingly from just behind his shoulder, and he entered the room to encounter a snapshot, the adults frozen around a large table, all with papers and plans in front of them, all peering at him, Olof Petter with the fury still etched on his face, and Hanna, at the top of the table, her mouth half-open, about to put him in his place. None of them looked quite the same as he remembered them, perhaps because he'd never seen them like this, so serious, so business-like, a committee struggling through disagreements to reach a majority decision. Henning no longer looked so old or incapacitated by his deafness, Ingegerd's glance had lost its kindness, and Gubbo was sitting still and frowning in concentration as he studied the papers in front of him. Elin scurried back to her place at the table and faced him stonily, Olof Petter controlled his anger with unsuspected patience and Hanna stood up hastily and approached him, blocking his view of the papers on the table.

"How can we help you?" she asked with a Chairman's formality, and her blue eyes, always so open, showed annoyance at the interruption and a lurking concern about the possible cause. Then, as if repenting of her coldness, she added, "Your visit's rather inconvenient just at this moment, Magnus. Is it so very urgent, or could it be delayed until tomorrow? I'd love to see you then, but now there's so much to be settled after August's death, and it involves us all."

"And some things have been settled already," Magnus said, lowering his voice so that only she could hear. "It seems August did have enough money after all to buy the open water, because he put in an offer shortly after Savchenko was killed. But that offer has just been withdrawn. By you, Hanna." He raised his voice, addressing all of them. "I'm very sorry to disturb you, but certain questions have arisen about August's business affairs which require some answers. I hope it won't take long, and I must ask you to stay in the area until I've completed my investigations as I may wish to speak to you."

He indicated that Hanna should follow him, and led the way outside where he could keep an eye on all the houses.

"Is it just August's business affairs you want to talk to me about?" Hanna asked him. "Or is there something else as well?"

She no longer seemed a young and sexually attractive girl. She was more poised, less simple, wary and defensive. She took a few steps out into the sunshine, a little further from the house.

"His suicide notes to you and me raise many questions," said Magnus. "Was the meeting I interrupted about the sacred trust he passed to you?"

Hanna nodded. "It's not a secret. I told you about the open water, and August was desperate to get it. He wanted me to finalise it."

"And against his wishes you've withdrawn instead. I assume it was that decision which angered Olof Petter?"

"You know already he and Gubbo put money into August's plans because they wanted to carry on the fishing. It was natural he'd be annoyed, more for Gubbo than himself. He's a strange man, but he really cares about Gubbo's happiness."

"Why did you act against August's wishes?"

Hanna sighed. "Because he's dead, and I have to do what is right for my son, and for the community. I didn't hide from you that I disagreed with August's dreams – I think he was making a prison for Jon, just as he did for Daniel, but while he was alive I always supported him. Now I must follow my own beliefs. I don't think there's any future in fishing here, or farming, or logging either. The future's all around us, modernisation, grasping the opportunities UNESCO has offered by declaring this a World Heritage site. Elin wants to open a jewellery shop here, Henning longs to show his goats to visiting children, running a little farm animal park, and Ingegerd will help him, making pastries and selling them. It's tragic in a way, but none of them really wanted August's dream."

"What do you want?"

"You're not to laugh, Magnus, but I want to have a little restaurant. I love cooking, I'm good at it, and I'll make it a success, I know I will."

"And all of this can be done here at Frisks?"

"It's the perfect site. There'll be walks by the water, views of the Baltic, picnic sites, perhaps even boat trips around the little lake our inlet will become."

"Everything August fought against, everything he hated."

"Do you think I'm wrong?"

He shook his head. "No, I think you're right. And I think you're very brave. But what about Olof Petter and Gubbo?"

"I don't think they'll want to stay. I'll have to give Gubbo back his investment, but I'm sure they'll both be able to find a fishing boat to work for someone further down the coast. Perhaps it'll be good for all of us to start again, if we're allowed to."

She stared at him, seeking the answer he was not ready to give her yet.

"You know I care for you, Hanna," he said quietly. "But I can do nothing unless I know the truth. August didn't have the money to buy the open water, not even with Gubbo's investment, or he'd have clinched the deal when the price was lower. But suddenly, after Savchenko's death, and just before his own, August was able to make an acceptable offer. You will need all that money to set up what you've planned, so I understand why you withdrew the offer, yet you talk of paying Gubbo back a million kronor. You're at a crossroads in your life, Hanna, and I'm terrified you're about to overcome the reluctance August sensed, and do something from which I cannot save you."

"And the murder?"

"We'll talk about that later. But the same harsh rule applies. If you want to stop the investigation, as August wanted, then you'll have to tell me all you really know."

Hanna looked at him for a long time. "I want the best for Jon, and for the others, and for me as well. Is that so wrong? And if it isn't, why are you destroying it?"

"You know why, Hanna. You've always known. Because the basis on which you're building your dream is morally wrong, and that will destroy it, not me."

"Why did you have to come into my life?" she asked him bitterly; but he did not reply, knowing she'd reached her decision, and these were only words, requiring no answer. But as she turned away from him he put his hand on her arm, holding her back. "Soon we have to talk of something else," he said sadly. "You know I want to help you, but you have to help me too."

She stared at him. "Are you promising me something?"

He shook his head. "I can't do that," he replied awkwardly. "But if you'll show me the truth, and it's what I think it is, there may be a way."

Hanna freed herself from his hand and went back into the house. After several minutes she returned with a large and obviously expensive briefcase, the black leather tooled with an intricate design, the fittings gilded.

"Is this what you want?"

"If it belonged to Savchenko, and the contents are untouched, then yes, it is."

She handed it to him. "It's chock-full of little packets of crack cocaine, and none have been removed. If I'd given it to Olof Petter, who knows his way around the drug scene, he and Gubbo would probably have got more for it than their original investment. That's how I would have paid them off."

"You can't go to a birthday party without a present," murmured Magnus, recalling Sonja's words the night before. He looked up at Hanna. "I assume Savchenko brought this with him as a little sweetener to start you all on your new career as drug smugglers?"

"Yes. And to implicate us, so there could be no going back."

"How very confident he must have been in his powers of persuasion. However determined you were at first to have nothing to do with drugs, he realised that in the end you'd all give in to him."

"You'd have done the same if he'd got hold of something or someone you loved. It's easy to sneer when you haven't had to face it, but if it had been your Johan…"

"I wasn't sneering," said Magnus gently. "I'd have acted just as you all did, and I can understand how, after Savchenko's death, the drugs, or rather the money they'd raise, became the glue which held you all together. That's why you all agreed to say you'd never seen him before and knew nothing of the killing. But it wasn't August who stabbed him. I think August died to preserve his dream, to end the investigation and so keep the drugs safe from discovery until they could be sold; and I'm sure he also died to protect whoever did kill Savchenko."

"Do we have to go on standing here in full view of everybody?" said Hanna with sudden irritation. "You're holding a bloody fortune in your hands."

"Let's walk towards my car then," replied Magnus, and as he said it he realised he'd be relieved to get the briefcase safely locked away in his office.

"How will you pay back Gubbo's money now?" he asked as they set off down the track.

"We'll have to do it over a period of time, and our great plans for this place will have to be a lot more modest. Maybe we'll even be able to persuade them to stay on and run the boat trips But we'll manage somehow." She looked at him fondly. "Oddly enough I feel relieved, though I ought to want to kick you in the balls."

When they reached the car Hanna smiled at the way he'd parked it. "You really are a bastard, Magnus. You pretend to know so little, but you weren't going to risk anybody escaping with the drugs. Or were you worried the killer would make a dash for it?"

"No," said Magnus, and his eyes were fixed on her. "I never thought the killer would try to get away."

"You'd better take me in then, because, as you well know, I'm the one who did it."

Magnus opened the door for her, ignoring the thin wrists stretched out for the handcuffs.

"Will Jon be all right without you?"

"He's used to my wandering off and doing my own thing, just like he does. Ingegerd's his second mum, so he'll be fine. And this won't take long; it was a sort of self defence, not murder."

She got in, closing the door with firm decision. Magnus settled himself beside her and drove away from Frisks.

"How do you think Daniel would have felt about all your new plans?" he asked, wanting to keep her talking.

Hanna gave a short laugh. "He'll be doing a jig up and down the corridors of heaven, chuckling himself silly. It'll be everything he ever wanted; a new start for Frisks, not a vestige of the past remaining, a final smashing of the shackles that destroyed his life."

"But wouldn't he want something of the family tradition to remain for Jon? A lot of fathers would."

"You're probably right," replied Hanna, and there was something in her voice that made him glance across at her. She was staring straight ahead, and he noticed the knuckles of both hands had turned white where she was grasping the strap of the shoulder bag on her knee. "Or you're as wrong about that as you are about other things at Frisks. You think you know so much, Magnus, and in many ways you do, but you know fuck all about the depths of life at Frisks, at least as it affected me." She turned to look searchingly at him. "Do you *really* want that truth you keep on talking about?"

Magnus concentrated on his driving, but he felt the tenseness in his body. "I have to have the truth," he said.

"All the truth, even though you won't like it?"

He nodded.

"Even though you won't like me either, because it'll destroy a lot more illusions than the sea serpent's skateboard did?"

He nodded again, her words conjuring up memories of her among the blueberries; and he noticed his knuckles, too, were white as they gripped the wheel.

"I'll tell you then. Daniel wasn't Jon's father. August was."

CHAPTER 23

Magnus did not know how he kept driving so steadily, but it was his only comfort, to keep faith with his Volvo. Remembering her assurances in the forest about her relations with August, he felt betrayed, emptied of all the trust he'd had that although she might lie to save others she would never deceive him about herself.

"You told me there'd never been anything between you," he said finally, when he felt he could speak calmly, but there was no hiding the bitterness in his words.

"There never was, not in the brothel which was what we were speaking of then, and never since until that one crazy moment before Daniel died."

"Before he killed himself," Magnus corrected her harshly. "Killed himself, I assume, because he'd found out you were betraying him with his own father."

"Poor Magnus," Hanna said, and there was real sorrow in her voice. "You're such a simple man yourself you can't imagine the twisted complications of other people's lives. Yes, it's true Daniel's boat had engine trouble that day, he came back unexpectedly as husbands always do in farces, and he found us just finishing our few minutes of joyless, guilty but, as it proved, effective coupling. And of course it spurred him to his death, not just because of what we'd done, but more I think because he blamed himself for driving us to act in a way that was so awful for us all. A man must find it hard to understand how desperate I was for a baby, and that I saw it as the only way of staying with Daniel. I didn't love him, I told you that, but I was very fond of him, more, I realise now I've been without him, than I understood even then. But he was incapable of giving me a child, and I often wonder whether he went to his death almost hoping one might have been started, the nearest thing he'd ever have to a son."

The desolate sadness in her voice dissolved his entirely selfish bitterness. "He was impotent?"

"In his own immensely complicated way I suppose you could say that. Perhaps he thought he'd killed his mother because she died when she gave birth to him; perhaps he came to think it because August loved his wife so much that deep, deep down he blamed Daniel for her death. How can one know these things? He was so sensitive he picked up on every feeling, however slight, and always blamed himself. That's why I know he would have blamed himself even for what I did that day. August heard me sobbing in my room, which I did sometimes when I thought I was alone. Somehow he extracted from me exactly what our problem was, and then came up with the usual idiotic solutions like IMF, or prostituting myself again, with no understanding of Daniel's fear and loathing of the thought I'd die when I gave birth, or of my longing to have a child who'd be a Frisk, as much a part of Daniel as was possible for us. But it was all so much more complicated than that, though I won't tell you any more, because it's things I share with only Daniel in my memory now. But at that one mad moment, when I'd just poured out my heart to August, and he'd said angrily he'd force Daniel to make me pregnant, like that would be helpful, we each suddenly seemed to see the same solution, and we acted. But it was an unforgiveable sin, and we were not forgiven. It drove Daniel to his death, it drove August to his, and my punishment is to be left alive to live with what I did."

They drove the last few kilometres in silence, but Magnus steered with one hand only, his other gripping Hanna's and expressing all he could not say; and by the time they arrived at his office both were a little calmer. He ushered her in and asked her to sit down.

"You have the right to ask for a woman police officer to be present," he said formally.

Hanna smiled. "She might be embarrassed by my language, and you might be even more embarrassed by my references, in front of her, to the way you lusted after me when we were together in the woods. If you didn't forget yourself then, you won't now, so I'll risk being alone with you. Am I under arrest?"

"No."

"Is this place bugged?"

"No."

"Prove it. Say you care for me."

"I care for you."

"And when this is over you'll forget me and only think about Sonja and your children."

"I'll only think about Sonja and my children."

"You didn't say you'd forget me."

"No."

She shook her head at him in exasperation. "Then for God's sake just accept I've come to confess, and don't dig any deeper. I can't think why you always seem to feel the need to do that."

"Because I'm not in charge, the prosecutor is, and I have to be certain any recommendation I make to him through Inspector Amrén is for the right reason, and not the wrong one."

"And I'm the wrong one?"

"Yes."

"Can you really take this case further, or did August's death effectively end it?"

"If there are good reasons to suspect there is something wrong in August's financial affairs the prosecutor can seize all the papers and freeze the accounts; but you've removed all possibility of that by voluntarily surrendering the drugs as soon as you found them after going through August's effects."

Hanna raised her eyebrows. "You certainly have your own way with the truth, Magnus."

"You said I was a simple man, so I suppose I'm sometimes rather innocent in how I view things."

"But what about the killing?"

"I believe the evidence, if closely considered, may show that August didn't do it, and his confession was to protect somebody else. That would mean re-opening the case and much more searching questions would be asked of everybody involved. The prosecutor and Inspector Amrén would take charge, I'd be in my proper place in the background, and with August dead, and the drugs handed in, they'd certainly get answers that would show what really happened. But for the moment I'm still here, and I still believe that hearing the truth from you is the best way forward. I'm pretty certain you agree with that or you wouldn't have turned yourself in."

Hanna looked round the room, interested by all it told her about Magnus. It was so neat, the papers on his desk stacked tidily, the pens and pencils in a circular plastic holder, the pictures on the wall all hanging straight, the mats unwrinkled. Nothing was uncontrolled, except, perhaps, his emotions. She picked up the framed photo of Sonja and the children and stared at it as if it helped her to see the way to go. It had been taken by a lake, and Johan was holding a tiny perch he'd caught, and Angelica was laughing at him while Sonja smiled down on both of them with a mother's protective pride she recognised so well. "The admissions I've made so far, and what I may say now, must at this stage be between the two of us. Jon's lost his father, and unless it's absolutely necessary he's not going to lose his mother as well. So if you attempt to report what I say, I'll deny I ever said it. Is that understood?"

"You're not under arrest, I haven't cautioned you, and nothing will be recorded at this stage."

Hanna looked at him suspiciously. "You're being too reasonable, it worries me."

Magnus smiled, clenched his fist and showed it to her. "I want the truth, the whole truth, and one way or another I'll get it out of you. Does that make you feel better?"

"Much better," said Hanna. "Now you're like the policemen I used to come up against in Stockholm, no agonies of conscience, just brutality and demands for sexual favours in return for better treatment."

"You're not afraid of men, are you? And you were the only one who wasn't afraid of Savchenko. Did you make that clear to him?"

"I don't like swaggering brutes. I was concerned about what he might do to Jon, but when he started to threaten me I told him to fuck off."

"And he didn't like that?"

Hanna shrugged. "I can't help it if men are so sensitive. But he buggered off, anyway, and after we'd all been to see August and told him about the threats, I got Jon out of the house."

"Was that where Savchenko was going to sleep?"

"Yes. August had given him the spare room, and that's why I'd no intention of hanging about there with Jon. I guessed Savchenko would be demanding a response about the change to drug smuggling, and August's so stubborn it wasn't likely to be satisfactory. Knowing Jon and I would be the obvious targets if Savchenko decided to up the pressure on August, we got out of the back window with our sleeping bags and went to our secret camp among some rocks near the Devil's Field. We'd slept there before, it was a treat for Jon on very hot nights, and I always enjoyed it too."

"What happened?"

"Savchenko wasn't the fool I'd taken him for. He must have been expecting us to get away, kept watch, and saw where we went, and only then went in to talk to August. When everyone had gone to bed and was asleep, as we were, he came to get us."

"What did he do?"

"Gagged me, tied me to a tree, so I could watch what he was going to do to Jon."

"What was he going to do to him?"

"Cut him, I suppose. It made me so desperate I was filled with violent rage and felt I could do anything. I managed to drag my right hand free, and as he turned to Jon, stooping to get at him, I snatched out his knife and plunged it into his back."

"And then you freed yourself?"

"Jon helped me. We ran back and met August coming out in search of us with his shotgun. He'd been worried Savchenko might do something to us so he'd checked our room, found we weren't there, and come out after us. He did whatever was necessary, wiping off my fingerprints, clearing Savchenko's pockets, cutting off the knife sheath and burying it in an ant heap well away from the area. Then he called us all together and we agreed a story for the police."

"Did he tell the others you'd killed him?"

"No. he was very protective, as he always was. He just said Savchenko had been disposed of, and let the others assume he'd done it himself. Everyone was so overjoyed I don't think they cared who'd done it, just relieved the fear was over."

"Was that when he told them about the drugs?"

"Yes. I wasn't worried if the truth came out because I'd killed in defence of my child, so I was in no danger of prison. But we all agreed to a conspiracy of silence because we wanted the money."

"Wasn't there more to it than that? Weren't you all afraid the smuggling would be discovered?"

Hannah shrugged. "Yeah, that too."

"You said you thought Savchenko was going to cut Jon? There wasn't any indication he might have been going to sexually assault him?"

Hanna stared at him, astonished. "God, no. I'd seen from the first he liked women, he was ogling me even while making threats, that's why I'd told him to fuck off."

"I understand," said Magnus thoughtfully, thinking how right Amrén had been to tell him to hold back some information. "And it was very brave of you to face me and make your confession, especially when you hadn't had enough time to think it out properly and so it was more ludicrous than any confession I've ever had to listen to."

Hanna jumped up angrily. "I came here voluntarily, and I don't have to stay if you're going to call me a liar."

Magnus smiled at her. "I need a coffee," he said, "and I'll bet you could do with one after all that make-believe. We can go on talking while I prepare it, if you don't mind following me into my kitchen. There are a few gaps in your story we ought to plug, and some glaring inconsistencies we need to tackle."

He led the way, and was relieved when she followed him. While he put the coffee kettle on the stove, set the cups and saucers out and put some *pepparkakor* on a plate, she leant against the door jamb, arms crossed over her breasts, her face sullenly defiant, a pupil caught out in a lie and awaiting the consequences.

"Tell me why Savchenko *stooped* to get at Jon," said Magnus, concentrating on taking sugar lumps from the packet and putting them into a blue and white bowl. "Was Jon kneeling or lying on the ground?"

"He was just half-crouched in misery. He wouldn't leave me, wanted to protect me. Anyway, big man, little boy, of course he had to stoop."

"Maybe it would seem more natural if he'd just picked him up, held him in front of him with one hand and had his other hand free to get at his knife and hurt him. But you were so certain about his stooping before you put the knife in that he obviously behaved in an odd way. Unless, of course, he was stooping for a very different reason,"

Magnus put imitation Lapp silver teaspoons on the two saucers. They were engraved with reindeer and had tiny silver rings suspended on each side of the handle. "You were asleep among the rocks when Savchenko woke you. How did he stop you running away?"

"He held his knife to my throat, gripped my arm, forced me to get up, took me to the tree, gagged me and tied me there."

"Did Jon wake up too?"

Hanna's eyes narrowed, and she glared at him. "Of course he did, and he was terrified I was going to be hurt and he followed me, crying; then, once I'd been secured, that vicious beast turned on him."

Magnus poured the coffee. "Savchenko would have been used to tying people up, he'd tortured lots of them before. So you must have had to struggle desperately hard to free your right hand, especially as it was against rough tree bark."

"I'm a lot stronger than I look."

"I'm sure you are. Nevertheless the bark would have grazed you and the rope left awful weals. May I see them?"

"I'm lucky, I heal quickly, and the marks have gone."

"But there were some?"

"All this questioning is pointless, and I'm not answering any more."

He handed her the cup of coffee, put the milk jug, sugar and biscuits on the little circular table, and sat down, pointing to the chair opposite him. Grudgingly she joined him.

"You don't need to show me the marks," he said understandingly. "As you've just realised, and I can't forget, I first saw you when you opened the door to me the morning after all this happened. You were wearing a skimpy little sleeveless top, and there wasn't a mark on you. I saw everything, I was stunned by you, I can still see you standing there, I probably always will, and your skin was unblemished, smooth and golden, and I wanted to kiss you all over."

She wouldn't look at him, and after a gulp of coffee he went on, "As you know, I have a little boy, too, you've seen him in the photo, and Johan's very like your Jon. He's been brought up to hunt, to handle knives and axes, to know about guns, to be self-reliant and utterly at home in the forest. If Johan had been sleeping out and his mother had been seized and threatened with a knife, he wouldn't have stood around and waited, he'd have run to get help, run to the person who'd taught him about shooting, the person who in his young eyes was invincible, who had a gun, who'd save his mother. In Johan's case that would be me; your Jon would automatically have run to August. Lively boys like ours don't hang around in emergencies like that, nor do they keep silent. They run, they shout, they act instinctively. It's mothers, Hanna, loving mothers like you, who are helpless once their child has been seized and threatened. They stay close, protectively, waiting for a chance, ready to sacrifice themselves to save their young. And that's what happened. Savchenko wasn't a fool, he seized Jon, and then he had control of you as well. It was Jon he tied to the tree, by one leg, and the next day I saw the rope burn round his ankle. And that was where

Savchenko made his only mistake. He'd been brought up in a city, he didn't understand the capabilities of a child like Jon. So, despising his youth, and ignoring such puny little hands, he believed tethering him firmly to a tree by one ankle was quite sufficient. He probably made sure the knot was behind the trunk, where Jon couldn't reach it, but that was enough because he was too eager to get to the main course, paying you out for treating him like dirt. The sexual assault was to be on you, Hanna, and we know there was going to be one because forensic evidence proves he was sexually aroused just before his death. I imagine he was planning a particularly nasty rape, in front of your son so it would be especially dreadful for you. At some time he pushed you down on the ground and that was when he had to stoop to get on top of you."

Hanna was looking at him now, but there was a cold resolution about her and she would not speak.

"As to what happened next, I can only guess the detail. And I hope you'll help me with it. I think you realized none of you, not even Jon, would ever be safe while such a man lived, so, before he grabbed you and threw you down, you used the one weapon you had, your sexuality, to render him helpless. You knew how quick and neat Jon was, and I guess you distracted Savchenko by rubbing yourself up against him, pushing him nearer to Jon, telling him how you'd misjudged him and how you adored a well-hung man, and putting your arms round him so you could indicate to Jon exactly where the knife was. Am I right?"

Hanna took a deep breath, seemed to gather all her strength to keep herself calm, and then she nodded.

"It was his eyes," she said. "They'll haunt me all my life. I was asleep, with Jon snuggled up beside me, and I was dreaming it was the last time we'd been there, some weeks before, and we were lighting a fire, and cooking food on it, and having fun, and I was so content, so safe, so utterly relaxed. And then I felt a hand on me, shaking me awake, and when I opened my eyes, his were staring down at me, full of cruelty, mocking me, savouring what he was going to do to me now I was at his mercy. I felt my heart stop because he had his knife raised in his other hand and idiotically I prayed he wouldn't notice Jon curled up so small against me. But as if he could read my thoughts he deliberately moved the blade down close to Jon's sleeping face. I'm not afraid of much, but I was fucking frozen with fear, could scarcely breathe. He didn't hurry himself, but watched me for a while, his tongue gently moistening his lips as he enjoyed his triumph. Then he grabbed Jon with his free hand, forcing him awake and jerking him up so roughly he yelled out for me, kicking and struggling. Savchenko put him under one arm, carried him to the tree and tied him firmly by the ankle. He still had his knife in his hand and I was helpless, running after him, begging him not to hurt Jon, to do anything to me but not to Jon. It's just like you said, a mother's bloody useless when her child's threatened."

She paused, looking at him, wanting him to say something so she would not have to continue. But he remained silent and would not meet her eyes.

"Jon was so brave, he made me ashamed of myself. He didn't sob or anything, and once he'd got over his first shock I could see he was looking for a way to help me, straining at the rope and watching me for any signal. Savchenko had slipped his knife back into the sheath, but it was dangling clear of his jacket in case he needed to get at it quickly. He was so sodding confident it made me furious, and that decided me. I wasn't going to let him do things to me in front of Jon, and I wasn't going to risk him doing anything to Jon in the future. He just wasn't going to be in Jon's future because I was going to kill him. So I acted exactly as you said, touching him, exciting him, squirming against him and pushing him back closer to Jon. I got one arm round him, pointing to the knife and desperately urging Jon with my eyes to pull it out and pass it into my hand while my other made sure Savchenko couldn't think of anything except what I was doing to him. It was one of the few times in my life I was thankful for my early training. But I must've excited him a bit too quickly for suddenly the bastard ripped my blouse open, threw me down, and stooped over me to pull my knickers off. I'd hurt my hip when I hit the ground and I couldn't stop myself crying out. That's when Jon whipped out the knife and stuck it in him."

"Did you actually see him do it? If a large man like Savchenko was over you he must have obscured Jon."

"Yeah, whatever," Hanna muttered, tears running down her cheeks now, and for a moment she was so involved in what she was re-living she could not go on. But then she burst out quickly, "Of course he only wounded him, and then August arrived and finally made sure of him."

Hanna had spoken with feverish intensity and Magnus, aware of the extraordinary sharpness of the blade and that two attempts to force it in would almost certainly have been discovered in the autopsy, said nothing. He knew now all he needed to know, all he had suspected, all he wanted to know, all that had been confirmed by Hanna's confession about Jon's real father. August would not have died to save Hanna, but he would have done, and did, to protect Jon from any public suggestion he'd killed a human being. He leant towards her and took her cold hands in his, saying gently, "So Jon feels no guilt, he doesn't think he killed him?"

"No. He's proud of what he did, proud of saving me, but he's never believed he'd have been strong enough to kill an adult and was glad when August finished him off. We made a lot of what he'd done, said how wonderful he was, hugged him, kissed him, told him how brave he'd been, how horrible the man was, how he deserved to die. And I truly believe it's left no emotional scar, and that's how it has to stay."

"Because of Daniel?"

"I saw what childhood guilt had done to Daniel, and the past had screwed August as well. I wasn't going to let that happen to Jon, and that's the reason, when I got the chance, I took Frisks into the modern world. Jon will be among real people now, the mass of humanity, trippers and opportunists. He can be whatever he wants to be, with none of the family pressures on him that Daniel had. His was a ruined life, and though I tried to make him happy, in the end I just contributed to his death. And that's the trouble, however good the intention, evil can so easily come of it. If the scientific evidence shows it was Jon's thrust which killed him, he'll get to hear about it, the press'll make sure of that. And for all the safeguards to shield children of his age, there'll be unscrupulous people who'll remember and then bring it up when he's older and less-well protected, and the guilt will become embedded and gradually its poison will spread through him. August killed himself to prevent his second son being afflicted as his first son had been, and if you force me to, I'll protect Jon in the only way I can, by confessing to the killing; and this time, thanks to you, I'll tell almost all the truth but add Jon put the knife into my hand, as I'd wanted him to do, and that was when I stabbed him. So that's your choice; August's confession, or mine."

She got up suddenly, her chair overturning, and knelt beside him, her face on his knees. "I'm not afraid to beg, Magnus, I'll do anything for Jon. And you owe me. I could have seduced you when you were at my mercy, when you were prepared to wreck your marriage and career for me, but I didn't do it. I knew I should've done, it would have put you in my power, and August wanted that. But something got in the way, an emotional something, and so I saved you from yourself. Now it's payback time, and I'm begging you, please, please Magnus, save Jon."

He longed to tell her none of this was necessary, that he would do anything to help her, that she did not need to plead, go on her knees; but knowing it was not a decision he could take, he remained silent. He touched her hair, untangling it behind one ear and smoothing it into place. "I have to make a phone call," he said. "Do you want to wait?"

She nodded, looking up at him, and he went into his office and closed the door.

He rang Amrén, telling him how Hanna had found the drugs and handed them in, and criticising himself for not realising sooner that Savchenko would probably have brought some with him.

"There's something else," he added. "August's confession left one loose end, the fact that Savchenko was in a state of sexual arousal when he was killed. It now seems he was trying to rape Hanna, and she thinks her eight year old son may have defended her by wounding Savchenko with the knife just before August finished him off."

"Is there any proof of this?" asked Amrén in his calmly penetrating way. "Did Hanna actually see her son do it?"

"No, Savchenko was between her and the boy, and the only other possible witness was August, who's dead. As for the autopsy report, it refers to a single stab. My guess is that the boy was so desperate to help his mother he actually believes he did do something. Eight year olds have a lot of imagination."

"We're just muddying the waters, then, and nobody will thank us for that, least of all Vessberg. We've got August's confession, and, even if there's any truth in this other stuff, he was still the last one to push the knife in."

"So leave it?"

"Hold on a moment."

Magnus waited, knowing Amrén would have switched to another line to talk to Vessberg and that everything now depended on a prosecutor he'd never even met. He imagined him as thin and worn, generally amenable but sometimes stubborn, always ready to put a junior policeman in his place if he'd exceeded his authority; and as each moment passed Magnus became more and more convinced he *had* taken much too much upon himself. But when the answer came it was exactly what he hoped to hear.

"Vessberg wants to keep it simple. He's glad you informed him because it shows you're not keeping anything back, or trying to take decisions on your own, but he says there's no value in pursuing it, and I agree with him. Everybody's better off without a vicious thug like Savchenko, we've got the drugs, August's out of it, it was probably justifiable homicide anyway, so we can heave a sigh of relief and get on with other things. And by the way, Lennart's back from holiday and I'll send him out tomorrow to take over from you for a few days. You've been away from Sonja and the children quite long enough, so you'll take three days' leave. Do I have to make it an order?"

"No," said Magnus. "I think I need a break."

"You're learning sense at last," said Amrén cheerfully, and he rang off.

Magnus went back to Hanna, but there was no feeling of triumph, just a great tiredness. "It's over," he said. "The prosecutor likes tidiness, so does my inspector, and so do I. A vicious thug's been taken out, a dead man's confessed, and the drugs have been recovered. So everybody's happy, and the case is closed."

Hanna stood up and seemed about to come to him and hug him, but then she didn't. "Thank you," she said, and he thought she'd never looked so lovely. "I know it's not quite true that everybody's happy, not you, not me; but you soon will be, because you've got your family, and so will I, because I've got Jon. It's a lot to be thankful for, Magnus, and we just have to get on with our lives. Come and see me sometime when I've opened my restaurant."

He said he would, but knew he wouldn't; and he knew she knew it too.

END

COMING SOON

THE THIRD BOOK IN THE MAGNUS TRYGG SERIES

'FINISHED'

In the Swedish town of Sundsvall the female owner of a basement flea market is killed by a single hammer blow. Magnus Trygg is away on an Inspector's Course, and so the case is reluctantly given to his rival for the post of Head of Homicide, Lennart Haverdal. An unlucky man, struggling to cope with the death of his wife, he does uncover one vital clue: although the murder weapon is beside the body, another hammer has been removed from a display unit. Unable to make much more progress with the first murder, he is soon investigating a second. Magnus, when he returns, is asked to guard the woman Lennart believes will be the third victim. Magnus has his doubts, but another hammer is missing and time is not on their side.

Robin Porecky's 'FINISHED' will be published by Austin Macauley in 2014